MW01119648

Also by Rita Kroon:

Letters from the Past (historical fiction)

*You Have Cancer – a Journey through the Valley
of the Shadow of Death* (memoir)

Praying the Scriptures (prayers from Scripture)

Womanhood: Becoming a Woman of Virtue (women's Bible study)

40 Days in the Wilderness (devotional)

40 Days of God's Encouragement (devotional)

40 Days of Assurance (devotional)

Kiss Your
Mommy Goodbye

Deb + Judd,
May you have fullness
of joy!
Rita

Psalm 16:11

RITA KROON

CROSSBOOKS

CrossBooks™
A Division of LifeWay
One LifeWay Plaza
Nashville, TN 37234
www.crossbooks.com
Phone: 1-866-768-9010

Author photo by Rick Busch

First published by CrossBooks 09/26/2014

ISBN: 978-1-4627-5297-3 (sc)
ISBN: 978-1-4627-5298-0 (hc)
ISBN: 978-1-4627-5296-6 (e)

Library of Congress Control Number: 2014915756

Printed in the United States of America.

This book is printed on acid-free paper.

DEDICATED TO

My husband with whom I share life and faith to the fullest,
My daughters and sons-in-law, who inspire me to persevere,
My grandchildren, who are my delight,
My sister, Gayle, who truly has a servant's heart,
And
To My Savior and Lord Jesus Christ, whom
I desire to honor in all that I do.

ACKNOWLEDGEMENTS

With deep appreciation I say thank you to:
My daughter, Rene´ Maleski, for all her
helpful comments and suggestions,
Debbie Christensen for her expertise with syntax,
My daughter, LaDawn Stalboerger, for keeping a
copy of the original manuscript from 1995,
My daughter, Shelly Smith, for her availability to listen,
My grandson, Michael Maleski for his willingness
to appear on the cover of this book,
Amanda Korpi for her participation on the cover of this book,
And to Rick Busch, the photographer who brought it together.

CHAPTER 1

Storm Clouds on the Horizon

They faced each other at the dinner table like two people sinking in quicksand—unwilling and unable to reach out to the other, powerless to reverse the inevitable. Tension, their faceless guest, sat between them, pretending not to be there.

Mike stared at Lisa. He looked at two-year-old Maddy sitting in her high chair next to where he sat. Her round, innocent eyes looked up at him. With his fingertips, Mike brushed her hair back from her face and kissed her forehead.

He looked back at his wife. Suddenly he felt a whisper of terror in his soul. "You want a divorce, don't you?"

Lisa seemed to weigh his words carefully, as if they balanced on a sliver of glass. "Yes," she said.

***

Several months and a fistful of failed attempts at reconciliation later, twenty-six-year-old Mike DiSanto sat in the last bench row of room 224 of the county court-house. He pressed his elbows into his knees and clasped his hands loosely together.

Just then, Lisa entered, wearing an outfit the color of a gun barrel. She took her seat next to a young man in a navy-blue pin-striped suit— every inch the lawyer—holding an attaché case on his lap. She flicked a flat glance at Mike.

1

Mike let out a long, hard breath. He focused on the old wooden floor as though it had power to wake him from this bad dream. However, it only creaked and groaned with every footstep of those entering the courtroom.

He, then, turned his attention to frosted-glass windows—anything to avoid looking at Lisa. Then, a heavy wooden door closed with a thud. He tried to shake the ominous feeling he had that his life was about to change forever.

"Case number 47-F2-91-3040, DiSanto versus DiSanto," the female court attendant called. "The Honorable Judge Blackwell presiding."

Mike and his lawyer, and Lisa with her lawyer, approached the judge's massive elevated bench. Beads of sweat dotted Mike's forehead.

The burly judge peered over his black reading glasses at the four people standing before him. He cleared his throat and read, "After several unsuccessful mediation sessions, divorce is hereby granted to Michael David DiSanto and Lisa Marie DiSanto on this tenth day of August, 1991, by the Court of Meeker County in the state of Minnesota." He banged his gavel sharply on the base.

After four years, Mike and Lisa's marriage vows meant to join two people for a lifetime of love and commitment echoed down the empty halls of time. Their family shattered, and no one could put the pieces back together.

Judge Blackwell turned his attention back to the papers in front of him. The terms and conditions of the divorce are as follows." He glanced from Mike to Lisa. "The house and all its contents, excluding Mr. DiSanto's personal belongings, are awarded to Mrs. DiSanto."

Mike's shoulders slumped, and he bowed his head. His stomach felt tight, as though his black leather belt had instantly shrunk.

"In addition," the judge continued, "I hereby order $300 monthly alimony, to cease only if petitioner should remarry, and $400 per month child support until child is of legal age."

Mike shut his eyes and expelled the air from his lungs with a heavy breath.

"This could get costly." The words of his lawyer mocked any sense of justice.

Lisa gave no response other than a thin smile.

Mike, on the other hand, shifted his body from one leg to the other as his jaw muscles twitched. He rubbed the back of his neck, twisting his head from side to side.

Mike's lawyer placed a calming hand on his shoulder. "Easy," he cautioned in a hushed tone.

Judge Blackwell adjusted his glasses. "Regarding your only child, I hereby award full custody of Madison Marie DiSanto to the child's mother, Lisa DiSanto with father visitation rights two weekends a month."

Mike's shoulders collapsed completely, and the blood drained from his face. His fingertips felt cold. Nothing mattered anymore—not the divorce, not the alimony, not the child support, not even losing the house. But when he heard full custody of their daughter being handed over to Lisa like a piece of merchandise exchanging hands at a local department store, a sharp spike seared into his heart.

However, Lisa stood tall like a princess, though she'd lost her kingdom.

"That's all." Judge Blackwell said and banged his gavel.

Mike heard his heart beat in his ears.

"Really tough break," his lawyer said with useless, sympathetic pats on Mike's back.

Mike's eyes stung, and his heart ached. Rage began to rise like molten lava about to spew. "She gets custody of Maddy. I get visitation rights to see my own daughter a lousy twice a month? Are you kidding me?" he mumbled through clenched teeth. *This is insanity.* He swallowed hard to stifle the roar that threatened to explode.

Lisa stood ramrod straight. A smug smile played at the corners of her bright red lips. A look of triumph trickled into her brown eyes, which glistened like the fur of mink. Her lawyer snapped his attaché case shut and gave a victory nod to Lisa and a sharp look of disdain to the opponents as he escorted Lisa from the courtroom.

***

3

Outside the courthouse, Mike felt like a combatant emerging from a Herculean defeat. He caught up to Lisa as she walked toward her car. "Why did you do it?" His jaw muscles twitched.

Lisa stopped and faced him, her eyes fixed, steely, and arctic. "Do what?"

"Go for the jugular?"

"Is that what you call it?"

"Yeah." Mike stepped in front of her, forcing her to stop.

She turned her head to the side, slowly crossed her arms, and tapped her fingers against her upper arm. She did not say a word, but neither did she move.

He rubbed the sweat from his forehead on the shoulder of his sport shirt—the blue-striped shirt Lisa had given him from Madison for Father's Day, an obligatory gesture, no doubt.

Without looking at Mike, she said, "As for Madison, rather than have you come to our—to *my* house," she corrected herself, "I'll bring her over to my parents' house. You can pick her up there."

"Look at me," he said his brows furrowed in a deep frown. "You can't deny me from seeing my own—"

She faced him, her arms at her side. "Oh, yes I can, and I have the court's backing." Her voice rose like an approaching siren.

He held his palms up, arms apart. "So?"

"So weren't you listening to the judge? Two weekends a month!" She held up two manicured fingers. Her red-polished nails flashed like a matador's cape in front of a snorting bull.

Mike glared at her.

"Are you about done?" She folded her arms, drummed her fingers against her arm, and tilted her head.

Mike recognized her all-too-familiar gesture that signaled the end of a conversation.

She turned to unlock her car parked at an expired meter. A parking ticket stuck under the windshield wiper caught her eye. She yanked it out and flashed an angry look at Mike.

"That's not my fault! And your parking tickets are no longer my responsibility!"

"Whatever."

"I have to get back to work."

"Of course. What else do you do?"

"You know very well why I had to work so much." With his eyes riveted on her, he said, "I'm done arguing!"

"Don't forget to have the child support to me by the tenth."

Dark storm clouds loomed on the horizon. A rumble of thunder sounded in the distance.

CHAPTER 2

Lisa

"**C**an you come in for a bit? Madison won't be up for another half hour."

"I'd rather not. Could you just go get her?"

"Please stay. She'll be up soon."

"I suppose." Lisa kicked off her white sandals at the door and plodded barefoot across the hardwood floor to the kitchen.

Betty Barrett poured iced tea in two tall glasses. The ice cubes crackled in protest as Betty set the glasses on the table. "Come, sit," she invited. She pushed the loose chair cushion back in place on the wooden chair.

Lisa ran her fingers up and down the frosted glass before poking the ice cubes under the cloudy liquid. She watched them bob to the top again. She took a sip of the fruity, sweet tea and looked at her mother. She was kind and still beautiful, with brown eyes and dark-blonde hair that she wore swept up in a messy fashion. She looked at her mother and felt nothing—as usual. Her mother's voice interrupted her thoughts.

"Do you want to talk about it?" Betty asked, sitting opposite Lisa.

"About what?"

"Court. The divorce. How you are feeling."

"How am I supposed to feel?"

"I don't know. I'm just wondering how you are doing." Her voice was soothing.

Lisa took a sip of her tea. "Good tea."

"It's peach. Not my usual raspberry. I'm glad you like it." She moistened her lips. "Lisa, you seem so, I don't know, detached from talking about the divorce—"

"Tell me about my adoption again."

"But why? That was long ago."

"I don't care. I just want to hear it again."

Betty sighed. "You were your birth mother's second child. You were just a few months old, and Annie was two when your mother placed you girls in an orphanage. She simply could not provide for you and Annie."

Betty blinked several times. "You were two years old when we started the adoption process, but international adoptions take time, and Sweden is no exception." She took another sip of the iced tea and set the glass down slowly.

"Did my birth mother ever come to visit me at the orphanage?"

"I don't know, Lisa. But, if she didn't, I'm sure she had a good reason."

"What would be a good reason?"

"Maybe she was ill. Maybe she had to work—"

"Not all the time."

"Why are you bringing this up now? We've talked about it before—"

"I don't know. I just am."

Betty reached over and cupping Lisa's hand, asked, "Does this have anything to do with the divorce?"

Lisa let her mother hold her hand for a few seconds. Then she pulled it away. "No, why would it? And why didn't you adopt Annie? What about her?"

"Because she had behavioral problems. A wonderful couple adopted her a few months before we adopted you. You were four—"

"Why did my birth mother reject me?"

"Lisa, I told you why your birth mother—"

"I know what you said. You always give everyone the benefit of a doubt. Tell me the truth. Why did she reject me? And why didn't my birth father know I existed?"

Betty sighed. "All I know is what the adoption agency told us, so I don't know why your birth father didn't know about you."

7

Lisa leaned forward, clasping the glass with both hands. She looked steadily at her mother.

"Maybe it was partly our fault. You see, the day your dad and I brought you home, we were thrilled that we would finally be a family." She looked tenderly at her daughter. "But, you seemed withdrawn, almost as though you were protecting yourself from being loved and loving in return."

Betty looked out the kitchen window beyond the lilac bushes to the old play house that had been abandoned so many years ago—Lisa's playhouse where she spent hours at a time. Lisa drew pictures, stick-figure pictures of two little girls walking hand-in-hand in front of a large square building with blackened windows.

"We were told that being cautious in new relationships was normal for adopted children," Betty said still gazing out the window, "and to just give it time." She sighed as though thinking of the lost years and looked at Lisa. "Time evolved into months, then into years."

"Go on." Lisa sat back and crossed her arms.

"We longed to hold you, but, even as a very young child, you did not want to be held. It seemed the only way we could get you to respond to us was if we bought you something—something special that would let you know how much we loved you. But, you simply took your gift and would go either to your room or to the playhouse." Betty shrugged her shoulders.

Lisa waved her hand for Betty to continue.

"When we adopted you, it was commonly believed that adopted children just needed to adjust. And, most do so in their own way." Betty brushed a strand of hair from her forehead. "Now, they say there may actually be something that inhibits some children from connecting—some form of attachment disorder—"

"Who's 'they'?"

"What?"

"They. You said 'they said some children have an attachment disorder.' Who's 'they'?"

"I don't know. Experts in the field of adoption, I suppose."

Lisa pushed her hair behind her ear and raised her chin. "Nobody's going to hang a label on me!"

8

"Lisa, I'm not saying you have attachment disorder. It's possible, but I don't think so. I think you felt rejected by your birth mother all your life. Maybe you convinced yourself that if your own mother didn't love you, no one could. I think it's more of a self-protection thing than attachment disorder." Betty looked compassionately at her daughter. "Lisa, do you feel rejected by Mike?"

Lisa crossed her legs. "Divorce was my choice."

"I know it was your choice, and I understand that life can sometimes be difficult. Nevertheless, life is a time of learning, and making choices is part of the process."

"What's that supposed to mean?"

Betty sighed. "Well, what if we could interpret life from God's perspective? Would that change your way of thinking?"

"Don't preach. You know how I hate that." She glanced at the clock. "I have to go."

Betty pushed her empty glass aside. "Before you go, can you tell me a little about the divorce hearing?"

"What's to tell? I got the house and custody of Madison. He has to pay alimony and child support. Mike got angry, and I left. By the way, he has visitation two weekends a month. I told him I would bring Madison over here, and he can pick her up at your house. OK?"

"Well." Betty hesitated. "Yes, I suppose so. But do you think that was wise?"

Her eyes locked unflinchingly on her mother. "It's the way it is."

"Lisa?" Betty's tone was soft. "What did you like about Mike more than the other boys you dated, the reason you married him?"

Her mother's question caught her off guard. She shrugged. "He was tall, dark, and handsome."

"And beyond that?" her mother prodded.

"I don't know," she hedged. "I guess his quietness, maybe the way he loved to work, and probably his determination. But, they were the things that sometimes made me the angriest at him, as well." She jabbed an ice cube plunging it to the bottom of her iced tea, only to poke it down again when it bobbed to the surface. "Maybe it was his new pickup truck. "I don't know." She rolled her eyes. "Why? What difference does it make?"

"Do you mean his good looks and his pickup were the safest things to love? Could that be possible?"

Lisa looked into her mother's perceptive eyes, but said nothing.

"Did you love Mike?" She paused for an instant. "Or, were you in love with the idea of being in love?"

Lisa looked down at her painted toes. "I liked him. What's not to like? But, I wasn't in love with him." *What's love, anyway? Who needs it?* She thought.

"You and Dad never pushed to know if I loved you or not, but Mike always wanted me to tell him that I loved him."

"That's not unreasonable," Betty said softly. She shifted in her chair, crossing her feet beneath her. "Lisa, can I ask a personal question?" Her tone was cautious.

She shrugged her left shoulder. "I guess."

"What did you and Mike argue about mostly?"

"Money. It was always about money." She gave an exasperated sigh. "Living with him was like having a perpetually expired credit card. I'm sick of it!"

"When did all this start?"

"After I quit working."

"Were you struggling financially? Because if that was the prob—"

"I didn't think we were, but apparently he did. Every time I wanted to go shopping, or get a pedicure or go to the spa or whatever, he would tell me to keep it under $100.00. 'Keep it under $100.00,'" she mocked, rocking her head from side to side.

"I see." Intimate talks with her daughter were far and few between before Lisa would put up her invisible wall, and this time was no different.

Just then, a muffled sound came from the hallway leading to one of three bedrooms.

"I hear Madison." Lisa sounded relieved for the interruption.

Two-year old Madison toddled around the corner, rubbing her eyes. She yawned, crawled up into Betty's lap, and snuggled against her chest. Lisa could see that Betty loved the feel of Madison's small frame nestled against her.

Lisa couldn't remember being held as a child and, for a split second, she felt the tug to be embraced by her mother.

"Madison, your mama is here," Betty said and turned Madison toward Lisa.

Madison yawned, climbed down, and waddled to Lisa, still rubbing her eyes.

Lisa picked her up, turning Madison's back toward her in one swooping motion as she set Madison on her lap and proceeded to put on the toddler's shoes.

"Is there anything I can do to help?" Betty asked.

"No. And thanks for taking Madison."

"She's no trouble at all." She bit her lip. Then, she asked, "Would you like to stay for supper? We could make spaghetti."

"No. I really have to get going. I've got plans."

"What about Maddy?"

""'I've got a sitter."

"She could stay here."

"No. I've got it covered."

Lisa gathered up Madison and her things, slipped into her sandals and rushed out the door. She buckled Madison in her car seat, slid behind the wheel and sped off.

CHAPTER 3

Mike

The ominous storm clouds that had bullied their way across the summer sky dumped a short, drenching rain—enough to make the sky milky white with heat and humidity.

Mike stopped at his parents' house, where he had been staying since he and Lisa had decided to divorce. By the time he changed from his sport shirt and slacks into his work clothes and headed to the job site, it was nearly 1 p.m.

The job site was an older, two-story house that looked as though several architects designed the house, but had never met to discuss the plans. Mike and his boss accepted the challenge to complete the house in order to flip it before winter.

Even before Mike got out of his pick-up truck, he heard the thwack, thwack, thwack, of the nail gun. He spotted Karl up on the roof. Mike forced a mirthless smile. "Hey old man," he hollered with a wave, "Do you think you're a roofer?"

Karl laughed and, with a single up nod of his head, yelled back, "I must be! I'm up here nailing shingles!"

Mike hoisted a bundle of shingles to his shoulder and climbed the ladder to the steep-pitched roof. He dropped the shingles down with a flat thud.

Karl, soaked with sweat, grinned. "Glad you decided to show up for work." And then in a more serious tone asked, "How'd it go at court, son?"

Mike hesitated for a moment, his eyes moist. "Not the way—" He cleared his throat.

"You look upset."

Mike nodded. "Yeah."

"Mike, I wish I could do something to make things right for you. But, just know that Katie and I are praying for you," Karl said and went back to nailing shingles.

Mike nodded and went back in time. *How did it come to this?* he wondered.

***

As a young boy, Mike thought his relationship with his dad had been a good one. But, one day, his third grade teacher said, "Your son needs extra help with arithmetic." Mike got extra help, but still, he continued to struggle with math.

That's when his dad became distant towards him and his mother, and Mike secretly shouldered the responsibility. *Surely I had disappointed my dad hadn't I?* He wondered. He tried hard to win his dad's approval, but to no avail. After his parents divorced, he never saw his dad again.

During his freshman year in high school, his basketball coach, after hearing Mike repeatedly invert the numbers of the games' final scores, suggested Mike get tested for a learning disability—one that affects a person's capacity to work with number concepts.

"Your son has dyscalculia," the high school psychologist said. "But, with intense assistance, and if Mike is determined, and concentrates, he should be able to function almost normally with numbers."

By the time he was in tenth grade, Mike had adjusted to having a stepfather and willingly took his stepfather's last name. Although he referred to him as Dad, he never considered him to be his dad. He wasn't sure why. Maybe his mother's detached influence? Maybe the stigma he felt coming from divorced parents? He didn't know. It's just the way it was.

During his senior year, he contemplated trying out for professional baseball.

Rita Kroon

"You have a good shot at it," his high school coach had said. "It's like the bat is an extension of your hand." His coach grinned broadly. "Like in the last game for the state championship. Bottom of the ninth, score is tied—three balls and two strikes. You were last man to bat."

Mike grinned. "Yeah, I remember."

"The way you swung that bat sent the ball into orbit! If it weren't for you, there'd be one less trophy in the trophy case! And those four scouts after you—"

"Nah, too iffy," he said.

After graduation, Mike considered staying on at his stepfather's hardware store. While the store was not a picture of order, it was a marvel of inventory—a place where many a townspeople said, "If DiSanto's doesn't have it, a body doesn't need it."

Mike knew the hardware business from years stocking shelves as a young teen. When he was old enough to work for a real salary, he promptly deposited most of his earnings into a savings account.

Mike liked the customers well enough, and they always joked with him. But he realized he wasn't interested in working at a hardware store. He wanted to work in construction—maybe even own his own construction company someday.

However, he decided to go to college. *I have to prove to myself that I can do it. Besides a business degree might help if I own my own company,* he reasoned.

Mike chose St. Cloud State, and he determined to stay focused. He was even more resolute to overcome his struggle with inverting numbers that had plagued him since grade school.

Mike attended college for two years and maintained a 3.0 grade average. But, he became restless. He talked to his long-time friend and college roommate about it. "I'm dropping out," Mike said. He knew his words landed like a bombshell.

"Dude! What are you thinking?" Ryan Summers asked.

"I want to go into full time construction."

"This isn't some snap decision you're going to regret, is it?"

"No, it's not. I'm thinking of going to trade school."

A slow smile ceased Ryan's face. "OK. I get it. And speaking of a change in plans, when are you going to find yourself a steady girl?"

Mike shrugged. "Haven't met the right girl yet."

"I'm going to Rachel's grad party next weekend. Why don't you come?"

"Nah."

"Give me one good reason."

"OK. I'll think about it."

"Good. I'll drive."

CHAPTER 4

The Meeting

Rachel Henderson lived in Shady Grove, a modest neighborhood with high arching trees on both sides of the street. Balloons of green, white, and black danced crazily from the front porch rails.

Ryan found a parking spot on the crowded street a short distance away. Rock music, talk, and laughter from Rachel's backyard filled the air.

Mike and Ryan weaved their way through the throng of guests to the volleyball net which stretched nearly the width of the backyard. Several energetic guys lunged, spiked, and smacked the volleyball back and forth over the net.

Rachel greeted Ryan with a hug and looked up adoringly. "I'm so glad you came."

"Me too," he said with a grin. "You remember Mike?"

"Of course. You guys grab a plate and get something to eat."

"You don't have to tell me twice," Ryan said.

The guys filled their plates, and Rachel led them to a shady spot where several young people sat around tables.

"Everybody, this is Ryan, and this is Mike," she introduced. "This is Julie, Shelly, Becky, and Lisa."

Mike nodded to each of the girls, but his eyes lingered on Lisa.

Ryan noticed.

"Uh, oh. I saw that look!" he side-mouthed to Mike.

"She looks familiar. That's all."

"Yeah, right. Uh-huh."

"There's pop and sparkling water over there," Rachel said pointing to a couple of huge ice-filled tubs.

Her dad stood at the grill turning sizzling brats and flipping juicy burgers while her mother brought out more trays of bars and cookies to add to the table already loaded with pasta salads and fruit platters.

Although Mike didn't get an opportunity to talk with Lisa, he smiled at her frequent glances in his direction as she sat with a few unattached girlfriends.

Rachel's high school graduation party lasted well into the evening ending with a huge bonfire with all the fixing's needed to make s'mores.

"I know why Lisa looks familiar," Mike said to Ryan as they sat on make-shift benches around the bonfire.

Ryan nodded as he stuffed a roasted marshmallow into his mouth.

"I saw her in the halls in high school." He glanced at her again. "She's still hot."

"Yeah, if I weren't so in love with Rachel, I probably would've looked her way myself."

"Is she dating anyone?"

"Not that I know of." Ryan shrugged. "Rachel says Lisa's never been serious with anyone. She just dates casual."

"Well maybe, I'll be her Sir Galahad!"

"Go for it," Ryan said popping another gooey marshmallow into his mouth.

Mike walked over to where Lisa sat and stood a short distance away. He smiled as he watched her try to put a marshmallow on the end of a stick—her brows pinched together in concentration.

"Aww," she groaned as the golden sweet morsel fell into the burning coals.

Mike grabbed a forked stick, jammed a few marshmallows on each prong, and stooped down near Lisa. He held the stick over the coals until the marshmallows bubbled to a golden brown.

Someone threw another log on the fire sending a crackling burst of sparks heavenward.

"I've got extra marshmallows. I'll share if you don't have any."

Lisa turned to face him.

In the bonfire's blazing glow, Mike noticed Lisa's eyes flick from mild interest to flirtatious.

A smile teased the corners of her red lips. "No thanks."

CHAPTER 5

Summer of Surprises

HELP WANTED. Construction worker needed. Dependable and hard-working. House remodeling. Carpentry skills a plus. Contact Karl Roberts at 555-4044.

"Dad, do you know Karl Roberts?"

"Don't know him personally. Why?"

"He's got an ad in the paper for a construction worker."

"Well, I know he's a fair man. He's a hard worker and does a good job, but that's all I know."

"That's enough. I'm going to call him about the job."

***

That evening, Mike went to an unpretentious house with white siding and a wide front porch. A single dormer perched itself comfortably above the porch roof. A giant cottonwood spread its arms wide as though to claim the entire front yard as its own—its cottony tufts quietly collected themselves along the sidewalk's edge. An older Ford pickup sat in the driveway

Mike rang the doorbell and glanced at his watch. Exactly 7 p.m. Right on time.

A tall man about his height, maybe ten pounds heavier, and about twenty-five years older with graying hair at his temples, bushy eyebrows and a cookie duster moustache opened the door.

"Mr. Roberts?"

"Call me Karl. You must be Mike." He stuck his large calloused hand out and Mike gripped it firmly. "C'mon in."

Mike liked him immediately.

Karl led Mike through the living room, the dining room and into the kitchen. Yellowed wallpaper with tiny clusters of faded pink roses and variegated dark green leaves covered all four walls in the dining room. The tired wallpaper seemed relieved to be able to hide behind a heavy-looking dark china hutch. It was like stepping into a century past.

The kitchen reminded him of his grandmother's old farm house on the south side of town. The only thing missing was a hot apple pie cooling on a rack on the counter.

Just then, he got a whiff of warm, spicy apple and cinnamon. He glanced at the counter and chuckled to himself. There sat the best-looking pie he had ever seen.

"Mike, this is my wife Katie. Honey, this is Mike," Karl introduced.

After pleasantries were exchanged, Karl invited Mike to sit down at the kitchen table. A bouquet of daisies in a glass vase sat in the center of the table.

"Would you like a cup of coffee and a piece of pie with ice cream?" Katie asked

Katie had a genuine smile that creased into deep laugh lines around her thin mouth. Her brown hair with streaks of gray looked like she had just come from getting a perm at the beauty salon. She seemed like the perfect match for Karl.

"I sure can't turn that down!" He looked around the kitchen. "You have a nice home."

"We plan to remodel it and bring it up to date," Karl said with a broad smile.

"That's what he does best." Katie filled Mike's coffee cup. "He brings new life to old houses. I design—mainly kitchens and baths—and he does the hard work."

Karl looked tenderly at his wife. Mike felt a twinge of longing to be in a relationship where each one loves the other—like Karl and Katie. His mother and stepfather seemed more like casual co-workers who shared the same clothes hamper. *If it weren't for the hardware store, there probably wouldn't be any relationship at all,* he thought.

"We inherited this old' house from Katie's folks. It was built in 1910."

Mike nodded. *That explains a lot,* he thought.

"I'll leave you two to talk. Nice to meet you."

"Same here."

Karl winked at her and turned his full attention to Mike. He stroked his chin as though thinking, studying the young man sitting opposite him. "What kind of experience do you have?"

"I worked some construction—mostly laboring for a masonry outfit—for the past two summers, but I'd really like to get into full-time construction."

Karl smiled. He had deep laugh lines around his dark blue eyes. "Do you have any carpentry skills? Ever build anything?"

"Well, I built new cabinets for my folks' kitchen last winter," Mike said not wanting to put too much emphasis on what he thought Karl may consider measly projects. "And I put in a store room at my dad's hardware store. And a dog house. I built my dog a house for shop class in high school." He looked Karl squarely in his eyes. "That's about it."

"Still got your dog?"

"No. Boone was hit by a car."

"Boone? What kind of dog did you have?"

"He was a Brittany. He was pretty young when I rescued him from a bad situation."

"Yeah? What was that?"

"He was chained to my neighbor's tree. No one took care of him except to give him food and fill his water dish every couple of days."

Karl nodded. "Good hunter?"

"Yeah, he was. I haven't been hunting since he died."

Karl took a swallow of coffee. "Did you ever go to trade school?"

"I took a four-month, on-line course for home remodeling my last year at St. Cloud State. Before college, I pretty much worked at my dad's hardware store." He ate a bite of pie followed by a gulp of coffee.

"How are you at learning on the job?"

Mike hesitated slightly. "Never had a problem."

"Long hours bother you?" Karl continued to stroke his chin.

"Nope. I like to work."

"Son, I like you. You seem to be exactly what I'm looking for!"

"I don't have much experience—"

"Perfect. That way I won't have to undo all the worthless short cuts most workers have learned." He laughed a deep laugh.

Mike grinned and finished the last bite of pie.

For the next hour or so, the two men talked salary, different aspects involved in construction, and the long hours needed to remodel a house before flipping it.

"When can you start?"

"When do you need me?"

"Tomorrow would be good." He raised an eyebrow.

Mike nodded.

"Can you be here about 7 a.m.? Oh, I almost forgot, do you have tools?"

"Yes to both questions," Mike said.

"See you in the morning."

"I'll be here."

Mike couldn't help but to grin as he started his truck. "Yeah!" he said out loud.

***

After the first week on the job, Mike felt confident carpentry was a good fit, and Karl was a great boss, but what made a good situation even better happened that Friday evening. He had just finished a late supper when the phone rang.

"H'lo."

A female voice said, "Mike?"

"Yeah."

"This is Lisa. I met you at Rachel's grad party a couple of weeks ago—"

"I remember. You lost your marshmallows," he said chuckling.

"Yes, I, I did." She sounded nervous. "That's why I'm calling."

"Uh-huh."

"I owe you an apology. I was rude when you offered to share your marshmallows with me—" Her voice trailed off.

"I thought you were polite—you said 'thanks.'"

"You're making this difficult."

"Now, I'm the one to apologize. I didn't mean to sound sarcastic. So, if you'll accept my apology, I'll accept yours."

"OK."

A few seconds of awkward silence ticked by before Lisa said, "Well, I guess that's all I wanted to say—"

"Ah, I hate to waste a good apology," Mike countered. "Would you like to go to the July 4th parade?"

"Um, I work."

"You work on July 4th?" Mike switched the phone to his other ear. "Where do you work?"

"Freedom Travel, but I get off at noon." She sounded hopeful.

"Well, we could hang out at the celebration at Lady Bird Park, eat ourselves stupid, and stay for fireworks?"

"Um, OK." Then as an afterthought, she added, "Maybe we could see if Rachel and Ryan want to go."

"Yeah, I haven't seen Ryan since Rachel's party. I'll call him. How does 2:00 o'clock sound?"

"That would work."

"I guess I need to know where you live so I can pick you up," he said grabbing a pen and paper.

I live at 756 Elm Avenue."

Mike scribbled her address on the yellow note paper. "OK, I got it."

***

The sun's rays fanned against the pale blue sky. It was early in the morning—so early the neighbor's sunflowers still had their heads bowed when Mike hit the pavement for his daily run. Flags waved proudly from front porches and the homes seemed to stand at proper attention this particular July 4th. Or, did it just seem that way?

Mike washed his truck and cleaned the inside. He showered, shaved, trimmed his mustache, and splashed on an extra dose of Drakkar aftershave.

Mike turned onto Elm Avenue scanning the house numbers for 657. He read 651, 653, 655, but then the street ended at the edge of a small woods. He looked at his piece of paper— 657 Elm Ave. He drew his brows together in a frown of recollection. He glanced at his watch— 2:05 p.m.

He made a U-turn to head to the next street to skirt the woods. But, before he had driven one block, he came upon barricades blocking all thru traffic as emergency city workers repaired a water main break.

"Aw, man!" he mumbled as he turned around and headed to Oak Street. This street cooperated. Mike turned left at the intersection only to discover that he was one block shy of clearing the wooded area. "For Pete's sake!"

Again he turned around and re-traced his route. This time he found a street that took him to the other side of the woods and back onto Elm Avenue.

He read the address of the first house—657. He pulled up glancing at his watch—2:15 p.m.

He jogged up the sidewalk, taking the porch steps two at a time and rang the doorbell. No answer. He rang again. He ran his hand over the back of his neck. *Of course! Everyone's at the celebration—everyone except Lisa and me!*

He drove down Elm Avenue wondering what he should do when he spied a mail box with the name BARRETT painted on the side above the address—756.

Figures! He eased his truck to the curb in front of a modest one-story house with brown shake siding and yellow trim. Its wooden stoop looked worn at the edges like an old bar of soap.

He glanced at his watch—2:20 p.m. He gave an exasperated sigh.

He took the four steps two at a time and rang the doorbell. After what seemed like a long pause, Lisa opened the door wearing red shorts and a white top.

"Hi. I'm really sorry I'm late," he said taking in her long tan legs and sandaled feet with red painted toes.

"Hi," Lisa greeted him with something approaching cordiality.

"I, ah, ran into some trouble—"

"It's OK. I just got home from work. Problems with the computers."

His eyes explored her eyes, her lips, her ears with dangling blue earrings. He grinned. "You look—patriotic."

Her smile turned saucy over the back door compliment. "Thanks, I think."

"Seriously, you really do look great."

Just then, a man and a woman appeared behind Lisa.

"Ah, Mom and Dad, this is Mike," she introduced.

Mike shook the man's hand. "Glad to meet you, Mr. and Mrs. Barrett."

"'Name's Bruce and this is Betty."

"Bruce. Betty." Mike nodded.

"I have to grab my sunglasses," Lisa said turning to step back into the living room.

There was an awkward silence. Then, Lisa reappeared, and the silence was chastised with hasty good-byes.

Lady Bird Park was crowded with festive throngs of people, food vendors, craft booths, and trinket stands. Rock music blared from the band shelter. On the far side of the park, children of all ages laughed as they jumped on trampolines, rode ponies, and got their faces painted. Crowds of people strolled throughout the park eating corndogs on a stick or mini donuts from greasy paper sacks.

Mike spotted Ryan and Rachel by the cotton candy machine.

"What's up?" Ryan greeted.

"Hey," Mike replied. "'Been waiting long?"

"Not unless you count almost an hour as long."

"Sorry about that, man. I was late."

"You're forgiven if you buy the popcorn. Extra butter."

"Deal, if you buy something to drink."

The two couples walked the entire park talking and laughing and stopped at every food booth. They sat on park benches listening to the music.

Lisa peeled waxed paper from a caramel apple on a stick, took a bite, and offered the mouth-watering fruit to Mike. He took and ate, savoring the sweet candied morsel.

***

The clear night sky proved a perfect backdrop for the spectacular fireworks display. A whisper of a breeze skimmed across Lake Ripley. With each boom, a burst of brilliant fireworks evoked "oohs" and "aahs" from the throng of people sprawled on the grassy beach area.

"I love fireworks," Rachel, said as the finale boomed staccato-like, drawing applause and cheers from the spectators.

"Must be a girl thing," Ryan laughed.

"Oh, stop. You know you like fireworks," Rachel scolded, rolling him over from his sitting position.

"OK. OK. I like fireworks!" He glanced at Mike.

"I like fireworks," Mike yelled before Rachel could bowl him over too.

The drive to Lisa's house was spent in a comfortable quiet except for country music playing low.

Lisa ran her fingers lightly across the dash. "Nice truck. Is it new?"

"Nah. I bought it last year." He stole a glance at her. "I had a good time," he said as he pulled up in front of her house.

"I did too."

"I'd like to see you again."

"I would like that."

He walked her to the door. She stood alluringly near in the dark shadows as she fumbled in her purse for the house key. Mike put his arm around her waist drawing her breathlessly close. She looked up expectantly. The silvery moon cast its lover's magic on Mike, and he leaned down touching her lips ever so lightly with his.

"I will call you," he whispered.

CHAPTER 6

Handyman Special

I t was mid-October—the days when trees start getting sad for no reason. The leaves were raked and bagged, and the lawnmower was emptied and parked in the garage. Mike leaned against the railing on the deck of his parents' home resting his coffee mug on his outstretched legs.

"I saw a house for sale on my way to the job site this morning," Mike commented to Rick and Irene. "It's listed as a 'handyman special' and the price is right."

"Buy it. Fix it. Sell it?" his dad asked.

"No, Dad. Buy it, fix it, keep it."

"Did you think this through?" His voice had the all-too-familiar, sharp sound of criticism.

Mike forced a smile. "Yeah, Dad. I thought this thing through."

"Do you have enough money saved for the down payment?"

"I've got enough."

"Oh, Mike," Irene fretted. "It seems so quick. Are you sure?"

"Mom, it's not like I'm moving out tomorrow! I'm almost twenty-one. I need to be out on my own."

"But with your job, and if you get this house, how will you have time for—?"

Mike grinned. "You mean Lisa? I'll make time. Don't you worry."

Rick looked skeptical. "It might work."

"Richard, you don't need to encourage him—"

"Why not? He's a hard worker. Plus, he's got my business drive." His tone morphed to that of a man who was bordering proud. He turned to Mike. "What's the house like?"

"It's a four-bedroom, two-bath, with a picket fence. That's for your benefit." Mike winked at his mother. "It's got a detached three-car garage."

Rick nodded.

"Well, it does sound interesting," Irene said.

Mike leaned over and gave his mother a quick kiss on the cheek. "I knew you'd come around. I'm meeting the realtor Saturday at 10:30 a.m. He said he's got a 9:00 o'clock showing."

"Well, I guess it's settled then," Irene conceded.

"Besides, I have to start thinking about the future."

"What does that mean?" Irene raised her eyebrows.

"I'm getting pretty serious with Lisa, and I'm just thinking ahead."

"Don't be in a hurry to climb fool's hill," Rick warned.

"It won't be for a couple of years—"

"Does Lisa feel the same?"

"Mom. Neither of us is dating anyone else. That should tell you something."

***

Mike pulled up in front of a once-proud, white colonial house—a house that time forgot. Eight pillars stood on the wrap-around porch as though the changing of the guards had just taken place, and yet, the chandelier in the entryway hung in shame at the array of junk piled high all around.

A shepherd's hook with two baskets of faded plastic flowers leaned precariously as though bowing to the mailbox that drooped over the picket fence. One hinge of the fence gate had broken off, leaving the gate loose and looking like a bird's broken wing.

Mike drummed his fingers on the steering wheel as he surveyed what most people would probably have considered a lost cause. A saying he once heard snapped to life in his mind. 'If you believe you can do something, you're probably right. So is the man who believes he can't.'

He sprang from the truck and jogged up the narrow, cracked sidewalk nearly obscured by tall weeds and wild flowers huddled together like long-lost cousins at a family funeral.

A thin man with dark wiry hair and John Lennon glasses opened the door. "Hello. My name's Ben Wright, realtor," he said nodding toward his name plate that dangled beneath the For Sale sign.

"I'm Mike." They shook hands.

The realtor's handshake was wimpy, at best.

"I just want you to be aware, my 9 a.m. show made an offer. I haven't presented it to the owners yet, but they'd be crazy not to accept any offer." He uttered a short, dry laugh.

Mike nodded.

"I can show you the house, if you want."

"Yeah, I'd like to see it."

The man sounded monotone as he described the house—as though he was reading the ad for the hundredth time. They walked through the living room furnished with a blue faded couch and a lone table with a lamp. Light flowing from the heavily fringed lampshade cast a soft yellow glow on the dull hardwood floor. The focal point, a red brick fireplace framed by shelves on each side, drew Mike's eye. He could almost smell glowing embers left by a roaring fire.

"How's the construction?"

"Solid." He picked up enthusiasm, and his words began to flow like water from a cleft rock. "It was built in 1940, has 2,300 square feet, and sits on a 1.5 acre lot. The basement is dry—never had any water in it. Windows are good. The kitchen needs a makeover, but—" He shrugged. "A plus is a four-seasoned porch facing south."

Mike nodded as they climbed the central stairway leading to the bedroom area.

"The bedrooms are pretty good sized. You married?"

"No."

"Seems like a lot of house for someone young as yourself and not married." He gave a rubbery smile.

"Someday," Mike said scanning the ceilings for water stains. A small yellow stain had crept onto the ceiling where the chimney was housed in one of two walk-in closets of the master bedroom. "Must be the flashing around the chimney."

"Could be."

"I'd like to check the basement and a few other things, if you don't mind."

"Go ahead. I'll be in the kitchen if you have any questions."

Mike walked into each bedroom, checking for squeaky floors. All the bedrooms were empty except the smallest one. A simple antique desk with a drawer in the middle and four drawers on the right side sat beneath a window with dingy curtains. A tiny bundle of correspondence neatly tied with a pink ribbon sat on one corner of the desk. An old straight-back chair with a tooled leather seat was turned out as though the former owner had just stepped out and intended to return shortly. A rocking chair sat in one corner of the room.

Mike walked over to the desk. He stared at the bundle of letters. The handwriting on the top envelope looked like a woman's script. It was addressed "To my dear child."

He reached for the stack of letters. But, suddenly, they felt sacred. Forbidden. He immediately withdrew his hand and wiped it down his pant leg. *What?!*

He pulled the curtains back and looked out to a spacious backyard. Other than a red wagon with a missing wheel and a weathered, wood play gym, the yard was empty.

Had it not been for the alley with its hollyhocks on the civilized side, the meadow beyond would surely have crept into the yard.

Mike scoured the entire house looking for any signs of structural damage. He checked the garage, the wiring, and the plumbing. With every step he took, he pictured Lisa in each of the rooms—sitting at the vanity applying make-up, hanging curtains in the bedroom, snuggling next to him on the love seat in front of the fireplace.

When satisfied with his inspection, he returned to the kitchen. "I'd like to make an offer."

"It sells 'as is.' I just want you to be aware of that."

"I understand."

"If it doesn't work out for the first party, I'll call you." He looked at Mike skeptically. "You realize you must qualify for a loan—" his voice trailed off.

***

That evening, Mike drove to Lisa's to take her to Macaluso's, a favorite restaurant. *I can't wait to tell her about the house, but what if the other offer is accepted? Maybe I should wait. Besides, she might think it's too early in our relationship to talk about a house. But, I'm too excited not to tell her. I wonder if she likes openness or neighbors right next door. Does she care about meadowlarks? Or flowers?* His thoughts ran together.

He envisioned Lisa wearing blue jeans and a white top kneeling on the grass planting multi-colored petunias along the sidewalk.

Mike took the steps two at a time and knocked his usual three knocks.

Lisa answered the door wearing blue jeans and a white sweater.

"Dé·jà vu!" Mike said slowly

"What?"

Mike shook his head. "Ah, nothing." He kissed her tenderly. "You look beautiful."

"Thanks. I just bought this sweater today."

"I like it."

Once in the truck, Mike said, "I'm curious about something."

Lisa looked at him with raised eyebrows.

"Do you like flowers?"

Lisa laughed, but there was a touch of seriousness in her brown eyes. "Not unless they're delivered. Why?"

"I was just wondering." *So much for flowers along the sidewalk,* he thought.

***

As dawn crept over the horizon the following Monday, Mike jogged his usual five miles. He liked the feel of the cool air in his lungs.

Maple and birch leaves, like copper and gold coins, had lost their grip, and fell to the ground to swirl like she-devils in the street. Dew hung on a cobweb at the bottom of a fire hydrant, each drop sparkling like a jewel in the rising sun. He had to admit, when he ran with Boone, he had never noticed such detail.

He veered off his usual route to go past the house on Meadow View. He grinned to himself, convinced this was the right house to buy.

***

At noon Mike and Karl straddled a plank laid on two sawhorses. Their lunch boxes sat between them.

"We're about done on this job," Karl said surveying their efforts with much satisfaction.

"Hope it sells before winter," Mike said taking a big bite from his sandwich.

"Yeah. Me too. I've got another one in the wing."

"Speaking of a house in the wing—I saw a house and put in an offer over the weekend."

"No kidding. Where's it at?"

"It's on Meadow View. A real fixer-upper. Someone already put in a bid, but if it doesn't work out for them, I have a shot at it." Mike shoved the last bite of sandwich into his mouth.

"I wonder how I missed that one!"

"So, where's our next job, boss?"

Karl stroked his chin. "Not far from here. It'll make a good winter project. In the meantime, we've got a couple of small additions to do."

Karl closed his lunch box, brushed crumbs from his jeans, and said, "Well, let's finish up."

Thursday evening, Mike found a note on the kitchen table. "Mike, at the store. Back about 8 p.m. Supper in fridge. Realtor called. Said he wants you to call him. Love, Mom."

Mike called immediately.

"I've got some great news, Mike. The first party withdrew their offer so if you still want to make your offer—"

"Yeah, I do."

32

"You're going to have to bump it up a few thousand."

"How come?"

"It's lower than the first offer, and the owners don't want to go any lower. Can you swing it?"

"Yeah, I think so." He knew the money would be tight, but if he could borrow $3500 from his dad for the earnest money, it would work.

"I'll draw up the paperwork with your offer. Can we meet tomorrow about noon-ish to sign?"

"I'm working, and I don't like to take off unless it's really necessary."

"No problem. I could swing by your work if that would be OK."

"Sure. I'll be at the house on the southwest corner of Jackson and Cleveland."

"See you then."

***

"OK, DiSanto, you've been grinning all morning like a prophet who's just had a vision. Are you going to tell me what's going on?" Karl readjusted his cap and smiled broadly.

"I got a phone call last night," Mike said rounding up his tools.

"And—" Karl looked at him expectantly.

"And the people who made the offer on the house?"

"Yeah?" Karl nodded.

"They withdrew it. I have to bump my offer a bit, but I think I've got a shot at it."

"You don't say?"

Just then the man with John Lennon glasses pulled up in a beat up, blue Olds Cutlass.

"Think I'll load up my truck," Karl said.

Mike watched with a puzzled look as Karl hurried around the corner of the house.

"Is this a good time?" the realtor asked.

"Good as any."

Ben Wright spread the papers on the opened tailgate of Mike's truck indicating where Mike should sign. "I'll present your offer Monday— the owners are out of town for the weekend."

Mike nodded.

"They have three days to respond so I'll call you next week, and we'll go from there. If they accept your offer, we'll draw up the purchase agreement and set the closing date." He studied Mike. "Closing costs get spendy. You sure you're ready for this?"

Mike nodded. "I'm ready." *The worst thing that could happen is I would have to sell the house. Besides, if we get married, we'll need a place to live and renting an apartment isn't an option,* he reasoned.

The realtor folded up the papers and stuck them in his brief case, shook hands, and left just as Karl came around the corner.

CHAPTER 7

Financial Upset

E arthquakes never occur in Minnesota, but there was one about to shake Mike's financial world.

Mike, his dad, the home owners, the realtor and two gentlemen sat at a long table at the title company.

After congenial introductions, one of the gentlemen asked, "Do you have the check for the earnest money?"

"Yes, I do," Mike answered, pulling an envelope from his shirt pocket and handing it to the man in a grey suit and matching tie.

The man opened the envelope. Instantly, his stare, direct and sharp-edged as though it could cut through granite, focused on Mike. "The earnest money check is for $3,500. It is supposed to be $5,300. You're $1,800 short!"

Mike's cheeks burned as the man spoke. He ran his hand through his hair. There was no denying the irritation from the man and it was up to Mike to remedy the situation. But how?

His dad leaned over and whispered to Mike. "I don't have any more to lend you. Sorry."

Mike nodded. He didn't expect him to. "I'll have to talk to my banker."

"Didn't you check your figures?" The woman spoke in her high pitched voice. "This is unacceptable!"

Mike bounced his knee underneath the table and stared at the figures on the check. *How could I have made this mistake? Why with something so important, would I invert the numbers? Again!*

"Now, dear," her husband began.

"Would it be agreeable to postpone this meeting until Mr. DiSanto can make the necessary arrangements to secure the additional funds?" the realtor intervened.

"Certainly seems an inconvenience—"

"How badly do you want to sell the house, Mrs. Walrod?" the realtor asked. He turned to those at the table. "They've only owned the house a short time and are eager to sell," he said as though to soften her outburst.

"I think a different date would work just fine," her husband said patting his wife's hand with several quick pats.

***

"Come on in, Mike." A tall man with thinning brown hair stood with outstretched hand as Mike entered the glass cubicle of the bank.

"Mr. Summers," Mike greeted, shaking his hand.

"You know, Mike, just because you called me Mr. Summers as a kid, doesn't mean you still have to call me Mr. Summers." His smile was warm and genuine.

"You mean your first name isn't Mister?" Mike laughed.

Mr. Summers laughed as well. "What can I do for you?"

"I need to borrow an additional $1800. I could put my truck up for collateral—"

"If I didn't know you so well, I would hesitate, but I know your character and the extra $1800 should not be a problem. How soon do you need it?"

"Next week."

"I can do better than that. If you can wait a few minutes, I'll have a check cut for you now."

"Thanks, Mr. Summers. I really appreciate it."

***

The following week, the meeting with the same group of people at the title company transpired flawlessly. Papers were signed, checks distributed, keys exchanged, handshakes ensued. Even Mrs. Walrod

36

shook Mike's hand, although she extended only her fingertips. No matter. Mike owned the house with its meager furnishings on Meadow View!

He called Lisa while still in the parking lot. "I've got great news!"

"What?"

"I bought a house! I just came from the closing."

"Oooh, really?"

"Yeah. It needs a lot of work, but—"

"Why didn't you tell me sooner?"

"I didn't know what you'd think and I didn't know if they would accept my offer. I'm moving in as soon as I can and start working on it in my spare time."

"Well, that's good news, I guess."

CHAPTER 8

Winter Project

M ike drove straight to the house after the closing. He parked his truck in front, got out, and stood for several minutes in the cold mist looking at his house. And, he grinned. *If only Lisa were here to share the moment!*

He leaned against his truck and crossed his arms across his chest. Where to begin? With his savings account nearly depleted, how could he buy materials?

He jogged up the sidewalk onto the front porch. He inserted the key. His hand gripped the cold brass doorknob as he opened the door. He stepped into his own house for the first time.

Mike shivered from the chill inside. He turned up the thermostat, but, there was no response. Nothing. He went downstairs to check the lifeless furnace and soon realized it must be the thermostat.

"Welcome to the world of remodeling," he said to himself.

The short jaunt to DiSanto's Hardware proved more expensive than anticipated—a thermostat, cleaning supplies, trash bags, light bulbs and a table saw.

"You can work it off rather than paying it back," his dad said.

Mike installed the thermostat and turned it to 70 degrees. The furnace grumbled to life. "Sweet!"

Just then Karl and Katie stopped by.

"You got company," Karl called out, as he poked his head inside the front door.

"Hey! My first visitors! C'mon in."

"Should we sign a guest book or something?" Karl laughed.

Mike joined in the laughter. "Let me show you around."

The kitchen was the first room on the guided tour.

"Oh dear," Katie said with a frown.

"What? A little paint, a little cleaning. Good to go!" Mike teased, rubbing his hands together.

"Ha! Not if you intend to bring a woman into your kitchen," Katie replied.

"Oh, I intend to bring a woman into the kitchen, all right. Everything I do is with her in mind. This kitchen has to be the ultimate kitchen."

"Where she, whoever that may be, will create fabulous dishes for you, no doubt?" She shot a side glance at Mike. She pulled out a tape measure and notebook. "Poor Karl. I remember when we first got married. He had never eaten so much burned toast and biscuits in his life."

"I happen to like food that's dark," Karl said and smiled at her.

"It didn't matter what I burned, Karl would just smile and compliment me. He never complained."

Mike nodded.

Katie looked up from her notebook. "That certain woman you intend to bring into the kitchen wouldn't happen to be Lisa, would it?"

Mike grinned. "'Nough said. Let me show you two around."

"Karl's already seen it, and I'd like to spend some time in the kitchen."

Karl got one of those deer-in-the-headlights look. "What she means is that most of these older houses look pretty much the same. Isn't that right, honey?"

"Oh, yes, of course." Her cheeks flushed. "You know the old saying, 'You've seen one house, you've seen 'em all.'"

Mike was not quite sure if he bought her explanation, but before he could pursue the matter, Karl said, "I'd like to look around with you, Mike."

As the two men walked from room to room, Karl said, "I've got a proposition for you. I'll help you a couple days a week and we'll work on my winter project the other three days." He leaned against a bedroom doorway.

"What's your winter project anyway? You never did tell me."

"Well, remember when I first hired you and I told you I wanted to redo our house?"

"Yeah, I remember." He looked quizzically at this man he had come to love and respect. "That's your winter project?"

"I can't think of a better time to do it than now with business slowing down the way it is. I'll still pay for the time you work."

"I can't accept money to work on your own house."

"Sure you can. I've set aside money for wages to redo my house no matter who would work on it, and I can't think of a better worker than you. So what do you say? Is it a deal?"

Mike shifted his stance. "Pretty generous offer, Karl."

"Think of it as an investment," Karl continued. "It's a win-win situation."

"How so?"

"You get your house fixed up—I get my house redone—and neither of us has to look for work for the winter." Karl smiled broadly.

"You drive a hard bargain," Mike said stretching out his hand.

Karl clasped it with a vigorous handshake.

CHAPTER 9

The Jewelry Box

Mike had a plan—a two-part plan.

He would take the diamonds from the wedding set his grandmother had given him. "When you meet that certain someone, take the diamonds" she had said a month before she died, "and have a new wedding ring made that would be perfect for your bride." That was two years ago.

And, he would make a jewelry box for Lisa and give it to her for Christmas. This would be no ordinary jewelry box, but one with a secret compartment where he would put the diamond ring.

Mike took his grandmother's wedding set and headed down to Gephart's Jewelers. "I'd like you to put these diamonds into a different setting," he said to the male designer, who wore massive rings on several fingers of both hands.

The man put a thick eyepiece to his eye and examined the old ring set. "These diamonds are very high quality. Did you have anything in particular in mind? If not, we could look at some designs in our catalog."

Mike nodded as the jeweler flipped open a colorful booklet and laid it on the glass counter.

Almost immediately, Mike found the perfect ring for Lisa.

"Excellent choice," the jeweler said.

The price was more than he anticipated, but Mike was able to put it on three interest-free monthly payments.

"It'll be ready in a week."

Next, Mike headed over to Karl's.

"Do you mind if I pick through some of your scrap wood? I want to make a something for Lisa for Christmas."

"Help yourself. I'm glad to get rid these scraps. In fact, take the whole bin," Karl said. "You'd be doing me a favor."

Mike loaded the bin of different woods into his truck. He set up shop in the basement of his house and picked through the scraps.

He found a piece of oak, and one of mahogany with which he would inlay a heart on the top. He would line the drawers with black velvet and put tiny drawer pulls on each drawer with an upper part to hang necklaces.

He promptly set to work; measuring, cutting, and assembling, saving the inlaid heart until last. He liked the natural look of the wood and decided not to stain it. Instead, he would seal it and varnish it.

***

The following week, Mike swung by the jewelers.

The designer pulled out a ring box.

Mike leaned closer as the jeweler slowly opened the box. He gave a low whistle. A grin spread over his entire face as he took the box from the jeweler. He turned the exquisitely transformed ring set in all directions to capture its luminescence.

"She's a beauty, wouldn't you say?" The jeweler puffed his chest in pride.

"Excellent!"

CHAPTER 10

Christmas Eve

S tark branches of an ash tree scratched against the window in obedience to the cold north wind. But a glow of warmth spread itself inside the Barrett house on Christmas Eve.

A handful of aunts and uncles with their children, Bruce, Betty, Mike and Lisa gathered in a loosely knit circle around the lavishly decorated Christmas tree.

"Betty, you outdid yourself with that fabulous turkey dinner," one aunt tried to say above the loud chatter from excited children eager to open presents.

Bruce handed out the gifts. Instantly, the rustle of paper and squeals of delight filled the room. Amidst the ruckus, Mike slipped out into the cold, dark night to his truck to retrieve his gift for Lisa.

He quietly took his place next to her, sitting on the floor. She handed him a small gift box wrapped in red paper with a gold bow. "Merry Christmas," Lisa said with a smile.

Mike unwrapped the box. Inside the box he found a rugged, water-resistant watch with a black dial and black leather band. "Wow! Thanks, sweetheart. I really needed a new watch!" He kissed her and slipped his new watch on.

"You're very welcome."

Mike handed his gift to Lisa.

She tore it open. When she lifted the beautiful jewelry box out, her smile drooped like that of someone opening a treasure chest and finding it empty. She stared at Mike with a look that said, "That's it?"

Suddenly the room became quiet and all eyes focused on Lisa.

"Look inside," Mike coaxed.

She pulled open the drawers and the doors to the necklace compartment. She looked blankly at Mike.

"Look some more."

This time she examined the drawers more closely and discovered the hidden compartment with a small box inside. She retrieved the box and opened it. She gasped and caught her breath. Her hands began to shake.

Mike took the ring, got up on one knee, and looked into her eyes. "Lisa, I love you. Will you marry me?"

She nodded. He placed the ring on her finger and kissed her to an eruption of cheers and exclamations.

"I love it," she cried, wiggling her fingers up and down. "I can't wait to show it to Rachel!"

A barrage of women scrambled to see her diamond ring and to give both of them hugs and congratulations.

Bruce shook Mike's hand. "When you asked us for our blessings to marry our daughter, I said yes then, and I say it publicly now, you have our blessings." And with that, he gave Lisa a hug.

"You knew?" she asked.

Bruce nodded. "Mike asked us a week ago for permission to marry you."

Betty hugged Lisa. She hugged Mike. She wept.

Going to church was not a priority for either Mike or Lisa. However, the engaged couple did attend the 11 p.m. church service for their first and only time. A soft, magical snowfall had begun, giving the dirty snow-covered land a look of purity.

The minister read from Luke 2, "And there were shepherds living out in the fields nearby, keeping watch over their flocks at night. An angel of the Lord appeared to them, and the glory of the Lord shone around them and they were terrified. But the angel said to them, 'Do not be afraid. I bring you good news of great joy that will be for all the people. Today in the town of David a Savior has been born to you; He is Christ the Lord.'"

Lisa sat in the soft glow of candlelight admiring her diamond ring. Mike sat next to her thinking about the house. *Finally, the house will be ours!* He thought about their future and how perfect everything would be.

And the people sang "O Holy Night."

CHAPTER 11

The Letters

T he house on Meadow View that would soon become Mike and
Lisa's was far from finished, but it was warm and dry, and
living there gave Mike the extra time needed to work on it.

It was late when he finished hanging the last kitchen cabinet. That's
when he heard the howling wind outside. He turned on the TV to get
the weather.

The weatherman had just issued a blizzard warning with an arctic
blast of cold. "This storm is predicted to dump two feet or more of snow
with forty-mile-an-hour winds causing drifts and impossible driving
conditions. Temperatures are expected to hover around zero. Extreme
caution should—"

Mike shut the TV off and looked out his back door. He sucked in
his breath when he saw the garage completely obscured by a whirlwind
of snow.

Mike climbed the stairs to his bedroom weary, but content. As
he walked past the smallest bedroom, he flipped on the light. After
the downstairs is completed, this room is the one he is most eager to
finish—the room that seemed to call to him.

He walked over to the desk. The small stack of correspondence
tied with a pink ribbon remained on the corner of the desk, untouched.
He remembered how the letters had seemed forbidden and caused him
to recoil his hand the first time he noticed them. He sat down on the
squeaky desk chair still turned out. He stared at the letters for a moment.

He reached for the bundle fully expecting the eerie sensation to erupt again.

But, there was no strange feeling. This time, he felt curious. *Who would write letters and leave them on a desk? Were the letters meant for the owner of the house and not for a stranger just passing through? Why was there no address, just the words, "To My Child?" Why only seven letters?* He wondered.

He untied the pink ribbon and let it fall to the desk top. Without moving the stack, he took the top letter and studied the handwriting. *Definitely a woman's handwriting.*

He turned the letter over, slipped his finger under the flap, and pulled out a yellowed piece of stationary. He read:

> *My sweet baby girl,*
>
> *The day you were born, I promised I would write you a letter every year on your birthday telling you how much you are loved and the great joy you bring to our home. Today is your first birthday.*
>
> *This past year, I marveled at your contagious smile, the way you giggle, and the soft whispers of your breathing when you sleep. I would cradle you in my arms and rock you, singing softly so not to wake you.*
>
> *I was delighted when you took your first two steps before plopping down onto the floor. I laughed and coaxed you to come to me. And, you did.*
>
> *I cannot imagine what life would be like without you. You are truly a priceless gift from God, and I will do everything in my power to teach you about His love.*
>
> *Happy first birthday, sweet one.*
>
> *Love, Mama*

Mike carefully folded the letter and placed it back in its envelope. He looked at the rocking chair in the corner and wondered if that was the same rocking chair that the unknown mother had rocked her child.

He took out the second letter also written on yellowed stationary.

To the joy of my life,

This past year has gone by so quickly, and you are learning so many new things. I love to play hide 'n' seek with you, although I don't think you know to be quiet when you are hiding. If I don't find you right away, you call, "Mama, I here." Of course, I have to pretend to be surprised to find you hiding under a pillow with your feet sticking out.

You are learning to fold your hands when we say prayers, but I know you wonder why you should do such a thing. Someday, you will understand.

Happy second birthday, precious girl.

Love, Mama

Mike took the third letter and read the tender words of a mother to her child.

My little snuggle bug,

I love the way you snuggle on my lap when we read books. Your favorite book is "Poky Little Puppy." You know all the animals, numbers, and colors—even mauve, although you call it "muff."

My heart breaks when I hear you cry because you skinned your knee, but I know, and you will learn, that you must go through these times, too. You will discover that crying may tarry for the night, but then joy comes in the morning.

Happy third birthday, joy of my life.

Love, Mama

Mike settled more comfortably in the chair, leaning back rather than hunched over the desk and opened the fourth letter.

My precious princess,

Today, we went for a walk. We met a lady walking with a cane. You said, "Are you a queen with a magic walking wand?" She seemed to stand a little taller and said, "Why, yes, I am. And who might you be?" You replied, "I am a princess 'cause my mama always calls me that." You really are a princess and some day you will live in a real kingdom.

Happy fourth birthday, princess.

Love, Mama

Mike glanced at his watch. Although it was getting late, he did not hurry in reading the letters. He knew he would not be going to work tomorrow because of the blizzard. He was glad to have the time to work on the house and he assumed Karl would be working at his house, at least for the next day or two.

He carefully opened the fifth letter and smiled.

My rosebud,

Today, you got a tea party set of dishes with pink rosebuds all around each plate. You were so excited to serve your first tea. We dressed up with hats and necklaces and even real lipstick for the tea. You poured my "tea" in such a proper way that I smiled even bigger than I did when I watched you open your tea party set. We each got two cookies—chocolate ones with white filling in the middle. We talked in proper language, pretending to be aristocrats. You learned that word from a movie we watched. Remember? You truly have a servant's heart.

Happy fifth birthday, my little Martha.

Love, Mama

Mike wondered what it would be like to have a little daughter or a son. "I hope I'm a good dad," he said aloud and opened the sixth letter.

My little tinker bell,

You lost your two bottom teeth and one is loose on top. You are so excited to go to school to see if other children lost their front teeth. Your teacher told me how you are her little helper, and how she likes your giggle. I love that about you, too.

You are learning to print so well, and you have so much fun discovering who you are. You have such innocence about you, and that makes me want to protect you all the more. But, I can only teach you and love you the best I am able to do. You will always be my little tinker bell.

Happy sixth birthday, sweetness.

Love, Mama

Mike was a little disappointed that he was about to read the last letter. This letter had a pencil sketch. He stared at a sketch of a young girl putting on her dancing shoes.

My daughter, Faith,

Your name fits you so well. Even when you were a baby, I knew you would be a picture of what your name stands for. My heart grieves deeply since you left just a week before your seventh birthday. The school bus accident—I close my eyes to block out the image. Oh, how I wish I could have been with you to protect you. And yet, at the same time, I feel a strange joy because I know you learned to pray, believing. You don't cry anymore because all your tears are wiped away. You really are a princess in a real kingdom now, just like you and I believed you would be some day. And, I know you will sing and dance for the King.

I cannot bear to stay in this house any longer, my daughter. I sold everything except the desk where I sat to write the letters to you, and the rocking chair where I cradled you next to my heart and sang to you. I must leave quickly for I cannot bear this grief. I will see you again. Rejoice!

Happy seventh birthday, Faith.

Love, Mama

Mike laid the letter on the desk and noticed for the first time the small round water stains on the yellowed stationary. He swallowed hard, but the lump in his throat stuck.

He retied the bundle of letters. He stepped out of the room and closed the door behind him.

CHAPTER 12

The Wedding

Winter months plodded wearily into spring, spring dawdled into summer, summer stumbled into autumn, and autumn trudged back into winter. The cycle started all over again until their June wedding day finally arrived. Purple clouds edged in gold stretched along the eastern horizon. The fragrance of lilacs permeated the warm air that filtered into Mike's bedroom as mourning doves cooed from the electrical wires out back.

He called his bride. "Hi, sweetheart. I just wanted to say good morning over the phone for the last time."

"That is so nice," Lisa said sleepily.

"I hope your day goes good. I love you and I'll see you at 4 p.m."

"Hmm-hum. Me, too."

***

The crowded Chapel on the Hill carried an unpretentious intimacy for the 120 guests. White satin bows interspersed with purple ones decorated the rows of chairs. Colorful stained glass windows quietly relinquished their own splendid beauty to the bride and the groom.

Mike watched anxiously as Rachel, Lisa's maid of honor, escorted by Ryan, his best man, proceed down the aisle as the guitarist sang, 'Forever and Ever. Amen.'

The ushers unrolled the white aisle runner. People stood to their feet, craning their necks toward the double doors at the back of the chapel. The doors opened and there stood Lisa with her father. The guitarist sang the last verse. "I'm gonna love you forever and ever. Forever and ever. Amen."

Mike's heart nearly burst as Lisa and her father walked down the aisle. Lisa looked stunning in her white satin wedding gown with lace and pearl beads. The allusion to innocence teasingly obscured beneath her shimmering veil took Mike's breath away.

Lisa's father carefully lifted her veil revealing her short blond hair, brown eyes with pencil-thin dark eyebrows, and her flawless ivory skin. He kissed her softly on her cheek, bowed slightly, and gave her hand to Mike.

Mike barely breathed as he gazed at his beautiful bride. He offered her his arm and side by side, the bridal couple walked up the four steps to stand before the minister.

The minister spoke a few words from 1 Corinthians 13, "Love is patient, love is kind. It does not envy, it does not boast, it is not proud. It is not rude, it is not self-seeking, it is not easily angered, it keeps no record of wrongs. Love does not delight in evil but rejoices with the truth. It always protects, always trusts, always hopes, always perseveres. Love never fails." He looked at the bridal couple and continued, "Love covers a multitude of mistakes and is the most important element in any relationship, but especially in marriage. Remember, it takes love. Love. Love. Love."

They exchanged wedding vows, promising to love and to cherish one another until death. Mike placed his diamond-studded symbol of love on her slender finger and Lisa, in turn, slipped a plain gold wedding band on Mike's finger while repeating the vows of marriage.

The guitarist sang "Always" as Mike and Lisa presented a long-stem red rose to each of their mothers.

The couple faced their guests as the minister said, "I present to you Mr. and Mrs. Mike DiSanto. You may kiss the bride," the minister directed.

And Mike did kiss Lisa to the applause of everyone in the chapel.

Rita Kroon

As the chapel bell bonged, Mike and Lisa exited to the cobblestone courtyard to receive their guests.

Mike and Lisa were showered with hugs, "Congratulations!" and "Best wishes!" before heading to the country club for their first meal as a married couple.

***

The wedding reception at the Royal Oaks Country Club rang with merriment, good food, and great music until the ribbons of dark shadows and splashes of moonlight flooded the country club grounds.

"Our house awaits us, m'lady," Mike said with an exaggerated bow, and held the car door open for her.

"Yes, our beautiful house!" she said and took his hand.

CHAPTER 13

After the Wedding

***

A few days after their wedding, Lisa stood at the kitchen counter of their home. She grunted and sighed.

"Would you like some help?" Mike asked.

"No. I feel stifled with you in the kitchen hovering over me."

"I didn't realize I hovered over you—"

"Well, you don't really hover." She seemed to search for words. "It's just that I don't know how to cook."

"That's OK, sweetheart. We could work together—"

"I get too nervous with someone watching me. I'd rather work alone."

***

One morning, late in summer the following year, Mike returned from his daily run to find Lisa coming out of the bathroom still wearing her robe.

"What's wrong, sweetheart? You don't look like you feel good."

"I don't. I think I have the flu. I'm not going to work."

"Do you want me to stay home?"

Lisa shook her head.

***

"Lisa's got the flu," Mike told Karl. "I'm going to call her at break and see how she's doing."

Karl nodded.

"That's strange," Mike said after hanging up the phone.

"What's strange?"

"I called home and Lisa didn't answer, so I called her work. She was there and said she started feeling better, had some toast and went to work. How could anybody get better that fast?"

"Maybe it's not the flu." Karl had a twinkle in his eye.

"What do you mean?"

"Maybe it's morning sickness."

Mike stared at Karl.

***

The following week, Lisa bought a pregnancy test on her way home from work. The next morning, she said, "There are two lines on the test strip."

Mike's eyes met Lisa's. "What does that mean?"

"It means I'm pregnant."

Mike broke out in a huge grin. "Sweetheart, that's great!" He hugged her for a moment before she disengaged herself from his arms.

"You are happy, aren't you?" he asked.

Lisa shrugged.

"Maybe it's because you don't feel well."

"No. It's not that."

"What is it then?"

"I want an abortion."

"What?"

"I want an abortion!"

Mike felt his heart thud. "You can't be serious!"

"I'm very serious. I don't want to be pregnant."

Mike stared wide-eyed at Lisa. "I don't know what to say." He shook his head. He turned away from her, then turned back. "No. You can't do this."

"It's my choice."

56

"No. It's not only your choice. I have a say I this."

"I don't want this baby!"

Mike felt like a lead ball had lodged in his gut. "Lisa! What are you saying?"

She looked directly at him. "I do NOT want to be pregnant. I do NOT want this baby. I am getting an abortion. What's so hard to understand?"

"I won't agree to it."

Lisa stared at him.

"Are you afraid of having a baby?" he asked.

"No."

"Then, what—"

"I don't want a kid. That's all."

"Just because you don't want a baby, doesn't mean you can—" He swallowed hard—"kill it."

"You make it sound like murder."

"Well?"

"It's not even a baby yet."

"Really, Lisa? Are you listening to yourself? You just said you don't want this baby. Now you say it's not a baby!"

She glared at him.

"I'm telling you, if you get this abortion, we are through!"

"Big threat!"

"It's not a threat. It's reality!" He shifted his stance.

She pushed her hair behind her ear and raised her chin.

***

Two days later at mid-morning, Mike's cell phone rang.

"H'lo."

"Mike? This is Rene' at Freedom Travel. Lisa didn't show up for work this morning and she hasn't called in—"

The color drained from his face. "Did you try her at home?"

"Yes, but there was no answer. I hate to bother you, but I'm concerned."

Mike's heart raced. "I'll check it out. Thanks for calling." He sat down—visibly shaken.

Karl rushed over to him. "What's wrong? You look like you're about ready to pass out!"

Mike drew in a deep breath. "I think Lisa might be having an abortion."

"What?"

"I'm going home to see if she's there."

"I'm coming with you."

Mike didn't argue.

They locked the house they were working on and left in Mike's truck.

As they raced to Mike's house, he told Karl about the conversation he had with Lisa.

Karl sat in stunned disbelief. He closed his eyes and bowed his head. Only his lips moved.

Mike pulled up to his house. He opened the garage door. Lisa's car was not there. He turned to Karl. "Where would she go for an abortion?"

Karl shook his head. "I, I don't know. Maybe—"

Just then, Mike's phone rang.

"H'lo."

"Is this Mike DiSanto?"

"Yes." He jerked his eyes to Karl.

"This is the Camden Medical Center. Your wife is—"

"Did she have an abortion?" His throat was tight and his voice strained.

"That's the reason we are calling. She is here, but—"

"Did she have the abortion?" He yelled.

"No, Mr. DiSanto."

Mike shook his head at Karl.

"Your wife claims you are in agreement with this procedure, but, since you have a $5000 deductible, and you are the responsible party on your insurance, we need your signature.

"No. I am NOT in agreement with the abortion and I will not sign."

"Your wife is very insistent that she have the procedure, but unless you sign that you take responsibility for any money not paid by your insurance, we cannot proceed."

"I won't sign." His tone was stern.

"Very well. We'll make a note of that."

Mike hung up. "What am I going to do?"

Karl shook his head slowly and shrugged. "I don't have a clue. How about if Katie and I come over after supper. Maybe we can talk to Lisa."

Mike nodded. "I can't work, Karl."

"I wouldn't expect you to, son."

"Thanks for understanding. I'll give you a ride back to the job site and then I'm going home."

"We'll see you tonight."

***

When Mike returned home, he found Lisa curled up on the couch—waiting.

They stared at one another.

"You're a jerk, you know that?" she snapped.

"I told you how I feel about the abortion, and if I'm a jerk for not signing, then I'm a jerk." His jaw muscles twitched. He shook his head. "I don't understand you."

Lisa shrugged and looked away.

He thought about telling her that Karl and Katie were stopping over, but changed his mind.

***

At 7 p.m., the doorbell rang. Mike answered.

"C'mon in," he said to Karl and Katie.

Katie hugged Mike. Her eyes were red and swollen.

"Lisa locked herself in our bedroom," Mike said quietly.

"Would it be OK if I go talk to her?" she asked.

Mike nodded. He motioned for Karl to sit in the easy chair as he sat on the loveseat—in silence.

Almost two hours later, Katie came down the stairs followed by a subdued Lisa. They sat on the couch.

"I think I understand Lisa's motive for wanting an abortion."

59

Mike and Karl looked expectantly at Katie, but said nothing. Lisa stared at the floor.

"She says the main thing is the hurt she experienced when her birth mother placed her and her sister in an orphanage. Lisa says she felt rejected and doesn't think anyone should be subjected to a world that abandons its own." She glanced at Lisa and continued. "She also has a great fear of being responsible for a baby."

"But, I would help her," Mike said.

"I know you would, but Lisa says she feels totally inadequate. She says she's not sure she will love the baby, and, I think having morning sickness just pushed her over the emotional edge." She put her hand on Lisa's forearm and gave a gentle squeeze. "She's overwhelmed right now."

Mike got up and sat next to Lisa and put his arm on the back of the couch. "I'll try to do whatever I can to help," he said softy.

Lisa nodded, but never took her eyes off the floor.

"I told Lisa that I would come over more often while she's pregnant," Katie said, "And when the baby is born, I hope between her mother and me coming on a regular basis, Lisa will soon feel comfortable taking care of the baby."

Katie stood up. "I think a wonderful therapy would be to fix up the baby's room—fun things in anticipation of the birth." She glanced at Mike. "What do you think, Lisa?"

Lisa looked up for the first time. She sighed deeply. "OK, I guess."

After Karl and Katie left, Lisa said, "I don't want to talk about this anymore." She got up and retreated to their bedroom.

Mike sat quietly on the couch. *How could she not want our baby? Why would she want an abortion? What if she decides to get the abortion in a couple of days or next week? How can I trust her? Is she cold and calculating or really just overwhelmed?*

CHAPTER 14

The Baby

Although Lisa's morning sickness continued for three months, she did not mention an abortion again. They had passed the crises when Lisa threatened to abort their baby, and yet, their relationship continued to hang in a delicate balance—somewhere between anticipation for the future and dread of tipping the scale to disaster.

Mike asked Lisa, "Do you want to go shopping for things to fix up the baby's room?"

Lisa wasn't enthused, but agreed to go. They picked out Winnie the Pooh decals with Piglet, Tigger, Rabbit and Eeyore. Lisa found small Winnie the Pooh and Tigger stuffed animals that she put on a corner shelf above the crib. Mike painted the rocking chair white to match the crib and dresser and got a light green cushion for the rocker.

"Should we move the desk to a different room?" Mike asked.

"Yes. It's old. What are you going to do with those letters?" She asked.

"Keep 'em."

"What for?"

"I don't know. It just seems the right thing to do," he said as he picked up the bundle of letters tied with a pink ribbon. "I've been thinking of names for the baby," he said as he placed the small bundle of letters in the desk drawer. Have you?"

"No," she answered, adjusting the stuffed animals on the shelf.

"I was thinking Madison for a girl," Mike said.

"What if it's a boy?"

"Jacob. Jake for short. What do you think?"

"What do we call Madison for short?" she asked.

"Probably Maddy."

"I like Madison."

***

Mike was in the delivery room with Lisa when Madison Marie DiSanto was born one month before they celebrated their two-year anniversary. Mike's heart burst with love at the sound of her first tiny cries.

The nurse wrapped the baby in a pink blanket and gently laid her in Lisa's arms. Mike and Lisa unwrapped the blanket from her tiny body to count her fingers and toes.

"God blessed you with a beautiful daughter," the nurse said.

Lisa looked at Mike. "She's got your dark hair."

Mike could not speak. He gazed from Madison to Lisa and back to Madison again.

"Do you want to hold her?"

Mike held out his arms, like one holds their arms when carrying a load of fire wood.

Lisa placed Madison in his arms. It felt awkward at first. His arms felt stiff as he held his daughter, his little princess.

"Let her rest on your arm and put your other arm over her," the nurse prodded.

Mike got the hang of it almost immediately. It felt like the most natural thing in the world. He beamed as he cradled his squirming daughter. A sense of amazement overtook him as Madison opened her mouth making squeaky noises in search of food.

"She's so helpless," he whispered in awe.

Much too soon he heard the nurse say, "I'm going to bathe your little one, and the doctor needs to check her over."

Mike reluctantly allowed the nurse to take the baby.

"I'll bring her back shortly."

Mike sat close to Lisa on her bed. Gently, he put his arm around her shoulders as the doctor tended to her after-birthing necessities. "You did great, sweetheart." He kissed the top of her head.

Lisa looked up at him, her nose dotted with perspiration.

"Smile, sweetheart. You just gave birth to our beautiful daughter. She looks just like you—except for her dark hair."

"I need a day at the spa."

He grinned. "You deserve it."

He heard the nurses' muffled laughter.

CHAPTER 15

Trouble Brews

few of weeks after Madison was born, Mike sat at the kitchen table balancing the checkbook. He sat in silence for a long time.

Lisa sat opposite him, thumbing through Macy's catalog.

He rechecked his figures again and again making sure he had not inverted any numbers. He put the calculator aside. "Lisa, now that you're not working anymore, you've got to cut down on spending. We're getting deeper and deeper in the hole."

Lisa closed the catalog and looked directly at Mike. "Are you saying you want me to go back to work?"

"No, I'm not saying that."

"Are you telling me that I can't get my hair done or I'm not supposed to get manicures?" Lisa's eyes flashed.

"I'm not telling you can't. I'm saying you have to cut down on spending—way down. Shopping. Getting your hair—"

"Oh, now you're telling me I can't go shopping, either?"

Mike's jaw muscles twitched. "Sweetheart," he said in a controlled tone. "I didn't say that."

"Oh? What exactly did you say?"

"I said you have to cut down."

"What do you mean 'cut down'?"

"Keep it under $100—"

"You're being unrealistic."

They stared at each other with animosity hovering between them.

Just then, Madison woke up, crying.

Lisa glared at Mike, grabbed a bottle of formula from the refrigerator, smacked it down on the counter, and huffed out of the kitchen.

Mike crumpled up the paper with his figures and threw it into the waste basket. As he was about to tie the trash bag shut to take it out to the garbage can, he noticed an unopened credit card statement. He took it out and sat down at the table just as Lisa reappeared carrying a fussing Madison. He held up the envelope. "What is this?"

She stared at him with unflinching eyes.

"We can't just throw bills away. We have to pay them, in case you didn't know!"

"You always rant about paying bills and I'm sick of it!" She grabbed the bottle of formula and turned to go into the living room.

Mike drew in a deep breath. "I'll feed Maddy," he offered.

She handed Maddy to Mike and huffed upstairs.

Mike held Maddy—loving the feeling of holding his daughter. But then he began to think about Lisa. *If only she didn't spend so much. Am I being too unreasonable? I don't think so. Where do I draw the line? Why does money cause so much trouble in our lives? Why is it such a big deal? But if spending money is what makes Lisa happy, where does that leave us? Our marriage? Our family? What about Maddy? I hate what all this fighting and arguing does to our family.*

***

For the next two years, Lisa's spending spiraled out of control forcing a constant financial struggle. Tension and arguing became the norm. Mike worked extra hours at the hardware store in addition to working with Karl. But there was no peace.

It seemed the more Mike stressed cutting back on spending, the more Lisa spent. They sought counseling, but after several sessions, nothing could be resolved.

They would put on their masks when out in public or at family gatherings, but in private, they left their masks of all-is-well at the door.

The inevitable happened. After four years of marriage, their dysfunctional family, a man, his wife, and their two-year-old daughter, shattered into splinters.

CHAPTER 16

After the Divorce

One day late in fall, a little over two years after the divorce, Mike called Karl on one of his off weekends. He referred to those times when he did not get to see Maddy as off weekends because everything seemed off then.

"Karl, do you mind if I stop over before I go to the hardware store? I'd like to talk to you."

"C'mon over. I'll put the coffee back on and ask Katie to cook some breakfast."

Mike drove the short distance to Karl's house. *I should've seen this coming before we even got married. All her new clothes. Always wanting to go to fancy restaurants. All her spa appointments. And now, never any time for Maddy. What was I thinking?*

Katie had a pan of bacon frying and the griddle heating for blueberry pancakes when Mike arrived.

Mike joined Karl at the table

"I don't even know where to start."

"Well, why don't you start by telling me what's bothering you the most."

"The fact that almost every time I call Maddy to say goodnight, a different sitter answers the phone, for one thing. That and all the money I have to pay Lisa. I'm glad to pay for Maddy's child support. Don't get me wrong. But, I resent the fact that Lisa spends the money for other things."

"Do you know that for certain?"

"Karl, I saw her driving a brand new Ford Taurus, and Ryan told me she just had the whole front yard re-landscaped."

Karl nodded slowly. "Fret not yourself, Mike, it tends only to evil."

Mike looked questioningly at his strange words.

"Someday you'll understand."

"Easy for you to say." He ran his hand along his jaw. "And, every time I pick up Maddy for the weekend, she either doesn't have shoes, or her clothes are too small or she doesn't have a jacket. When I ask why Maddy doesn't have shoes or clothes or whatever, I get the same answer. 'I forgot to pack them' or 'I was running late and didn't have time.' Who knows what she's feeding Maddy? It's like Lisa is incapable of taking care of Maddy and it's tearing me apart."

Karl looked at Mike with genuine concern.

"I end up buying Maddy what she needs. I don't mind, but what am I paying Lisa $400 a month for?"

Karl shifted in his chair. "I feel terrible to hear this. I can imagine how you must feel."

Mike barely touched his food, although blueberry pancakes was one of his favorite breakfasts. Instead, he paced back and forth from the kitchen table to the sink and back again. "She needs stability. She needs to know she is loved."

He sat back down at the table. "And Lisa told me Maddy is doing things."

"Doing things? Like what?"

"She said, 'Your daughter is wetting the bed.'"

"Lisa said that?"

"Those were her exact words."

"That's not good."

"Tell me about it. She said Maddy complains about stomach aches, and that it must be because I'm not feeding her right. And, Maddy runs and hides either in her closet or under her bed whenever the sitter comes. But that's my fault, too, because I don't expose her to enough different people."

Karl stroked his chin pensively. "I don't know what to say other than there is something seriously wrong here."

68

"Oh, and Maddy is having nightmares because I don't let her watch TV when she goes to bed. The list goes on and on."

"How long has this been going on?"

"I guess for the past year, but I just heard about it this week because Maddy is getting worse."

"Do you notice any of these behaviors on the weekends you have Maddy?"

"She complains of stomach aches when I take her back to Lisa's, but I haven't seen any of the other stuff she talks about."

"Why do you think Lisa waited so long to tell you?"

Mike shrugged. "I don't think she would have told me at all except Betty took Maddy to the doctor and I had to pay the copay."

"What did the doctor say?"

"He said there was nothing physically wrong."

"Sounds like emotional problems setting in."

"Big time."

"What about getting custody of Maddy?"

Mike looked squarely at Karl. He felt defeat as he heard himself say, "You know how many times I've tried—always ending up going nowhere."

The last time Mike had contacted his lawyer flashed through his mind. "What do I do to get full custody of Maddy?" he had asked the lawyer.

"For starters, you have to show probable cause why you should have full custody," his lawyer said.

"What does that mean?"

"Has your ex-wife ever physically abused your daughter?"

"Well, not physically. But, certainly emotionally."

"Doesn't count. Was she guilty of child endangerment? Neglect? Withholding basic needs; food, clothing, shelter?"

"Not totally. Lisa feeds her, but I don't think its healthy stuff."

"Can you prove that?"

"No, I can't really prove it."

"Then give it up. Without any proof that your ex-wife is an unfit mother, and that's what it takes, your chances of getting custody of your daughter are as likely as finding a snowball in Hades."

"How did it go?"

Mike snapped back to the conversation with Karl. "He said I have to prove that Lisa is an unfit mother according to the court's definition—which I can't prove. He also said that even if I got full custody of Maddy, I'd have to hire a sitter while I worked, and that I should seriously consider that aspect. I can't do that to Maddy. Lisa's got all her bases covered, and that leaves me on a dead-end street with nothing."

"That's a little harsh, don't you think?"

"Maybe so, but—"

"So, what are your options?"

"I don't know. I need to figure out something. Soon."

CHAPTER 17

The Plan

T wo weeks later, Mike and Karl finished a small addition. An upcoming remodeling job would carry them through the winter. Karl got a phone call, so Mike finished loading their trucks. Mike watched curiously as Karl hung up the phone and sat down.

"Bad news, Mike."

Mike waited silently.

"The big job just fell through. The owner had a heart attack and he's in the hospital. He and his wife decided not to go ahead." He looked up at Mike. "I'm really sorry. That was our bread and butter for the winter."

Mike exhaled through pursed lips, like he was blowing out birthday candles.

"You and I are out of work." Karl stroked his chin thoughtfully.

It's now or never. If I'm going to do something to protect Maddy, I've got to do it now. I've got to get my plans together, Mike thought.

***

The next day, Mike put an ad in the Minneapolis newspaper to sell his truck. He figured chances to sell it were far greater in the Twin Cities than in a small town. And he needed cash. He read the classifieds and went online for jobs, local and otherwise. He made phone calls. By the end of the next day, Mike had a job interview lined up for the following Saturday as a maintenance man at an apartment complex. *My weekend with Maddy,* he thought. *Perfect.*

CHAPTER 18

Kiss Your Mommy Goodbye

arly the following Saturday, Mike jotted a note to his parents. "Don't look for Maddy and me tonight. I'll call you tomorrow. Mike" He propped the note up on the kitchen table and left.

He drove to the Barrett's house to pick up Maddy. The autumn air felt cool and pleasant. He inhaled the earthy scent of a new season deep into his lungs. He jogged up the steps of his former in-law's home and rang the doorbell.

No answer.

He checked his watch, exactly 8 a.m. He pushed the button again and heard the chimes vibrate their melodious tune.

This time, the door opened slowly. Bruce Barrett regarded Mike with a half-hearted smile that needed no explanation.

Mike knew it meant another apology for Lisa's late arrival with Maddy. His heart sank.

"Mornin', Bruce." He tried to sound casual. "Is Maddy here?"

Bruce shook his head. "Not yet. Maybe Lisa is running a little late this morning." He clearly struggled to offer an excuse for Lisa's habitual late arrivals that sometimes meant no arrival at all.

Mike leaned against the aging pillar of the porch. "Mind if I wait?"

"Not at all." Bruce stood in awkward silence, his long arms dangling at his side.

Shoving his hands in his jean pockets, Mike walked down the steps and then back up. He sat on the top step of the familiar old house as Bruce stepped back inside and gently closed the door.

He looked at the tire swing dangling from the huge oak tree. He could almost hear Maddy giggle with anticipation.

"Higher," she would call to him, and he would push her over his head.

He looked at the bright yellow and orange mums crowding together in the narrow flower bed. There was a time when he thought Lisa was what made the yard, the house, the street beautiful, but that was long ago.

The door opened and Bruce and Betty stepped out. "I have some warm apple strudel and fresh coffee. Won't you come in? I'm sure Lisa will be here—"

Just then, Lisa pulled up behind his truck.

Maddy jumped out and ran toward him. Tucked under one arm were her Raggedy Ann doll and her pouch of agates that she brought with her nearly every place she went. Her pony tail swished from side to side. "Daddy! Daddy!"

He scooped her up and hugged her tight before hoisting her to his shoulders. "Hi, sweetie. How's Daddy's little girl?" He cocked his head and looked up at her.

"Good," she giggled, hugging his neck. "Hi, Grandma! Hi, Grandpa!" she called from her six-foot perch.

"Did you bring stuff for Maddy?"

"I didn't have time to do laundry," Lisa answered flatly.

But, Mike anticipated that and had shopped for Maddy the night before—pants and tops, socks and underwear, nightgowns, shoes and jacket, hairbrush and toothbrush, and a pink tote to put everything in. He also bought a bag of reading books, color books, and crayons.

"New outfit?" Mike asked, noticing Lisa's studded jeans and white angora sweater.

"As a matter of fact, it is. Not that it's any of your business."

Mike nodded. "New car?"

Lisa ignored his obvious sarcasm.

"Come in for some strudel," Betty invited.

"We really have to get going," Mike said.

"Maddy hasn't had breakfast." Lisa looked at Mike with cold, dark eyes.

Mike looked at his watch. He nodded a quick nod and followed them into the house.

Mike heard the rattle of dishes from the china hutch. He knew his former mother-in-law would never use one of the chipped cups from the kitchen cupboard to serve a guest. *And that's exactly what I am here—a guest who picks up Maddy on weekends,* he thought.

Betty's butter knife easily cut through the fresh coffee cake, but there wasn't a tool around that could cut the fibers of emotional tension. She placed a piece of strudel on a plate with a glass of milk for Maddy and dished up strudel for the others.

"I can't stay long," Lisa said. "I'm meeting Cindy. We're going to the Cities, shopping." She looked candidly at Mike.

He swallowed hard and turned his eyes to his plate.

"Must you spend your time with the likes of Cindy?" Betty asked.

"Don't start."

"But, she has no—"

"Tie downs?" Lisa finished. "Well, neither do I."

Maddy jumped down from her chair and Mike seized the opportunity to make their escape.

"We really have to go," Mike said. He took Maddy by the hand. "Say goodbye to your grandma and grandpa." Mike waited for Maddy to finish and then he said, "Thanks, Betty, for everything." He nodded to Bruce. "Bruce," he said with a smile and a handshake.

Am I doing the right thing? It's got to be right. Then, why am I sweating and my gut tied in knots?

"Kiss your mommy goodbye," he said.

CHAPTER 19

The Journey

"We're going to do something very special this weekend," Mike said buckling Maddy into her booster seat. "What are we going to do?"

"It's a surprise. You'll have to wait."

"Aww." Her disappointment tugged at his heart strings.

"OK. I'll give you a hint. There'll be lots of other people there."

"Shopping?"

"No, not shopping."

"What then?"

"We're going on a trip." Mike felt his adrenaline surge wildly in anticipation of what he was about to do.

"Where?"

"A place where you have never been before." He pulled away from the curb and didn't look back. His need for justice made him blind to the risks ahead.

Maddy persisted in asking questions. "Do they have ice cream there? And do they have monkeys and lions and tigers and polar bears and—"

"Whoa, little girl. I'm sure they do somewhere, but I'm not sure they have them where we're going."

He saw disappointment creep into her dark eyes. She had his eyes, but her petite features were Lisa's. "Tell you what. We'll find a zoo and spend a whole day there soon. Would you like that?"

"Yaay!" She clapped her hands, her curiosity satisfied.

Mike drove down Sibley Street to Holcombe Avenue where elm trees formed a golden arch. He drove past Litchfield High School where he walked the noisy halls, where he played baseball, and where he noticed a beautiful blonde. It seemed like a lifetime ago.

The traffic light ahead was green. "Stay green," he whispered. If it turned red, he would have to stop and if he stopped, he might change his mind and go back. *Back to what? Futile payments and an unstable environment for Maddy? Emotional problems that may scar her for life?"* Not on my watch," he mumbled.

The green light turned to amber, warning motorists to proceed with caution, as he sped through the intersection. Without hesitation, he said farewell to the small town where he grew up and had come to love.

Mike glanced at his watch—9 a.m. He was to meet the potential buyer for his truck in Minneapolis at 10:30 a.m. *What if the buyer changes his mind? What if he doesn't think the truck looks like it did in the ad and decides not to buy it? Then I'm back to square one.* He looked up at his visor. The envelope with the truck title peeked out. A denial or a confirmation? Since he hadn't heard anything to the contrary, he reassured himself that it was still a go.

Maddy seemed content to look out the window at the passing farmland with its brown fields and horses standing with their noses to the ground. She clutched her Raggedy Ann doll and her bag of agates in her left arm. *Did she crave the love of her mother? Does she even know she is loved? Was his love given on two weekends a month enough to give her security and stability?*

Mike reached over and tugged her pony tail.

She looked at him with her round eyes and smiled the sweetest smile.

It's up to me to do my best for her sake, he reasoned.

He reached inside his lightweight jacket. He felt the envelope tucked behind his cell phone. "What do you think about flying on an airplane?"

"Really?" Her eyes widened and danced with merriment.

"Really." *Maybe I should've waited. I don't want to disappoint her,* he thought.

***

The neighborhood on Minneapolis' south side where the potential buyer lived was an older neighborhood with small houses crowded together on narrow lots. But, it looked like a nice area where everyday folks did everyday things.

He followed the directions, arriving at his house at 10:35 a.m. A man about his age was raking leaves when Mike pulled up.

The man leaned on his rake, studying Mike's truck. He grinned, dropped the rake into a pile of leaves, and walked to meet Mike.

"Well, it looks like it's everything you said it was. My name's Tony," he said as he held out his hand.

"I'm Mike." He shook the stranger's hand.

Tony looked under the hood and the body of the truck, and checked the tires and gauges.

"Mind if I take it for a spin?"

"Not at all." Mike unbuckled Maddy and lifted her from her booster seat.

"And how old are you, young lady?" the man asked.

"I'm four, 'cuz I was born on my birthday," she said holding up four fingers.

"I've got a little girl about your age and a boy two years younger. "Do you have any brothers or sisters?"

"No, but I have Raggedy Ann," she answered, holding up the doll to Tony.

"She's a mighty fine looking Raggedy Anne," he said with a smile.

Mike glanced at his watch and tried not to look impatient.

Mike, Maddy and Raggedy Ann sat on the step while Tony took the truck for a drive. Ten minutes passed and Mike began to pace. Maddy wanted to run from tree to tree while Mike counted how long it took for her to run around five boulevard trees and back again.

"Thirty eight seconds," he called out.

Just then, Tony drove around the corner. "I'll take it. Let's go inside."

Mike grabbed the envelope with the title from the truck visor, took Maddy by the hand, and followed Tony inside.

Tony plunked down the payment on the table while Mike unfolded the title for him to sign.

"Is someone picking you up?"

"No. Actually, I'll call a taxi. We're heading to the airport."

"Shoot. We're only ten minutes away. I'll give you a ride."

Mike hesitated.

"I could get you to the airport and be back home for lunch in less time than it takes for a taxi to get here."

Mike nodded. "Thanks. I'm mighty grateful to you."

CHAPTER 20

At The Airport

Minneapolis-St. Paul International Airport bustled with four lanes of taxi's and cars, dropping off and picking up passengers. Horns honked, tires screeched, and a few people shook fists at one another.

Tony pulled the truck to the curb. Mike lifted Maddy and her car seat out, grabbed her tote, fun sack, and his duffle bag.

"Thanks a lot," he said.

Tony nodded. "Take care." He pulled back into traffic.

Mike looked at his watch again—just enough time to check luggage, and grab lunch at McDonald's. He grasped Maddy's hand.

"Hold on," he said.

"I am," she said clutching his hand tighter.

Gate 37 was filling with passengers, many laughing, some crying, and a few quiet with blank faces.

Mike glanced at the departure board on the wall. *Flight #736 to Los Angeles departing at 12:30. On time.*

He found two empty seats close to the window at the boarding gate so Maddy could watch airplanes take off. Several children pressed their noses against the window overlooking the runway, chattering and squealing with delight as each passenger jet took off. But, Maddy began to look sad.

Mike picked her up, put her on his lap, and held her.

"What's wrong, sweetie?"

Maddy shrugged.

"Are you hungry?"

She nodded, brushing her tears from her cheeks.

"How about if we eat our hamburgers. I got you a strawberry malt."

Maddy perked up.

After they finished their lunch and a trip to the restroom, Maddy asked Mike if she could sit by the window with the other children.

She watched the planes, and Mike watched Maddy. *I wish there was some other way*, he thought. *What if I'm doing the wrong thing? What if she's too young and can't adjust to a different way of life? What if? What if? I wish I knew. Man, I wish I knew. OK, I'll give it a month and if she isn't happy, we'll come back*, he reasoned with himself.

Maddy stared wide-eyed as plane after plane took off. She looked at Mike. "They look like giants!"

Mike smiled and nodded.

He looked around at the other passengers waiting to board.

He noticed a middle-age woman wearing khaki slacks, and a brown-and-white-striped blouse sitting across from him. She was sipping a Pepsi and reading a paperback book. He noticed two soldiers talking quietly.

The PA cracked. A shrill female voice said, "May I have your attention. Flight #736 to Los Angeles is now boarding general seating at gate 37. Please have your boarding pass ready."

"C'mon, Maddy. Let's go."

Maddy scrambled from her ring-side seat and grabbed Mike's hand as he led her down the hallway to the waiting 747.

Mike buckled Maddy into the window seat and buckled himself in the seat next to her. A lady with white hair and brown spots on the backs of her hands sat in the aisle seat next to Mike.

She looked at her seat partners. "Why, your little girl is pretty as a picture."

"Thanks." He put his hand on Maddy's forearm. "Her name's Maddy."

"Hello, Maddy. I have a granddaughter in California just about your age."

Maddy smiled and went back to looking out the window.

The lady turned to Mike. "My son and his wife sent me a plane ticket to visit them for a week. Land sakes! I'm so excited, I almost forgot. My name is Gladys."

"I'm Mike."

"Do you have a wife?"

Mike thought the conversation bordered on awkward. But why? It was a perfectly legitimate question. "No. We're divorced."

"Such a shame." She tsked, tsked.

CHAPTER 21

The Flight

Four hundred passengers made last minute adjustments to seat belts and settled against high-back seats. Six cordial flight attendants in navy blue skirts and jackets walked the two aisles adjusting backrests and securing overhead compartments.

The double engines beneath each wing revved to a high timbre whine.

Maddy looked at Mike with frightened eyes. Her normally pink cheeks turned white as she grabbed his arm.

He put his arm around her. "Everything's OK, sweetie. It's supposed to sound like that."

As the 747 taxied down the runway, it gained exhilarating speed. The engines roared in a surge of power. Mike felt a rush of anticipation. The engines screamed in a high pitch as the captain pushed the throttle forward until it seemed the engines would explode. The plane rose from the ground winging its passengers into a transparent blue sky.

Maddy clung to Mike. He grinned and squeezed her hand. "Look out the window and tell me what you see."

Maddy looked down. "Oh, Daddy! I see little trees and little blue puddles." She squealed and clapped her hands. "This is funner than Tykes Park."

"Are you still scared?"

"Uh-huh," she said swishing her pony tail from side to side.

Not long into the flight, a deep voice spoke over the plane's intercom. "This is the captain. Welcome to Southwest Flight 726. We are over Sioux Falls, South Dakota. If you would like snacks or something to drink, please let one of our flight attendants know. We hope you enjoy your flight."

"Daddy, can I color?" Maddy turned to Mike as a flight attendant brushed past.

"Sir, would your little girl like a coloring book?" she leaned in to Mike.

He nodded.

"I'll be right back." She smiled. Her red lips said far more than her words did.

Mike ignored the obvious gesture.

The flight attendant reappeared and reached across to Maddy with a coloring book and a box of eight crayons. "Here you are, pretty girl." She lingered in her reaching position a bit longer than necessary.

"Thank you," Maddy said in her small voice."

"May I bring either of you two something to drink?" She focused her attention solely on Mike and all but ignored Gladys.

"I'll have black coffee and a small juice. Thanks."

"I'll have tea," Gladys said dismissing the flight attendant to do her duties. She looked at Mike, and asked, "Have you ever been to California?"

"Once. When I was a kid, my folks took me and one of my friends to Disneyland for a vacation."

"Don't you just love Disneyland? Why, I'd go there again in an instant."

The flight attendant reappeared with a small tray of refreshments. She smiled as she handed the tea to the elderly lady and black coffee to Mike. "I have apple juice for the little lady," she said stretching across to Maddy. Her charming smile faded into her professional expression as she moved to the next row of seats.

An hour into the flight, the intercom cracked. "Ladies and Gentlemen, we are directly over North Platte, Nebraska. We are flying at an altitude of 39,000 feet, cruising at a speed of 530 miles per hour. We may experience a little turbulence in a few minutes. Nothing to worry about, but we do ask that you remain in your seats with your seat belts buckled."

Mike put Maddy's empty juice glass inside his coffee cup and set them on the tray in front of him. He secured Maddy's seat belt and then his own. Gladys didn't seem concerned as she paged through the *Ladies Home Journal*. Then, Mike noticed her hearing aid. He tapped her arm and motioned to buckle up.

Suddenly, the plane bumped, jarred and vibrated.

"Land sakes! It's a wonder these planes don't shake apart," Gladys scoffed.

Maddy looked at Mike with terrified eyes.

He tightened his arm around her. "Everything's OK."

The turbulence subsided as abruptly as it started, and the plane settled into a smooth flight once again.

Gladys settled back and before long, she sat with her head against the seat, mouth gaping open, like a baby robin waiting to be fed.

Maddy curled up as Mike adjusted her small pillow and tucked Raggedy Ann under her arm. As her eyes fluttered in the early stages of sleep, her long, dark eyelashes brushed her pink cheeks.

Mike gently stroked her bangs. *You deserve a chance. I love you, Princess. How do I protect you? I don't want to fail as your daddy.*

He rested his head back and closed his eyes.

CHAPTER 22

Thinking Back in Time

Mike's mind drifted to back to when he first knew Lisa. She was beautiful and mysterious. The saucy way she walked down Main Street turned many heads—both male and female. Men looked with desire and women stared with envy. She was at ease with her own good looks and evoked a self-confidence that daunted many of her would-be pursuers.

Mike and Lisa dated for almost two years when Lisa announced to her parents, "We want to get married and have a big reception someplace nice."

"Your mother and I have been tucking a few extra dollars away for a little trip, but I guess that can wait," her father said.

"Yes, yes, of course," Betty chimed in. "We would love to give you a nice wedding reception. The VFW hall is nice and reasonably priced—"

"I was thinking more of Peter's on the Lake," Lisa interrupted.

Betty arched her eyebrows. "Peter's on the Lake? Well—their dining room is lovely at night—" She began to flounder and looked to Bruce.

"I'll pay half," Mike said.

"We can't let you do that," Bruce said. "She's our daughter. We'll work it out."

"I'll pay half," Mike said firmly. And so it was settled.

I should've seen it coming right then and there.

More than a year later, Mike was still captivated by her beauty. He remembered one of their rare romantic walks in Memorial Park when

Lisa was first pregnant. They strolled over the wooden footbridge that crossed the creek toward the picnic area. Weeping willow trees with thick hanging vines crowded along the water's edge.

As Lisa leaned against the weathered railing of the footbridge, Mike gazed past her white cotton top and red shorts, down her lean and firm legs to her sandaled feet. He admired her youthful, trim body that carried his child.

The moon splashed a silver reflection on her head and body, but the shadows of the night hid her eyes.

He inhaled the intoxicating fragrance of her perfume. He bent his head toward her, feeling her warm breath on his lips. He kissed her tenderly, then passionately.

She tilted her head back and looked at the polished moon that silhouetted them like black ghosts against the evening sky.

He followed her gaze, resting his chin on the top of her head, while his heart returned to its normal rhythm.

They listened to a rhapsody of frogs and crickets, and watched eerie, blinking signals of fireflies dotting the darkness like the marquee lights of an old theater.

"Are you going to be able to afford to take care of me after the baby is born?"

Mike leaned back from their embrace. "What kind of question is that?"

"Well, you're just a carpenter, and I don't want to work after the baby is born."

Mike let go of Lisa altogether.

"I'm just trying to be practical," she reasoned.

"Being practical is if we don't have enough money, we don't spend. If we can't pay off the credit card every month, we have to cut down."

"You're beginning to sound like my mother. Every time I suggested going shopping in the Cities, she would say, 'What's wrong with Penney's? They have quality clothes at decent prices.'"

"Hey, c'mon Lisa. We both know your parents love you. They would've sold everything for you—"

"They don't have anything. That's the point. I don't want to live like that."

I should've seen the writing on the wall, but how was I to know that the only thing that made her happy was spending money? Mike pinched the cleft in his chin and exhaled slowly.

And, what about the time Karl and Katie ran into Lisa and Maddy at the grocery store? Katie had remarked to him, "Maddy has such sad eyes." I had to do something to protect her. I know my motives are right—for her sake.

"Ladies and gentlemen." The voice on the airplane's intercom jarred into Mike's thoughts. "You will notice the beginning of the Grand Canyon. You should be able to see Zion Park, Arizona, and in ten minutes, we will be flying over Lake Mead in Grand Canyon National Park. You won't want to miss this view!"

Mike looked down at unique rock formations and deep crevices. Pastel shades of pink and beige blended together as far as he could see. Blue-green pine trees peppered the lower parts of the canyon and seemed to cling to bare rock for their stingy existence. Mike traced the course of the drab brown Colorado River winding its way through the giant stone walls.

He sat quietly searching the strange beauty of the world below, fingering the cleft in his chin. He glanced at his watch. Barring any delays, he would make it on time for his interview as the maintenance man at Green Tree Complex

The deep voice from the cockpit spoke. "Lake Mead is on your left."

Mike glimpsed a long, cool splash of blue near Grand Canyon National Park. He was tempted to wake Maddy, but decided to let her sleep.

The pilot continued, "Las Vegas is coming up on the right and Hoover Dam is below."

The startling white spray of the falls looked like it was tumbling through giant, opened elevator doors. What a contrast from the Colorado River.

Like dating and marriage, he thought.

CHAPTER 23

California

The plane landed five minutes late and taxied to Gate 51 of the Los Angeles International Airport.

"Are we there yet?" Maddy rubbed her eyes and looked out the window.

"Yes, sweetie. We are here."

"Where?"

"We're in California."

Gladys woke up. "It felt good to rest my eyes," she said with a yawn. Mike nodded.

***

The people mover carried a full load of passengers to the escalator. The lower level was crowded with travelers scanning rotating turnstiles for their luggage.

Mike lunged for his duffle bag and Maddy's bulging tote on the second rotation.

They stepped out of the terminal into warm sunshine. The streets were lined with huge palm trees wearing brown, leafy underskirts. He felt exhilarated.

He had to stop so Maddy could look at the towering palm trees and think about them for a while.

"They look like twizzle sticks."

"Like what?"

"Twizzle sticks. Like stars on a stick," she explained.

"I think you're right." He tugged her ponytail. "The first thing we have to do is buy a newspaper and rent a car."

Mike bought the Star News and the last edition of the Pasadena Weekly left in the news rack.

"Let's go sit over there." He nodded toward a row of chairs along the wall. "You can color while I find us a place to stay."

Mike scanned the 'Apts. For Rent' pages. One ad stood out from the rest. "Immediate Occupancy. Newly Decorated. Reasonable Rates. Children OK. No Pets. Located at corner of Knott Avenue and Orange Street in the heart of Pasadena. Ask for Liz."

Mike called the number.

"Knott-Orange Apartments," a female voice answered.

"Well, if they're not orange, what color are they?" he said trying desperately to shake the vice-grip that tension had on him.

"How may I direct your call?" said the impatient voice.

"I'd like to speak with Liz about renting the two-bedroom apartment."

"This is Liz." Her voice softened. "That apartment has been rented, but I have a one-bedroom available."

"No. That won't work. Thanks anyway," he said and hung up. He looked at his watch.

He quickly fumbled in his wallet for the number for the job interview. A pleasant female voice answered. "Green Tree Complex. Rosie speaking."

"Hi, this is Mike DiSanto. I have an appointment for a job interview at 4:30 p.m., and I was wondering if you could give me directions from the Los Angeles Airport."

"Of course."

Mike jotted down the directions on the newspaper. "We should be there by 4:30 p.m."

After Mike hung up, he looked at Maddy hunched over her coloring masterpiece, both feet tucked beneath her. "Let's go, sweetie."

Maddy jumped up holding the colored comics for Mike to praise.

"Hey, good job!" He gave his sincere approval as he examined the scribbled picture.

The shuttle to the car rental took a few minutes and, then, Mike and Maddy were on their way to what Mike hoped would be a successful job interview.

CHAPTER 24

The Interview

M ike etched the flowering California freeway into his mind next to the image of high arching elm trees of Litchfield. Life will *be as different as Minnesota streets and California freeways,* he thought.

"The flowers look different," Maddy said. "Can I pick some?"

"No, sweetie."

"Why not?"

"Well, these are special flowers to look at, but not to pick."

"What are they?"

"I think they're called bottle brush." He remembered his parents talking about the red flowers that grew along the freeway. But that was a lifetime ago.

It wasn't long before all four lanes of traffic stopped. Mike inched along bumper-to-bumper gaining speed only to slow to a crawl again.

However, Colorado Boulevard afforded much less time to look at the sights than the freeway did. Every lane of traffic sped along as though each car was hooked together with a five foot invisible chain and pulled at frightening speeds.

Mike glanced at his watch—4:30 p.m.

"I hope Rosie doesn't think we're not coming," he mumbled.

"Who's Rosie?" Maddy seemed so engrossed in re-arranging her crayons in the box that Mike was surprised she even heard him.

"Rosie is a lady I have to talk to about a job."

Maddy shrugged and went back to placing her colors in order.

MONTE VISTA WAY 1 1/2 miles. The stark white letters stood out boldly on the green overhead sign. The afternoon sun nearly blinded Mike as he headed west on Monte Vista Way for the short drive.

Mike stopped in front of two white stucco buildings, each two stories high with red tiled roofs. They sat under palm trees about fifteen feet from the sidewalk. Globe-shaped shrubs and billowy ground cover with dark berries sprawled behind a black wrought iron fence with an opened gate. A white painted sign with black lettering stood in front of the fence.

GREEN TREE COMPLEX
Rosie Woods, Mgr.

"We're here," Mike said.

Maddy glanced out. She looked at Mike with eyes that asked a million questions, but said nothing.

Mike led the way to a door marked "Manager." A squat clay pot sprouting clusters of red strawberries sat at the bottom of two steps. A picture of a gray kitten with green eyes peeking from behind a bowl of berries on the welcome mat read, "You are Berry Welcome." He rang the doorbell.

A lady of about fifty with a mop of strawberry blonde hair cut above long ears opened the door. "You must be Mike," she greeted with a smile so big it revealed a gold-capped back tooth.

"Yes, I am. I'm sorry I'm late, but the freeway traffic was—"

"Oh, it gets worse," she said with a laugh. "And who is this pretty young lady?"

"This is my daughter, Maddy."

She bent down. "Hello, Maddy. My name is Rosie." Then standing upright, she reached out her hand to Mike. "Rosie Woods," she smiled. "Come in."

Rosie led them to her small office. "Please, sit down," she invited. "I have to turn down my oven." Rosie disappeared into the kitchen and the aroma of roasting chicken and baking powder biscuits swept out to where Mike and Maddy sat.

"I'm hungry," Maddy whispered.

"Again?" Mike laughed.

Maddy shook her head.

"We'll eat in a little while, sweetie. Can you wait a bit longer?"

"I'm **pretty** hungry and I have to go potty," she said rolling her eyes upward.

Just then, Rosie reappeared. "Say, would you and Maddy like to have a bite to eat before we get down to business?"

"Oh, no, ma'am. We'll eat later."

"Why, Daddy?"

Before Mike could say another word, Rosie said, "Call me Rosie and I would be so happy to have both of you join me for a bite to eat."

"No, we couldn't impose—"

"Nonsense. I've got plenty. I never did learn how to cook for one. My husband died several years ago, and my daughter is married and lives in Oregon, but I still cook enough to feed a field crew," she laughed.

"Can we, Daddy?"

Mike flashed a grin. "Well, OK. Would it be all right if Maddy uses the bathroom?"

"Certainly."

Mike felt strange sitting at a table eating a meal with a complete stranger, but he smiled gratefully at his hostess. "Please, help yourself to more potatoes," Rosie said to Mike. "And, Maddy, would you like some more chicken?"

"Just one more," she said in her small voice.

"Will your wife be joining you?" Rosie asked as she buttered a baking powder biscuit.

"No. It's just Maddy and me." He kept his eyes on his plate.

"We have several children at the complex. I love hearing them laugh and have fun."

Mike nodded.

"Are you staying anywhere?"

"No. We just flew in and I haven't had time to look yet. We'll probably just get a motel until I can find something."

Rosie smiled and nodded.

After dinner, Rosie suggested going into her office. "Can you tell me a little about yourself and experience?"

Mike relayed minimal details about his personal life, but elaborated on his years with Karl. "Our job ended and we would be out of work, so I thought it would be a good time to change locations."

When they had talked in length, Rosie said, "I desperately need someone dependable to do the maintenance here. I have one stipulation, however, and that is the maintenance man must live on site." She pointed to a white stucco building. "The apartment is just across the walk from my office. It's a two bedroom apartment, almost completely furnished. But, there's a whole assortment of furniture in the storage shed left behind from when people moved out." She looked steadily at Mike. "If you accept the maintenance position, you are welcomed to use whatever you need."

"You mean I have the job?"

"You do, if you're sure you want it." She paused. "We'll try it for a month before you sign the agreement. That way, if either of us is unhappy about the arrangement, neither of us will be obligated to stay in an unpleasant setting. Fair enough?"

"Fair enough," Mike said. He tried to smile, but an uneasiness settled over him like the choking dust of a passing car on a country road, so he simply nodded.

"I'll grab the apartment keys and give you a quick tour of the complex before getting you and Maddy settled in. We'll go over the job description tomorrow after church." Rosie paused.

Mike nodded, but did not say anything.

Rosie unlatched a redwood gate and closed it behind them. "There are forty-eight units in the complex. One of the smaller complexes, but plenty of work for the maintenance man. We'll cut through the pool area to Building D," Rosie called over her shoulder to the trailing hand-in-hand father and daughter.

Without breaking her lively step, Rosie gave a neighborly wave and her signature big smile to the BBQ chefs as she whizzed past them.

Two buildings on the back side of Green Tree Complex were newer, but smaller, than the two front buildings. Carports ran alongside and behind each building.

"Each apartment has one carport, and we have storage units to rent over there next to the laundry," she said waving her arm in a wide sweeping motion, "but there's a waiting list for them."

Mike nodded, taking in the flood of information. He looked down at Maddy. *Would she be lonesome for her mother? Had Maddy missed him between his visits every other weekend? Do little kids even have a concept of time and separation?*

He squeezed Maddy's hand, and she squeezed his in return.

"The laundry room is over there in that small building," Rosie explained, pointing to a low building nestled among tall bushes. "There are eight washers and twelve dryers. And, we do have a small country store with basic grocery items that's attached to the laundry building if you need something to tide you over until you can get groceries."

Mike nodded taking particular notice of the country store with grocery items.

The threesome meandered throughout the complex on sidewalks that wound among small rocks of various colors.

"Daddy?"

Mike looked at Maddy.

"They don't have any grass."

"Really? Are you sure?" Mike teased.

"How come?" Maddy persisted

"Maybe their hardware stores don't sell lawnmowers."

"Daa-ddy!"

"Sweetie, it's too hot and not enough rain to grow grass in California."

They stopped by the storage shed. "You'll need an end table and a lamp, for sure," Rosie explained. "And I have towels and extra bedding. Otherwise, you should have just about everything you need." She smiled. "I'll carry the lamp if you can carry the table."

"No problem. And, thanks a lot!"

"Sometimes the unexpected happens here at the complex," Rosie said. "Like the time I rented a corner apartment in Building C to a family. The couple had two young girls. They had six other family members living there, and none of them spoke English. I didn't know about the extra tenants until I got a complaint from the man downstairs."

"What happened?"

"The downstairs renter called to tell me he had a huge black stain on his living room ceiling and it was beginning to sag. Naturally, I went right over to see for myself and sure enough, just like he said. I hurried to the apartment above. When I knocked, an old woman answered the door. She must have been the grandmother. There were three other old people huddled on chairs in the kitchen staring at a TV with no sound."

"They were watching TV in the kitchen?"

"They couldn't use the living room."

"Why not?"

"They had a garden growing on their living room floor—dirt, water and all!

Mike burst into laughter at the absurdity of it. "I'm sorry for laughing, but was anything growing?" he asked between gasps.

Rosie laughed, too. "As a matter of fact, yes. This is the first time I ever laughed about it though," she hooted, wiping her watery eyes with the back of her free hand. "Vegetables on one half and marijuana on the other half."

Mike laughed so hard, he had to set the table down.

Maddy looked curiously from Mike to Rosie and back to Mike again.

Mike put his arm around Maddy. "Rosie told a funny story," he managed to say between peals of laughter.

"That was an eight-thousand-dollar garden!"

"What happened to the people?" he asked, trying to regain a serious tone.

"Two of the men were charged with illegal drug possession and drug trafficking and sent to prison. The rest were taken to a shelter until permanent living arrangements could be made." Mike picked up the end table again and started walking with Rosie leading the way to the front of the complex.

The unexpected laughter sent welcomed strains of relief to his emotionally charged brain. For an instant, the reality of moving to California without anyone in Minnesota knowing about it, drifted to the back of his mind and settled itself in a fog.

He felt a slight chill as the afternoon sun sank beyond mountain peaks casting deep purple shadows across the city.

Rosie unlocked apartment B2, and ushered Mike and Maddy inside. The corner apartment was not spacious, but certainly adequate for their needs.

"We're like a huge family here in the complex," Rosie said. "A mixture of people, but we all look out for one another."

Mike smiled. Family. The fog abruptly cleared from his head as he thought of what he knew he had to do. *I have to make phone calls.*

CHAPTER 25

Phone Calls

M ike woke early Sunday. He crept to Maddy's room and peeked in. She seemed so small curled up under her blanket with her rag doll hanging precariously over the edge of her bed.

He showered and dressed, feeling the strangeness of the apartment. He opened the patio doors and stepped out onto the veranda. He heard the hum of freeway traffic. He scanned the eastern horizon already clouded with a hazy orange ring.

"Hi, Daddy." Maddy stood in her ruffled, yellow polka dot nightgown rubbing her eyes.

"Hi, sweetie." He scooped her up in his arms.

She put her head against his shoulder and yawned again.

"We have lots to do today." He brushed her hair from her rosy cheeks.

"What things?"

"Well, first we have to go out for breakfast. We have to buy some groceries—"

"Can we go to the zoo?"

"Hmm. That would be fun, but today we have to do other stuff. How does sometime real soon sound?"

"I suppose." Then Maddy brightened. "Can we take Molly with to breakfast?"

"Of course. You go get dressed and brush your teeth and we'll go."

Maddy ran to get ready. She grabbed her Raggedy Ann doll and tucked it under her arm. "Ready."

As they walked the short distance to a fast food place for breakfast, Maddy skipped beside him chatting constantly about finding a zoo. "Do the animals look as silly as the trees?"

"Nah, sweetie. Animals look the same no matter where you are," he said with a laugh. "What's your favorite animal in the whole world?" he asked.

"A bunny. What's your favorite animal?"

"A lion."

"Why do you like lions?"

"Because lions eat bunnies." He growled ferociously. "Why do you like bunnies?"

"Because bunnies can hide from lions," she giggled.

Rosie returned a short time later, carrying two bags. "I stopped to get my groceries and got a few things for you and Maddy that the country store doesn't carry until you can get groceries," she said with a big smile.

"Rosie, you are an angel, but I can't accept the groceries."

"Why not?"

Mike shrugged. "Well, because—"

"That's not a very good reason. Here, take them." She plopped two bags into his arms.

Mike smiled. "I don't know how to thank you."

"You can give to someone else in need some time."

Mike nodded setting the bags on the counter.

***

That afternoon, Mike sat in Rosie's office discussing the details of what was involved in his job responsibilities while Maddy colored and munched on Rosie's peanut butter cookies.

Just then the office phone rang. "Green Tree Complex, Rosie speaking."

Mike couldn't help overhear Rosie's side of the conversation.

"A two bedroom? Yes, one left on the second level in Building D facing the front. $950 per month. 3:30 p.m. is fine. Detective and Mrs. Sherman, you say? Great. Well see you then," she said and hung up.

Detective? Hope our paths don't cross, Mike thought. *Why am I getting paranoid? He probably investigates unsolved murders—not missing persons. Besides, no one knows we're missing yet.* He swiped his sweating palm down his pant leg.

"We have a prospective resident coming this afternoon. If they take it, we'll have a full boat, as Noah would say." Rosie smiled. She seemed quite pleased.

"There are a few things I need to do this afternoon."

"Not a problem. Don't feel you have to stay at the complex 24/7. Just check the answering machine for resident messages and pick up any work orders you need to do. I'll go over work orders with you. Now, what can I do to help?"

"I need to buy a car—nothing fancy, just something to get us around."

"You might check the *Shopper* in the rack there on the wall or the bulletin board for residents that post sale items," Rosie said pointing to the opposite wall behind him that was littered with post-it notes, 3x5 cards and scraps of paper with For Sale items listed.

"Thanks. I really appreciate your help." After they finished discussing work orders, Mike checked the bulletin board. He found two possibilities right at the complex.

"C'mon Maddy, let's go look at a car."

"Aww." Maddy scrunched up her nose.

Mike cocked his head at her.

"Oh, OK."

"Hasta mañana," Rosie waved.

Mike and Maddy walked over to Building C to look at the first car. "Too many miles," Mike said.

They walked over to Building D to look at the second car. "Hmm. This one would work," Mike said to himself. The price was right so he bought the car.

To celebrate, Mike drove to the mall on Colorado Blvd. for double scoop ice cream cones for Maddy and himself. They arrived back at their apartment at 5 p.m.—7 p.m. in Minnesota—the time he was supposed to have Maddy back at Lisa's.

"Sweetie, do you think you could color a picture for Rosie while I make a phone call? Then, we'll make some supper."

"OK!" Maddy ran to her room.

Mike inhaled deeply. He stared at the phone. *Ah, man!* He rubbed the back of his neck. He took in another deep breath and punched in Lisa's phone number.

The phone rang. He swallowed hard. *What am I supposed to say?* The phone rang a second time. He looked out the patio door. *Ah, by the way, Maddy will be a little late tonight? How am I going to explain that she's not coming back?* The phone rang the third time. *I think Maddy has a better chance with—*

"Hello?"

Mike couldn't speak. He began to sweat profusely.

"Helloo?"

"Lisa?"

"No, this is the sitter. Who's calling?"

"This is Mike. What time do you expect Lisa?"

"I dunno. Is there a message?"

"Um, yeah. Would you let her know that Maddy will not be home tonight and that I'll call her tomorrow?"

"Is that it?"

"Yeah, that's it. Oh, tell her Maddy is fine."

"If Madison's not coming home tonight, do I have to stay here?" the sitter asked.

"It's up to you. Just make sure Lisa gets the message."

Mike felt relieved that he didn't have to talk to Lisa, but on the other hand, he knew he still had to talk to her the following day.

Next, he called his parents.

"Mom?"

"Yes?"

"This is Mike."

"I know that," she said with a laugh.

"I just wanted to let you know that Maddy and I have left town and—"

"Are you up on the North Shore?"

"No."

"Well, what do you mean you've left town? Where are you?" she asked with alarm.

"I can't tell you that. I've been thinking about this for a couple of weeks, and—"

"What are you saying?"

"Maddy and I have moved. We won't be coming home."

"I don't understand—"

Mike heard quiet sobs then a rustling.

"Mike, you've upset your mother. What's going on?"

"Maddy and I have left town, and we won't be coming back home. At least for now."

"Are you crazy?"

Mike stepped out onto the veranda. "Maddy needs some stability in her life. She doesn't deserve to be treated the way Lisa treats her, so I—"

"Have you lost your mind? You mean to tell me you just took Maddy?"

"Yeah, I guess you could call it that."

"I can't believe I'm hearing this! What does Lisa say?"

"She doesn't know yet. She wasn't home. I left a message with the sitter—"

"You left a message with the sitter that you kidnapped Maddy?"

"No, Dad. I told the sitter I would call Lisa tomorrow."

"She'll have the cops after you and rightfully so!"

"I just need some time. I've got to try to give Maddy—"

"Why didn't you tell us?"

"I didn't want to involve anyone."

"Well, where are you?" Rick's tone bordered on rage.

"I can't tell you that."

"And I can't tell you how disappointed I am in you!"

Mike stood there, his shoulders slumped. "I'm sorry, but I didn't know what else to do." He heard his mother sobbing more loudly in the background. "Will you put Mom on the phone?"

"Hello," she sniffled.

"Mom, I'll call when I can. Please don't worry. We'll be fine."

"But Mike," she cried.

"Don't cry." He covered the phone and stepped inside to check on Maddy who had three pictures spread out on her bedroom floor. "Maddy, do you want to color one more picture? It will make Rosie smile." He took his hand off the phone. "I'll be in touch, Mom."

"Um, OK. Just one more," Maddy called from her room.

Mike stepped back onto the veranda and called Karl.

"Hey! How's it going?" Karl asked, when he heard Mike's voice.

"Well, I got a job." Mike hedged around the real reason he called.

"That was quick. Where did you find work?"

"I'm doing maintenance work at an apartment complex."

"You don't say? You'd better hang onto it because there's nothing coming up for remodeling jobs. If this economy doesn't turn around pretty soon, I'll have to figure out a different line of work myself and at my age—"

"Ah, Karl, the reason I'm calling is, is to let you and Katie know that Maddy and I have moved out of town. I didn't say anything before because I didn't want to involve you. This way you can honestly say you didn't know anything about it."

Mike heard an eerie silence.

"Karl?"

"I'm here, son. I know you were backed into a corner with the situation with Maddy, but, do you think this was a wise decision?"

"Probably not, but I honestly didn't know what else to do, especially since I found out about Maddy's emotional problems. She would only have gotten worse and I figured if I could just give her some time to—I don't know—to be loved—to have security, she'd be OK."

"I understand. But, just because I understand, doesn't mean I agree. Can I ask you a question?" His tone was gentle.

"Yeah, of course."

"Do you remember telling me how you rescued your dog from a bad situation?"

"Yeah."

"Did you just take him?"

"No, I asked the owner. Why? What does that have to do with Maddy?"

"Did you ever consider going to Lisa and asking if you could at least share custody of Maddy?"

"She would never agree to that. She told me that right after the divorce. Besides, if she did, she would lose $400 a month in child support and she would never give that up. No, Karl, my hands were tied."

"I see. You know, Mike, I really believe you want what's best for Maddy, but—"

"What other choice did I have?"

"I wish I had the answer."

"So do I, but—"

"Well, for whatever its worth, Katie and I will be praying for you, and for Maddy."

"Thanks, Karl, for understanding. I'll keep in touch."

***

Mike and Maddy walked across the sidewalk to Rosie's.

Maddy held the handful of colored pictures up to Rosie. "I made pictures for you."

"Say, isn't that the most precious thing!" She smiled a big smile.

"You got sparkly teeth," Maddy said noticing the gold tooth.

"I've been told I have many things, but never that I had sparkly teeth," Rosie said with a laugh. "Thank you, Maddy. Say, I am making cookies tomorrow for a neighbor and they have a girl just your age, and it's Carla's birthday. Would you like to help me bake cookies and take them over to their apartment?" Rosie looked up at Mike. They live right there in Building C."

Maddy looked at Mike. "Can I? Please?"

"I think that would be fun."

"Yaay!"

"By the way, Detective and Mrs. Sherman rented the apartment."

Mike nodded.

CHAPTER 26

Call to Lisa

Mike got up early so he could call Lisa before Maddy got up. He had time to think things through during the night and felt confident that this was the only way to help Maddy. The court system didn't give him any options and talking again with Lisa to get shared custody of Maddy would have been ludicrous.

He showered and dressed, yet beads of sweat collected on his forehead. He wiped them away with his forearm, and called.

Lisa answered on the second ring.

"Lisa? Mike."

"What do you think you're doing? Who gave you the right to keep Madison another day?"

"I tried to call last—"

"I know. I got the message Madison would be home today."

"That wasn't the message."

"Oh, really? What exactly was the message?"

"I said I would call you tomorrow."

"Ok, so now you're calling."

"Lisa, I'm concerned about Maddy."

"The doctor said there's nothing wrong with her."

"Nothing physically. But, that doesn't mean she's not getting messed up emotionally."

"You don't know what you're talking about!"

"Don't I? How about her bed wetting? Or, the way she runs and hides whenever a sitter comes over? Or, her stomach aches? Huh, Lisa? Can you explain that?"

"What do you want?"

"I'm calling to tell you that Maddy and I have moved—"

"What do you mean you and Madison moved?"

"We moved out of town. Maddy is not coming back."

"You can't be serious," she said in a guttural tone.

"Yeah, I'm very serious. I'm going to try to give Maddy a life that won't make her run and hide or wet the bed or—"

"You won't get away with this," she screeched. "I'll have you arrested!"

"Do what you got to do, but this is the way it is."

"You'll pay for this!"

"I've been paying for the past two years and for what? So you could drive a new car and wear fancy name-brand clothes, and all Maddy gets is a sitter?"

"You think you're her hero on a white horse? Ha! Well, I'll be there to watch you fall off!" she yelled.

"Lisa! I just wanted you to know Maddy is OK. It's the way it is, and I'm done arguing. I'll call again." And he hung up.

He rested his cell phone against his forehead.

Just then, Maddy said, "Hi, Daddy."

Mike whirled around. *How long had she been standing there?* "Good Morning, young lady."

"Are you sad?" Maddy looked up at him with big, doleful eyes.

Sad? What does a four-year-old girl know about sadness? Mike knelt down to Maddy. "Yes, Daddy is sad, but you don't need to be sad, too. If you smile, I'll smile, and I won't be sad anymore."

Maddy smiled at him, and he smiled in return, but heartache gripped his entire body like a giant vise.

CHAPTER 27

Tuesday

Mike poured himself a cup of coffee. The phone rang and startled him.

Police? Don't be ridiculous! The police don't call for an appointment. They just show up.

"H'lo."

"Hello. This is Mrs. Doyle in C-10. I'm sorry to bother you so early, but my faucet is dripping. 'Kept me up all night."

"Mrs. Doyle, it's not too early. Sounds like it may need a washer. Would this afternoon be OK?"

"Oh sure. It's been dripping for the last two months."

"Two months? Why didn't you call sooner?"

"I just got my hearing aids fixed. 'Never bothered me before."

Mike smiled. "I'll be over after lunch." He jotted name, apartment number and complaint on the maintenance check list. Then, the phone rang again.

"H'lo."

"Good morning, Mike. This is Rosie. I hope I didn't wake you."

"No, I've been up for a while, besides Mrs. Doyle called. She has a dripping faucet," he said.

"Sweet Mrs. Doyle. She and Mr. Doyle are our pioneer residents. You will love them. I meant to tell you, all the tenants have direct access to the unlisted maintenance apartment. They all know not to call in the middle of the night unless it's an emergency."

"That's good." He felt relief that only the apartment dwellers had access to the maintenance phone.

"I'm calling to invite you and Maddy over for breakfast and a short meeting on the veranda. I'd like to go over some more of the job responsibilities and requests for replacement items. About an hour?"

"Yeah, that works for us. See you then."

Rosie's sundrenched veranda sported a white wrought iron table with four matching chairs. A green and white umbrella had its top pitched just enough to shade the table and its guests without blocking the view of the mountains.

Three glasses of freshly squeezed orange juice and a stack of hot French toast beckoned even the most meager of appetites to indulge heartily.

"This is the sweetest orange juice I've ever had," Mike said glancing at Maddy.

"Thank you, Rosie," Maddy said politely, wiping the tell-tale orange pulp from her lips with the back of her hand.

"Just squeezed it this morning," she said with a weak smile. "Now, down to business." She pulled out a stack of papers and explained repair reports, a list of places to get parts, daily and weekly upkeep, and grounds maintenance. "You'll receive a monthly check from the corporate office, but it's up to you to take out your own taxes. You can use this table to figure the taxes."

Mike looked over the paper work and grimaced.

"It's not as difficult as it looks," she said with a short laugh. "You'll catch on quickly."

Mike nodded.

She handed Mike a large key ring with several keys—a master key for all the apartments, one for the storage shed, another for the tool shed, and a key for the swimming pool pump house.

"All the tools needed to repair most everything are in the shed." She sipped her orange juice. She set her glass down slowly. "Stephanie, my daughter, called last night. She and Roger are flying down from Oregon early tomorrow for a visit."

"Hey, that's great!" Mike poured maple syrup on Maddy's French toast.

Rosie sat across from him clasping her hands and rubbing them back and forth. She seemed preoccupied.

Mike noticed and put his fork down. "You seem a little—"

"Apprehensive? I guess I am a little. Mothers sense things, you know, and I sense something amiss."

"Do all mothers sense these things?"

"Most do." She looked curiously at Mike, then to Maddy, but did not venture a comment. "Well, enough about my troubles." She laid her hands flat on the table.

Mike changed the subject. "I promised to take Maddy to the zoo sometime soon. Any suggestions?"

"The L.A. Zoo has hundreds of animals from all over the world. 'Course it's not like the San Diego Zoo, but there's more than enough to see for a fun day."

She gathered the empty breakfast dishes together. "If you really feel daring, they have elephant and camel rides," Rosie said with a laugh.

"Do they have pony rides?" Maddy chimed in.

"I don't think so, but they do have beautiful bird shows and wonderful cat shows. And, I know you'll love the koala house."

"What's that?" Maddy frowned as she scrambled to retrieve her flitting napkin from the gentle breeze.

"It's a gray, furry animal that looks like a little bear without a tail."

"No tail?" Maddy giggled. She tapped Mike on his knee and motioned for him to lean forward. "Cafiforna does have silly animals," she whispered.

"California," Mike corrected gently.

"Maddy, would you like to come over right after lunch and we'll make those cookies for Carla's birthday? She will be five years old."

"Yaay." Maddy clapped her hands. "Can I make a picture for her and can Molly come?"

"That would be wonderful and I bet Molly is your doll, right?"

"Uh-huh. How did you know?"

"When my daughter was a young girl just like you, she had a doll, too. And, do you know what else?"

"What?" Maddy put her elbows on the table and cupped her chin in her hands.

"I sewed lots of doll clothes for Stephie's doll. In fact, Stephie and her doll had matching outfits. I bet if I look real hard, I just might be able to find the trunk with Stephie's doll and the clothes. Would you like that?"

"Uh-huh!" She smiled so big her round cheeks pushed her brown eyes into sunny arches.

"Would Stephanie be upset if Maddy played with her doll?" Mike asked cautiously.

"Oh, goodness, no. I put the doll and all the clothes in a trunk when Stephanie grew up. I fully intended to give them to her when she had her first baby, but—" Rosie looked away briefly.

"I suppose you'll be going to kindergarten next year, right?"

"Uh-huh, 'cuz I'm this big already," Maddy said patting her hand on top of her head.

"You can practice buttoning, zipping and tying when you dress Molly and Lisa Lilly, OK?"

Lisa Lilly? Well this is awkward.

"Yaay," Maddy agreed.

Rosie turned her attention to Mike. "Would it be all right if Maddy stays with me to bake cookies and take them to Carla while you work on Mrs. Doyle's faucet?"

"Fine with me." He looked at Maddy. "OK?"

Maddy nodded.

How strange. Maddy would run and hide whenever a sitter came over to Lisa's, but she seems totally comfortable to go with Rosie. What was it about Rosie that a child would willingly go with her? Karl and Katie had the same quality, whatever it was.

"You'll be lucky to get out of the Doyle's before we get back," Rosie said with a smile. "I'm sure she'll offer you her famous crumpets with homemade strawberry jam. What a treat! Oh, I almost forgot. Detective and Mrs. Sherman will be moving in late today. Would you check their air conditioner? It made a strange clicking noise when I turned it on this morning."

"Will do."

***

The faucet in C-10 needed a washer, just as Mike suspected, and Rosie was right about Mrs. Doyle, as well.

Mrs. Doyle offered fresh, hot crumpets with homemade strawberry preserves and tea.

Mike accepted the tea only after he saw the look of disappointment trace its way across seventy-some years of lines on Mrs. Doyle's face.

She turned to the stove as a shrill whistle escaped the copper teapot.

Mike tried to imagine the proper way the English might eat crumpets and drink their tea, but he could not even begin to do so. He ate the crumpets like a bagel and drank his tea like a cup of coffee. He shot a glance at Mr. Doyle who looked as though he lived by an unwritten no-speak rule.

***

Afterwards, Mike stopped by the birthday party to check on Maddy. She, along with three other girls her age, sat around a kid-size table in front of Building C wearing party hats, giggling, and eating ice cream. Rosie and a young woman sat nearby, each with a tall glass of lemonade.

Mike wanted to meet Maddy's new friends and the mother where Maddy was spending time, but he did not want to intrude.

"Everything OK?" Mike called to Rosie.

"A-OK." Rosie smiled and made a circle with her index finger and thumb.

"Do you want to stay a little longer?" he asked Maddy.

Without any hesitation, she said, "Uh-huh."

He turned to Rosie. "Would that be all right?"

"Absolutely."

"I'm heading over to check on the air conditioner."

Rosie waved. "I'll bring Maddy home in a bit."

***

Mike repaired the rattling air conditioner and was replacing the cover when a moving van pulled up, followed by a beat-up, older Buick.

111

A heavy-set man dressed in a sport shirt and khaki pants with blue suspenders got out. His big neck squatted under the long, straight jaw line that resembled the stone faces of Mount Rushmore.

A smartly dressed thin woman stood on the walkway, shading her eyes from the afternoon sun. Even though she stood erect, she gave the impression of a cold, overcooked spaghetti noodle.

Mike met them at the door. "I'm the maintenance man here. I'm checking on a noise in the air conditioner." He stuck out his hand.

"I'm Detective Sherman and this is Mrs. Sherman." His voice filled the room. He did not reciprocate the hand shake, but only gave Mike a careful smile.

CHAPTER 28

Visitors

M ike trimmed unsightly Japanese shrubs and overgrown Camilla bushes in the courtyard as Maddy and her new friend, Carla, sat at a nearby table serving cups of water to their dolls.

"Yoo-hoo, Mike."

Mike spotted Rosie on her veranda as she motioned for him to come over. A woman and a man stood on either side of Rosie.

The man of medium height and build with brown hair and blue eyes flashed a warm smile. The slender woman at his side had chestnut hair bobbed just below her ears. She wore a white shell and white slacks tied loosely at the waist with a deep pink sash. She looked like she could be an advertisement for vitamins except for the worried look in her green eyes.

"I'd like you to meet my daughter and my son-in-law, Stephanie and Roger Sterling." Rosie flashed her typical large smile. "And, this is my maintenance man Mike DiSanto."

"Mother told us how fortunate she feels to have you here. She's been without a maintenance man for over two months and I think the stress was getting her down." She extended her hand to Mike. "I'm so glad to meet you."

Mike clasped her hand briefly. "I'm the one who's glad to be here."

Mike held his hand out to Roger. Roger shook his hand like someone clinging to a life line while in a sinking boat. Roger's eyes had the same grip, and for an instant, Mike felt Roger held a secret locked deep in the center of his mind.

Mike hoped his own eyes revealed nothing more than his words did.

"Where are you from?" Roger asked with genuine interest.

A prickly feeling ran down Mike's spine. He swallowed. He knew to answer truthfully might lead to the discovery of his flight from Minnesota, but to not answer at all would surely cast suspicion.

"I come from—"

Suddenly, Roger turned ashen and sat down, visibly shaken.

Stephanie grabbed for her husband. "Roger! Are you all right?" Alarm permeated her voice. Her eyes darted toward Rosie.

"I'm fine." Roger waved his hand in an upswing motion, obviously embarrassed by his sudden weakness. "It must be from the flight. I'm OK. Really."

Mike felt relieved for the diversion to Roger's question, but sorry for his misfortune. "I'd better get back to work." He looked from Stephanie to Roger. "I hope your stay will be a good one."

"I do, too," Stephanie said with a strange hesitation.

Three days later, Mike noticed Stephanie and Roger lounging by the pool. The sun shone unusually warm in a yellow sky rimmed with a brown haze like someone had inverted a brightly painted pottery bowl.

The pool teased those nearby to come enjoy its blue coolness, but Stephanie and Roger sat in somber silence staring absently at the glimmering water.

Stephanie wore her hair pulled away from her face with a green headband that matched her eyes. Mike noticed her almond-shaped eyes surrounded by tiny lines in tan skin were expressionless.

Roger had a gaunt look, as if he had slept poorly.

"Howdy," Mike greeted, and immediately sensed a strain in the air, and felt like he was intruding into their private world. Stephanie looked up and smiled, but it was only a polite smile. Roger didn't move except for a slight nod.

Mike continued his walk to Rosie's apartment with several folded papers sticking out his shirt pocket.

Rosie, eyes red and swollen, greeted him cheerily, but it did not fool Mike. Something was wrong.

"I brought over some maintenance reports and requests for—but maybe this is a bad time. I'll come back."

"No, no." She waved her hand in protest. "You don't know how much I appreciate you taking over the maintenance so competently, but I do; especially now." She lowered her voice to barely above a whisper. "Remember when I said I felt something was wrong when Stephanie called to say they were coming for a visit?"

Mike nodded.

"The reason they came to California is—" She sighed deeply. "...Roger had to see a specialist, an oncologist." She blinked rapidly and brushed her tears aside trying unsuccessfully to regain her usual cheerful composure.

"What is it?" Mike asked quietly.

Rosie took a long time to answer. She looked up at the ceiling brushing tears from her face. She looked frantically around the kitchen. She stared outside at her daughter and husband.

"Preliminary tests, CAT scan and MRI, confirm that—" She took a deep breath.

"Rosie, you don't have to tell me—"

"To not say the words out loud would be to deny the fact, and denial won't help face the reality." She turned to Mike. "Roger," she faltered, "Roger has been diagnosed with an inoperable brain tumor."

CHAPTER 29

The Reaction

Mike felt like he had just dropped into the eye of a hurricane. He didn't know what to say or how to comfort Rosie.

"He's scheduled for surgery tomorrow to relieve some of the pressure," Rosie said dabbing at her eyes. "But, the doctor said it would only give him a little relief for a short time."

"Poor guy," Mike said sympathetically, shaking his head slowly. He drew in a deep breath. "How's Stephanie taking it?"

"Not very well, I'm afraid. They've only been married five years." She wiped her eyes again and blew her nose. "They were planning to start a family soon, but, Roger has been getting such terrible headaches. They wanted to make sure everything was—" She covered her eyes and turned away.

Mike reached over, put a comforting hand on Rosie's trembling shoulder, and patted it gently.

"Anyway, they'll be going back to Oregon as soon as Roger is able to travel. They're going to put their house up for sale and take care of some personal things." She took another Kleenex. "They'll be moving back here." She blew her nose and wept silently with her head buried into the Kleenex.

"Is there anything I can do?"

Rosie shook her head. "It's in the Lord's hands." Her voice held a certainty as though taking deep comfort in her own words.

Mike squinted against the sun through the open patio door. He looked past where Stephanie and Roger sat holding hands, staring at nothing in particular, to where Maddy played and giggled with her new friend. "Why don't they want to stay in Oregon?"

"It was Roger's decision. He thought it would be easier on Steph to be here rather than to be alone with him at their ranch. You know, in case anything happens to him."

"Don't they have neighbors who could help?"

"Oh, they have wonderful neighbors, but the closest neighbor is three quarters of a mile away and the doctor is thirty-five miles away." Rosie stopped speaking as she rubbed small circles on her temples with her fingers.

"What does Roger do?"

"He works for Northwest Chemical Control. He studies the effects of pesticides and pollutants on the environment. That's one of the reasons why they live in the foothills of the Cascade Mountains. That, and it's one of the most peaceful and beautiful places on earth."

Just then, Stephanie shuffled into the kitchen. Her lively bounce from a few days earlier was gone. "I'm going to make Roger a sandwich."

"Nonsense. I'll make a plate of sandwiches and some lemonade and bring them out." Rosie washed her hands and set to work immediately.

"Let me help," Stephanie said taking tall lemonade glasses from the cupboard and two smaller glasses for Maddy and her friend, Carla.

Mike noticed Stephanie maneuver about the kitchen as easily as Rosie. The two women worked silently, but with a natural grace and obvious affection one for the other.

Mike slipped out and walked slowly to the table where Roger sat with his hands folded against his forehead. He sat down quietly next to Roger.

He thought about Lisa and the many times Betty had made sandwiches and coffee for him and Lisa after a date. *Come to think of it, Lisa never offered to help Betty,* he realized.

He thought about Maddy. *Will she ever know the caring love of a mother? Is she destined to grow up with a single parent? Me? The one who doesn't understand this complicated thing called love?*

"Hello?" Rosie waved her hand in front of Mike's trance-like eyes.

"Sorry," he apologized, shaking himself back to reality. "I guess I was a thousand miles away." He stood up. "I'll be going."

"Please stay. I made enough for you, Maddy and Carla." Rosie smiled as she held up a plate stacked high with chicken salad sandwiches.

Stephanie set a tray with a pitcher of lemonade and several glasses onto the table. "I'll get the fruit and chips."

Roger looked at Mike. "You better stay or I won't stand a chance here with Rosie and Stephanie fussing over me."

Mike nodded. He liked Roger and wondered if they would have become friends under different circumstances.

Mike called Maddy and Carla to come over. "This is my daughter, Maddy, and her friend, Carla," Mike introduced. "This is Stephanie and Roger."

Stephanie smiled a clone of Rosie's smile. "Hello, Maddy and Carla. I'm happy to meet two such happy young ladies."

"Hello, girls." Roger held out his hand.

Maddy looked up at Mike. He nodded, so Maddy timidly slipped her hand into Roger's

Mike looked sympathetically at Roger. *He'll never know what it's like to have kids.* Roger's eyes had lost their distant look as he turned his amiable attention fully on those around him.

How incredible to know one's fate and not be able to change it or to escape it, Mike thought, *and still exhibit such acceptance!*

CHAPTER 30

Phone Calls

---

everal weeks after settling in at Green Tree Complex, Mike
called Karl.

"Hello?"

Mike felt a deep stab of lonesomeness at the sound of his voice. "Hi
Karl. It's Mike."

"Mike! How are you? Where are you? How's Maddy?"

"I'm fine and Maddy is fine. In fact, Maddy is doing great. How's
Katie?"

"She has a bit of a cold, but nothing that will keep her down. She
just took an apple pie over to the neighbor's."

"Maddy wants to say hi." Mike put his cell phone on speaker and
handed it to Maddy.

"Hi, Mr. Karl."

"Hi, Maddy. Say, you don't have to call me Mr. Karl. You can call
me just plain old' Karl."

"Okee dokee, jus'plain old' Karl, but that's a lot longer to say than
Mr. Karl."

Mike grinned, and he heard Karl laugh on the other end.

Maddy said goodbye and gave the phone back to Mike.

Mike switched off the speaker. "How's Lisa doing?"

"Ever since the divorce, she didn't have much to do with us, but now,
never. The last we heard, she's still madder than a wet hen about you
taking Maddy. And, I guess she's started dating her lawyer."

"That doesn't surprise me. I'm gone a few weeks and he's on my doorstep."

"That should be the least of your worries."

"You're right. She's divorced and free to do what she wants."

"That's not what meant. Mike, you've got to come back." He sounded more pleading than commanding.

"I wish I could, but I can't. Maddy is doing good and I don't want to risk having her revert back to being emotionally troubled again. Or worse. Karl, as a father, there's something in me that will not condone the way my daughter is mistreated, not in a physical sense, but in every emotional sense of the word."

"I understand what you are saying, but I need to tell you, son, the police have questioned just about everybody in town about your whereabouts."

"I figured they would."

"There's a warrant out for your arrest, too. Kidnapping is serious. It's a felony, and you could wind up in prison. Then, what?"

"I don't know, Karl. I don't know what to do. I just know I can't put Maddy back in a situation that will destroy her."

After he hung up, he sat quietly at the kitchen table.

Maddy came out of her room. "I'm hungry."

"Should we call mommy and then make something to eat?"

"OK."

Mike punched in Lisa's number and handed his phone to Maddy.

"Hello. This is Lisa. Please leave a message."

"Mommy's not home," Maddy said looking at Mike.

"You can leave her a message," he coaxed.

"Hi, Mommy. We are having fun, but I miss you a little. I love you." She handed the phone to Mike.

"Lisa, Maddy just wanted to say hi. She is doing fine. We'll call again." He heard a beep and hung up. *Mistake to call?* He wondered. *Who knows?*

CHAPTER 31

Good News and Bad News

Roger Sterling was released from the hospital three days after his surgery to relieve the pressure from his brain tumor. He sat on the veranda amidst the morning newspaper, a pitcher of ice water, a plate of toast, a bowl of strawberries, and several pillows.

"Looks like you're set for the day," Mike greeted, setting down the pool vacuum.

"I guess Steph and Rosie didn't want me to starve to death while they went grocery shopping," he said with a dry smile beneath a gauze turban. "Sit down." He motioned toward an empty patio chair.

"How's it going?"

"Well, I have some good news and some bad news. Huh, that reminds me of a story about General Custer," he said with a short laugh. "Seems one of Custer's scouts came to him and said, 'Sir, I have some good news and some bad news.' General Custer asked. 'What's the bad news?' The scout said, 'Sir, we're completely surrounded with no hope. There's no one to rescue us. We're dead.' General Custer asked, 'What's the good news?' His scout replied, 'We don't have to go back through Nebraska.'"

Both men laughed, but then they became serious. "What's your news?" Mike asked.

"I have good news and bad news. The bad news is—" He paused as though trying to convince himself that the targeting arrows were only a mirage. "I'm dying of brain cancer. The good news, sir," he said holding up his first finger, "is that I have six months to spend with Steph instead of the three months they originally thought I had."

Mike nodded slowly and looked down at his feet. "My dad always said, 'We are the captains of our souls.' Then my mother would say, 'And, sometimes, it takes storm clouds and sunshine to make a rainbow.' I never knew what they meant." He didn't know what else to say.

"My mother used to tell me to be sure to always wear clean underwear in case I was ever in an accident."

Both men smiled.

It was Roger who spoke first. "I suspected the tumor even before—"

Mike nodded.

The two men looked each other with mutual respect hovering between them.

***

Ten days later, Stephanie and Roger returned to Oregon. Every week, Rosie received a letter from Stephanie and, sometimes, she read parts of the letter to Mike. One letter, in particular, evoked a huge smile from Rosie. "Listen to this," she said unfolding a two-page letter from Stephanie.

"We sold the ranch and most of the furnishings!" she read. "They want to close December 26th, so, would it possible for you to come on the 21st for Christmas and help us pack up our things? We plan to rent a small U-Haul and drive back after the closing. We will get your airline ticket, if you can come. Please come."

Rosie continued reading. "Roger is still working nearly every day, but seems so tired when he comes home. There is so much uncertainty with the move and Roger's illness that, at times, I'm overwhelmed. Even when Roger is sitting next to me, I sometimes feel so all alone. I'm losing a part of him each day. I cherish the times when we pray together, and am comforted when I hear him pray for me as I hope he is encouraged when I pray for him."

Rosie quietly folded the letter and tucked it back in its envelope.

"The apartment next to mine will be vacated on December 15th. I hate to ask especially so close to Christmas, but would it be possible for you to get it ready for them?"

"Not a problem," Mike said with a nod.

CHAPTER 32

Christmas Tree

T he next morning, Mike listened to car doors slamming, tenants calling out holiday greetings, and the monotonous hum of the early morning freeway traffic.

He sipped his black coffee while Maddy ate her usual bowl of Cheerios with sliced bananas. "Do you want to get our Christmas tree today?" he asked.

Her brown eyes brightened. She ran to the patio doors, pulled open the curtains and peered out. "But, Daddy, there's no snow. I think it's stuck in the air."

Mike got up and walked over to look. The gloomy sky seemed to creep to the ground. Fog and smog mixed with one another until everything seemed encased in a silver gray mist.

"Sweetie, it doesn't snow in California."

"Why?"

"Because it's too warm."

"Will Santa be too hot?"

"I think he wears different clothes when he comes to California."

Looking around their small living room, she asked, "How is he going to bring my presents?"

Mike walked back to the table and picked up his coffee mug. "He'll probably leave them on the veranda, but that's OK, right?"

"Yaay." She looked up at him with a big smile. "I colored a puppy for Grandpa and a kitty for Grandma."

"Well, that is great! Can you show them to me?"

She ran to her room and retrieved the pictures from the small desk Mike had rescued from the storage shed the week before and painted it white. She held up a picture of a puppy playing with a shoe in a yard of flowers. "See. This is for Grandpa." She held up a picture of a kitten chasing a butterfly. "And this is for Grandma."

"You did an excellent job! How about a special picture for mommy, and then we can mail them for Christmas?"

"I already did one for mommy. See?" She held up a picture of a family having a picnic under a tree.

Mike stared at the picture with its obvious display of a family—a mother, a father, and child together. *Did she feel the brokenness? Did she choose this particular picture because she wished she could have a real family? Does she miss her mommy? Her grandparents?*

"You did good." He nodded and forced a smile. "Do you want to see your mommy?"

"Sometimes."

"Do you like being here with Daddy?"

"Yes," she said nodding

"Are you sad?" he asked thoughtfully.

Maddy shook her head.

"OK, then," he said clapping his hands together, "let's go get our tree." His lame attempt at sparking excitement must have been enough for Maddy because she bounced up and down and squealed with delight.

The sky had turned a darker shade of gray and a steady, chilly rain began to fall. Scotch pine and blue spruce trees leaned against the temporary red fencing of the small, otherwise vacant, corner lot.

Mike dashed around brown mud puddles, but Maddy jumped into each one sending a grimy spray against her red rubber boots.

"Look, Daddy! I'm Rudolph!"

Mike sighed and dodged another messy splash.

By the time they found the perfect tree, sheets of cold stinging rain pelted down, taking no mercy on tree shoppers. Mike tied the tree to the roof of his car.

"We need lights," Maddy said.

Mike grinned. "That we do, young lady."

They stopped at a discount store that played a wavy version of "We Wish You a Merry Christmas" as shoppers jostled armloads of packages.

Weaving their way through the crowded Christmas decoration section, they picked out red, green, and white twinkling lights, tinsel, shiny red bulbs, and a lighted angel with golden hair for the top.

When they reached the car, the rope that had secured their tree hung limply down to the puddled ground.

"Aw, man!" Mike said under his breath.

"Daddy! Our tree is gone!" Maddy wailed.

"Who would take someone's Christmas tree?" he muttered.

"Daa—ddy!"

"Don't cry, sweetie. We'll get another one." He put their few packages in the trunk, picked Maddy up and held her as she sobbed.

***

The corner lot still had several trees, but the Scotch pine seemed a little more scraggly and the blue spruce a bit scrawnier.

Mike picked a little blue spruce and stood it next to him. "What do you think?"

Maddy shook her head.

Holding a scotch pine out in front of him, he asked, "What about this one?"

A smile scrambled across her face. "Yup."

***

Maddy, dressed in her pink flannel nightgown, curled up on Mike's lap with Molly under her arm. Mike clasped both arms around Maddy and Molly and, together, they gazed at their twinkling Christmas tree.

The pine scent lingered in the room, and somehow in the dimness, the spot on the tree with no branches didn't look quite so bare. Although the lighted angel could look up to Mike, she stood perfectly straight atop her perch. The tinsel danced, and the lights blinked their way around the tree.

"Daddy?"

"Hmm?"

"I love you."

"I love you too, sweetie." He squeezed his arms tighter.

***

The next morning, Maddy stood in front of the tree eyeing it from top to bottom. "Daddy, can we put cookies on the tree."

"What?" Mike called, above the buzz of his electric shaver.

"Carla has cookies on her tree. Can we put cookies on our tree?"

"Maddy, I don't know how to make cookies."

"Hu-huh. Daddies know how to do everything."

"Who told you that?"

"Grandma."

"Who makes the cookies at their house?"

"Grandma."

"Well, there you go. Grandmas make cookies. How about breakfast?" he asked, splashing spicy aftershave on his face and neck.

"Can Rosie help us?" Maddy persisted.

"We can't ask her to do that."

"But, why?"

"Because she's busy getting ready to go see Stephanie and Roger for Christmas. Remember we're taking her to the airport tomorrow?"

"Uh-huh. But if we bake cookies, she can take some with, and we can have some."

Mike knelt down to her. "Sweetie, sometimes we can't always have what we want."

"Why?"

"Because sometimes things happen that we can't control."

"What does that mean?"

"It means 'fix.' Sometimes, things happen that we can't fix."

"You mean like a faucet?"

"Not exactly. I mean people."

Maddy scrunched up her nose.

"Sweetie, listen. Grandma isn't here, and we can't fix that. Rosie is going away, and we can't fix that. Do you understand what I'm trying to tell you?"

"Uh-huh. We need to find a grandma to help us make cookies."

Mike breathed a sigh. "What would you like for breakfast?"

"Green eggs and ham."

Mike laughed. "I can't make green eggs and ham."

"Sam I Am can."

"Well, sweetie, I am not Sam I Am. How about cereal?"

"Can I have the kind that talks?"

"Rice Krispies coming up. Snap. Crackle. Pop," he said and tweaked her nose.

While eating, Mike said, "I have to do some paperwork after breakfast. Can you be a good girl and play in your room till I get done?"

"OK."

Mike focused on completing the maintenance reports. He scanned a copy of the form for reporting earnings as a self-employed contractor. Something caught his eye. He frowned when he noticed his Social Security number. He inadvertently switched two numbers and had already submitted the original. "I've got to take care of that," he mumbled, and put the paper in a drawer to do later.

Maddy seemed unusually quiet this morning. Typically, she would interrupt Mike for something every half hour or so to show him what Molly was wearing or what color she was using in her coloring book. He did not hear her customary chattering to Molly pretending they were friends having a tea party with tiny cups of water and a small dish of M&M's.

Mike pushed her bedroom door open to check on her. The room was empty!

"Maddy? Maddy." He looked under her bed and in the closet. "Maddy?" He searched the bathroom and even his room, but no Maddy.

He spied the door ajar. He ran out into the courtyard, looking everywhere, but no Maddy. He saw a small group of children in the play area. "Did you see Maddy?"

The children stopped playing and shook their heads.

He dashed to Rosie's apartment, but there was no answer to his frantic knocks. He ran to the laundry room, but there was only a Hispanic woman, folding clothes. "Did you see Maddy?"

"No, Señor."

He rushed outside. "Maddy! Maddy!" he yelled.

Just then Detective Sherman exited from Building D and said, "I think I saw her go in Building C a while ago. I thought it was strange she wasn't with—"

Mike didn't wait to hear what strange thoughts he may have had. He raced to the next building. He started banging on doors asking each occupant if they had seen Maddy.

"No, sorry," they answered.

He banged on C-10. Mrs. Doyle opened the door.

Before Mike could ask about Maddy, he spied her in the kitchen.

Maddy looked at Mike. She had flour on her cheeks. "I found a grandma," she announced triumphantly. She held up a plate of white frosted cookies sprinkled with red and green sugars.

He brushed past Mrs. Doyle and dashed into the kitchen. He didn't know whether to scold Maddy or to hug her. He decided to hug her and scold her later.

"I'm sorry, Mrs. Doyle. I couldn't find her."

"I thought you knew she was here. Otherwise, I would have called you on the tele. I am so sorry for your worry." She licked her fingers and wiped them on her apron. "She said she wanted to make cookies for your Christmas tree. I am truly sorry."

"No harm done, Mrs. Doyle. I'm sorry for being so abrupt." His shoulders relaxed and his jaw muscles stopped twitching. "Thank you for taking the time to make cookies with Maddy."

Mrs. Doyle wrapped aluminum foil over the plate of cookies and gave them to Maddy.

"Thank you, Mrs. Doyle," Maddy said.

"I had fun. I hope you can come again."

Maddy skipped alongside Mike seemingly unaware of the worry she had caused him.

"Maddy," Mike said as they walked to their building, "just because you're almost five years old doesn't mean you can do whatever you want to. You have to make sure it's OK with other people. Next time, ask Daddy."

His words left a hollow echo in his ears.

CHAPTER 33

Christmas in California

M ike and Maddy sat on the floor of their living room in front of the Christmas tree. A meager pile of gifts wrapped in festive paper lay beneath. Mike suspected the several crudely wrapped gifts scattered around the tree were some of Maddy's favorite play things she had wrapped for him. He smiled.

"Can we open presents?" Maddy asked, bouncing up and down on her knees.

"OK. Here goes!"

Mike handed her a large box with a big red bow. He read the tag, "To Maddy, love from Mr. & Mrs. Doyle."

Maddy tore off the gift wrap and lifted the cover. She pulled back the tissue paper and squealed with delight. A beautiful porcelain-face doll looked up at her. The doll wore an emerald green, satin dress and lace stockings. The eyelashes above big, blue eyes were hand-painted with exact detail. She had a tiny red mouth and brown hair fixed in long curls. A handwritten note was pinned to the doll's dress that read: "To Maddy, this doll used to live in England many, many years ago. Her name is Tiffany. My mother gave her to me when I was five years old. With Love, Mrs. Doyle."

Maddy held the doll on her lap. "Your turn, Daddy."

Mike picked a small box wrapped in green paper. It was signed, "To Mike with much gratitude, Love, Rosie." He opened the lid, looked inside, chuckled, and closed the lid again.

"What is it?"

"Something very special."

"What? Open it!" Maddy could hardly contain her curiosity.

Mike laughed and whisked off the cover. "We get to go to Disneyland," he said waving two all-day passes. He was about to toss the box, when he spied two more tickets. "And—" He gave a low whistle of amazement at Rosie's generosity. "Two tickets to the Rose Bowl game?!"

"Yaay! Can we go to Disneyland tomorrow?"

"How about we go when it's sunny and warmer."

"Why?"

"I think we'll have more fun if it's nice out, don't you?"

"I guess."

"Here's another one for Maddy." He made much of presenting a gaily wrapped gift to her.

Maddy ripped the paper off, and her eyes grew wide with excitement when she saw the Easy Bake Oven and four miniature cake mixes.

Mike read the card: "To Maddy. Now you can bake special cakes for your tea parties with Molly. Be sure to have your daddy help you, and then he can have some cake, too. Merry Christmas. I love you, Rosie."

"Oh, wow! Will you help me?"

"I sure will. How 'bout if we make one tonight and leave a piece for Santa Claus?"

"Yaay!"

Maddy picked one of the crudely wrapped gifts. "This is for you."

Mike shook the package. He squeezed it. "I wonder what's inside."

Maddy's little fingers tore at the paper.

"Hey! I thought this was for me."

"Daddy, you're too slow."

"Ah! My very own agates! Thank you, my little princess." *I'll have to be sure to remember to sneak these back into her pouch*, he thought.

Mike handed Maddy a box. "Last one."

Maddy squealed with delight when she opened a set of tea party dishes. "Read what it says."

"To my special girl at Christmas, I love you. Daddy."

"Thank you, Daddy. You're the bestest daddy ever!" She hugged him tightly around his neck.

"And you're the bestest daughter ever."

"Can we bake a cake now?"

"Hold on, princess. I have to read the directions first."

Mike and Maddy spent the better part of an hour baking a cake and cutting a piece to put on a plate for Santa. Mike helped Maddy write a note: "Dear Santa, this cake is just for you. I hope you like it. Love, Maddy." They placed the cake and note on the kitchen table.

"Time for bed."

***

Mike heard Maddy scramble from her bed before dawn on Christmas Day.

"Santa came! Santa came!" she announced.

Mike pulled on his jeans and walked into the living room.

"So he did. Go ahead and open," he said.

Maddy tore off the paper and looked at a plain cardboard box.

"Well, let's see what Santa brought." He lifted a child-sized cupboard from the box and set it on the floor. "Oh, wow! My very own cupboard. And, look! It matches my desk!"

The white painted cupboard had two glass doors on top with tiny hooks to hang cups, an open shelf, and two wooden doors with pink knobs below.

"Santa left you a note. It says: "Dear Maddy, thank you for the cake and milk. It was very good. Love, Santa Claus."

"Did Santa really write that?"

"That's what it says," he said giving the note to Maddy to examine.

"He must a run outta paper then."

"Why's that?"

"Cuz he wrote it on this," she said holding up a piece of brown paper torn from a grocery bag.

"Well, it's OK if he uses our paper, isn't it?"

"I guess so." She shrugged. "Can we call Mommy? I want to tell her what I got."

"We sure can. Do you miss Mommy?" he asked, as he punched in Lisa's number.

"I don't know," she shrugged. "Maybe sometimes."

"Sometimes, I miss her, too."

"This is Lisa. Please leave a message," the answering machine said.

Another one of the hundreds of pangs of guilt, and sadness stabbed him in the heart.

CHAPTER 34

Back Home

Mike awoke early, tired, yet unable to sleep. He got up to check on Maddy and smiled when he saw her curled up in footie pajamas amidst her dolls, pillow and crumpled blanket. He pulled the covers over her and brushed her hair from her face.

She stirred slightly as he crept from her darkened room and retreated to his room.

He lay stretched out on his bed with his arms behind his head and one foot crossed over the other. He thought about the return of Rosie, Stephanie and Roger later that Sunday.

He thought about going to church. It seemed important to Rosie. Stephanie and Roger talked openly about faith as did Karl and Katie, but he had never attended church except the one Christmas Eve when he and Lisa got engaged. Besides, he didn't know which church to go to or why he should go in the first place.

He contemplated the upcoming Rose Bowl game between the Michigan Wolverines and the Washington Huskies, and a flood of excitement ran through him. He hoped Roger would be up for it. He knew how much Roger enjoyed football, and he seemed eager to go when Mike told him he got two tickets as a Christmas gift from Rosie.

He closed his eyes and listened to the steady tick tock of the kitchen wall clock. He clenched his teeth. The rhythmic, loud ticking reminded him that morning was just a short time away. Finally, drowsiness settled over him into welcomed sleep. Then he heard, "Daddy, I'm hungry."

Late that afternoon as Mike and Maddy tidied up the courtyard, a car toting a U-Haul, pulled up to Rosie's building. Stephanie, looking weary, maneuvered the vehicle into a large parking space.

Mike saw her give an obvious sigh of relief and felt sympathy for both her and Roger at their plight.

After they exchanged pleasant greetings, they wholeheartedly accepted Mike's offer to help unload.

Roger tried to carry the smaller boxes, but for the most part, he had to sit on a chair and rest.

Mike was surprised at Roger's deteriorated condition from just a few weeks before. "Glad to see you, Roger. Was it a long trip for you?"

"Just the last couple hundred miles when I got too tired, and Steph had to take over." He looked away briefly.

"Are you feeling good enough to go to the game this Saturday?"

"You bet! I'd have to be in my casket before I would miss a golden opportunity to go to the Rose Bowl."

Mike unloaded the boxes and brought them to the newly cleaned and painted apartment. Stephanie and Rosie set to work unpacking boxes labeled "kitchen" while Roger emptied boxes of clothing in the bedroom.

Mike noticed the frequent smile exchanges between Stephanie and Roger, as though there were no death sentence hanging over Roger at all—just the continuation of life in a new setting for them. Roger did not seem to solicit any pity, and Stephanie didn't give him any. It was more of an acceptance of what must be for two people devoted to each other.

"I'm making a brunch at 11 a.m. for the Tournament of Roses Parade. You and Maddy are invited," Rosie said stacking plates on a shelf in the cupboard.

"Sounds good. What can I bring?" Mike asked.

"Just your sweet selves and your appetites. Steph and I will entertain Maddy, or should I say, Maddy will probably entertain us, while you're at the game."

***

New Year's Day dawned bright and sunny with the temperature predicted to be 55 degrees by game time. Mike thought about another

New Year's Day in Minnesota when he had to shovel over a foot of snow to get his truck out, and the temperature hovered around ten degrees with a wind chill of -23 degrees. He felt a chill just thinking about it.

The Rose Bowl parade created a festive mood. Rosie, Stephanie and Roger, Mike and Maddy enjoyed egg bake, fresh fruit and Danish rolls as marching bands and floats outrageously decorated with beautiful roses of every color and hue imaginable paraded down streets of Pasadena.

On their way to the stadium, Roger asked, "Has your home state ever played in the Rose Bowl?"

"Yeah. They lost to the Washington Huskies in '61 and defeated UCLA in '62."

"Ah, you're from Minnesota, huh?"

Mike looked sideways at Roger and nodded.

"I thought everybody in Minnesota had blonde hair, blue eyes, and said, 'yeah, sure.' You're not a Swede or Norwegian in disguise, are you?" he asked, with a wry chuckle.

"No, actually I'm a second generation Little Italy New Yorker. Although I was only a year old when my folks moved to Minnesota, so I don't remember anything of New York."

"Does Minnesota really have 10,000 lakes?"

Mike was impressed with the knowledge Roger had of places and things. "Those are just the good fishing lakes," he said with a laugh.

They settled into their seats on the twenty-yard line. "Not bad seats," Roger said with a huge grin.

Mike nodded and smiled.

Action on the field brought a deafening roar from over 100,000 fans as Michigan and Washington battled back and forth for the championship. Mike yelled for the Midwestern team and of course, Roger cheered for the west coast team

By halftime, Roger looked pale and haggard.

"Do you want to cut out early?" Mike asked.

"No way! I'm here to watch football."

Neither team dominated the game as they see-sawed back and forth in scoring. Roger took every opportunity to spout off his confidence in the Huskies.

Mike took the jabbing good-naturedly defending the Wolverines to the end. When the final score flashed on the screen, Michigan had won by seven points.

"Can I still get a ride home?" Roger asked.

"Yeah, sure."

And, life moved on toward spring.

CHAPTER 35

May

Maddy ripped the paper from the huge box and stared wide-eyed at the picture of a two-wheeled bike with training wheels. "Yippee! Can I ride it?"

"Yup! As soon as I put it together." Mike grinned and bent down to Maddy. "Happy birthday, five-year old!" he said and kissed her forehead.

"Do you want to open another present?" Mike handed her a small gift-wrapped box. "This is from Rosie."

Maddy tore off the paper. Inside the box were purple and white streamers. "Oh! I love 'em! And they match my bike, too!"

"One more present. Then, do you want to help me put your bike together?"

Maddy jumped up and down and clapped her hands. Her eyes sparkled, and her smile lit up her whole face.

She opened a box from Stephanie and Roger, although Roger was in the hospital. She pulled out a purple helmet and immediately put it on.

"You look just like a girl ready to learn how to ride a bike!"

A short time later, Mike finished assembling the bike. It had a little wire basket and a horn that sounded like a circus clown's horn.

Maddy swished the streamers that dangled from the handle bar grips and squeezed the black rubber bulb. She squeezed it again and again, and giggled each time she heard the horn.

She danced around the room and holding her arms outstretched, she said, "I love you a big bunch."

Mike held his arms out wide and said, "I love you a bigger bunch!"

"Uh-huh. I love you more."

"No, I love you more."

Early that afternoon, the pool area swarmed with glistening, tan bodies. Bikini-clad women lounged on beach towels and lawn chairs at the pool's edge. Boys cannonballed into the water sending cool sprays onto anyone sitting within ten feet of the pool. Startled screams and laughter permeated the area. The fragrance of coconut suntan oil drenched the air. Oily films collected on puddles, creating iridescent colors.

"Do you want to go swimming, ride your bike, or take Carla to a movie?" Mike asked.

Maddy became quiet and Mike could tell she was thinking seriously of the options. "Movie!" Maddy said with finality.

"'The Adventures of Winnie the Pooh' or 'The Rescuers'?"

Maddy made a big "O" with her mouth as she thought again. "'Winnie the Pooh!'"

"After the movie, let's stop by the hospital to see Roger."

"Can I ride my bike after?"

"Yup."

Mike and Maddy picked up Carla and headed to Mike's assigned carport. He noticed Detective and Mrs. Sherman sitting at a table under the shade of an umbrella, sipping on tall, iced drinks.

He avoided looking directly at the detective, but he could feel his penetrating eyes follow his every step. It made the back of his neck sweaty.

At the matinee, Maddy and Carla, like the rest of the noisy children in the crowded theater, sat on the edge of blue cushioned seats, munching buttered and salty popcorn, and laughing at the silly antics of Pooh and Piglet.

Mike watched the movie with unseeing eyes. He felt restless. Maybe it was because Roger lay in a hospital dying of a brain tumor, and he's sitting in a movie theater watching a children's movie?

He rolled a piece of hard watermelon candy between his teeth and tried to concentrate on the screen. Still, his thoughts trampled together like wild horses.

I'm twenty-eight years old and not even listed in a phone book, for crying out loud! I'm a man outside my trade with no real home to call my own. I have no connections to my past, except Maddy. There's a warrant out for my arrest for kidnapping, and I'm living in an apartment complex with a detective for a neighbor!

He glanced at Maddy sitting next to him, giggling.

***

After dropping Carla off at her apartment, they drove directly to the hospital. Once there, however, Mike was able to suppress his edginess. At least, for the time being.

They rode the elevator to the fourth floor. As the doors opened, Rosie greeted them.

"I was on my way to the cafeteria for a glass of iced tea," she said and smiled a thin smile. "Stephie and I take turns so Roger always has someone with him. I'm so glad you came."

"How's he doing?" Mike asked soberly.

"He slips in and out of consciousness. But he doesn't seem to be in any pain, and that's a good thing."

How could someone slip so quickly? Mike thought about the last time he spoke to Roger just a few days before. At that time, he was still able to mumble an acknowledgement to Mike. But now, only semi-conscious? How could this be?

"I'll take Maddy for a soda, if you'd like."

"Thanks. I'll meet you there after I see Roger," he said.

Rosie pointed to the hallway that led to the wing restricted to terminally ill patients. "It's Room 413."

Rosie and Maddy got into the elevator, and Mike headed down the hallway. He stopped at the closed wooden door of Roger's room.

Mike knocked quietly, then pushed the door open.

Stephanie looked up and smiled gratefully. She provided the only touch of color in an otherwise all-white room.

Mike nodded and smiled in return.

She motioned for him to sit on a beige chair with wooden arms on the opposite side of Roger's bed.

"Roger, it's me, Mike," he said quietly.

Roger turned his head slightly in the direction of Mike's voice. He gazed at Mike with eyes dark and hollow, sunk in bony cheeks the color of old ivory.

Mike took hold of Roger's hand in their usual thumb locking handshake, but it was like holding the hand of a sleeping child.

Roger lay with half-closed eyes. His breathing came in shallow spurts from a skeletal cavern that echoed in mockery of life.

Mike glanced at Stephanie sitting by her husband's bedside. *So young to be approaching widowhood*, he thought. *Too gracious to let it detract from her loveliness.*

"I'm glad you stopped by," she said just above a whisper.

Mike nodded. "Me, too." He returned his gaze to the floor, sitting with his elbows resting on his knees and his hands loosely clasped together.

"You seem preoccupied. Are you all right?" she asked.

"Yeah, a little restless maybe. How about you?"

"I'm all right. You see, this morning, I finally fully accepted what must be." She looked tenderly at Roger. "I think that's when I discovered what the Lord meant when He said, 'My grace is sufficient for you.'"

Mike looked blankly at Stephanie.

She gently smoothed the thin, white blanket covering her semi-conscious husband who had drifted off, never to wake again.

CHAPTER 36

To No Avail

Monday morning promised to be another hot August day when the sun baked the earth from a white sky.

Mike showered and slipped into his jeans and a green t-shirt. He walked, still barefoot, out onto the veranda sipping his coffee and admiring the view of the San Gabriel Mountains.

Today was going to be a big day for Maddy. Mike would register her for kindergarten at the elementary school a few blocks from the apartment complex.

Maddy needed no prodding to get dressed or to eat breakfast.

"Are you excited to see where you'll go to school?" he asked, slipping on his shoes.

"I am sooo excited," she said rolling her eyes in her typical fashion.

On their way to the carport, Mike noticed Detective Sherman approaching.

"Mornin'," Mike greeted. His tone lacked emotion.

Detective Sherman wasted no time with greetings. He faced him directly with his fat thumbs hooked under his suspenders. With gray eyes narrowed, he knit his brows together and stared icily at Mike.

Mike met the penetrating eyes of the detective with his own unwavering dark eyes. He rolled a piece of hard watermelon candy with his tongue letting the sweet, tangy juice trickle down his dry throat.

Detective Sherman seemed to be challenging Mike, yet at the same time, wetting his lips at some sort of victory.

Suddenly, the redwood gate behind Mike burst open. He turned—stunned.

Three police officers and a woman were running toward him. The woman wore a L.A. Child Protection Services badge pinned to her white cotton blouse.

Mike's face got hot, his chest tightened. He glanced at Maddy a few yards away.

"Are you Mike DiSanto?" the policeman, a stocky man with bushy hair, asked.

Mike bit the last of the hard candy into nothingness. "Yeah."

"You're under arrest!"

"Arrest?" Panic seized him. "What for?"

"For kidnapping and transporting a minor over state lines." The police officer put his hand, like a bear's paw with outstretched claws, on Mike's shoulder, and spun him around. He grabbed Mike's arms behind him and clamped handcuffs on his wrists.

"Read him his Miranda."

"You have the right to remain silent. Anything you say can and will be—"

"Daddy, what are they doing?" Maddy cried, running to him.

Mike instinctively tried to step between Maddy and the middle aged woman from Child Protection Services.

"Are you Madison DiSanto?" she asked. Her voice sounded starched.

'Uh-huh," she said nodding her head. She wiped her eyes with the back of her hand and looked up at Mike.

"Sweetie—"

"I have orders to return Madison to her mother. Immediately." The woman glared at Mike.

"Let me talk to my daughter," he pleaded.

The woman turned her back to Mike.

"Lady, just give me a minute to talk to her." But his plea fell on deaf ears.

The woman bent down to Maddy. "You have to come with me." She reached for Maddy, but Maddy slipped from her grasp and clung to Mike's leg.

"Daddy, I don't want to go. I'm scared." She began to sob loudly.

Mike twisted free from the husky officer and knelt down to Maddy, his arms locked behind him.

The woman grabbed Maddy's arm.

"Get your hands off her until I can explain." He glared at the woman who retracted her grip momentarily. "Maddy, listen to Daddy, you have to go with this lady."

"But, why?" Maddy cried, uncontrollably.

"It'll be OK. She won't hurt you."

"But, Daddy—" She choked on her own sobs.

"Sweetie, she has to take you back to mommy."

He touched his forehead to her forehead as hot tears stung his eyes.

"Hold me," she pleaded, trembling.

He looked up at the officer. "Please, let me hold my daughter—just for a second."

"Sorry, the only privilege you get is a phone call."

"Hold me," she cried, shaking.

His whole body shook as he wept. "I can't."

"But why?"

"I have handcuffs on."

Just then, Rosie raced over. "What's going on?"

"This is a police matter, lady. Go back to your apartment."

"I'm the manager here and this is my maintenance man. I demand to know what's going on," she said, her face rigid with anger.

"Well, lady, you're maintenance man is under arrest."

"Under arrest?" She looked down at Mike in disbelief.

"For what?"

"For kidnapping his daughter and transporting her over state lines," he said jerking Mike to his feet.

Rosie kept her eyes fixed on Mike. "I don't know what to say—" she mumbled, in shock. A rose hue blossomed up from her neck.

Mike looked at Rosie through watery eyes. He nodded a single nod.

"Dear Lord," she gasped.

"All right. Let's go," the burly officer said shoving Mike toward the waiting squad car.

Mike struggled between two police officers, straining to look over his shoulder at Maddy.

The woman from Child Protection Services grabbed Maddy's shoulder. "You have to come with me, young lady."

"Daddy! Daddy!" she screamed.

"I love you, Maddy." His last words were stifled as he was shoved head first into the police car.

Mike watched out the squad car's back window in horror as the woman led Maddy to the second squad car. Her terrified screams drew the attention of several tenants rushing to the area, but all they could do was watch in stunned disbelief.

The woman and her police partner placed the screaming, terrified girl in the back of the police car.

Mike watched Rosie cover her ears at Maddy's screams and cries, and watched helplessly at the two disappearing squad cars.

***

The police station buzzed with people shouting. Police barked orders, citizens clamored to be heard, and those arrested bellowed their innocence. Except Mike.

He was ushered into a glass enclosed room with a battered wooden desk littered with papers.

"Sit down," a husky man said and motioned with his opened hand toward one of two blue metal folding chairs. Rolling out a leather swivel chair for himself, he nodded to the arresting police officer who, then, unlocked Mike's handcuffs and left the office, banging the door shut behind him.

Mike rubbed one wrist and then the other.

"I'm Sergeant Holloway." He had friendly blue eyes. He wore his white shirt opened at the neck and his tie in a loose knot. "You're facing some pretty serious charges, Mr. DiSanto," he said matter-of-factly, reading the police report.

"Where's Maddy?"

"She's in good hands," he said without looking up from the report. "Ms. Huntington and your daughter are probably on their way to the airport by now."

"The airport? Man, she'll be terrified and crying—"

"Ms. Huntington may look hard. She has to. She has a tough job. But, that's just a shell. Actually, she likes kids."

"But—"

"Dee Huntington has never lost a kid yet. It's her job to return kidnapped kids to their parents and in this case, to your daughter's mother." He lit a cigarette and offered one to Mike.

Mike shook his head. "Don't smoke."

Sergeant Holloway leaned back in his chair and blew white smoke rings toward a yellow stain on the ceiling. "Stupid things. I should quit."

A small oscillating fan rattled hopelessly back and forth from a metal stand in the corner.

"What's going to happen?"

"You'll be extradited to Minnesota tomorrow."

"How did you find me?" *Not that it matters at this point*, he thought.

"Seems Detective Sherman's habit of running checks on practically everyone he sees paid off. Detective Sherlock—that's what we call him around here—even ran a make on me once," he scoffed.

"But how did—"

"You were of particular interest to him since he couldn't find any link to your past. He kept digging around, but it was your little girl that tipped him off."

"I don't understand."

"Seems she was showing off some rocks, agates, I guess, to some lady one day at the pool. 'Guess she wanted to show the lady how different agates look when they're wet. Detective Sherman was sitting nearby and asked if he could see them, too."

Mike stared at the floor as the sergeant rambled on.

"He recognized it as a Minnesota agate. He did some hard-nosed checking back in your home state and sure enough, a case a little over a year ago of a man kidnapping his daughter and disappearing without a trace. Everything fit—the time, the description, everything."

Mike shifted in his chair. He leaned forward, his hands clasped between his knees, his head down.

"There's just one thing that puzzles me," Sergeant Holloway said.

Mike continued to stare at the floor feeling numb from his head to his feet. "What's that?"

"Why'd you do it?"

CHAPTER 37

Back in Minnesota

"Madison!" Lisa called, when she spied Maddy. She stood at Gate 47 on the blue concourse of Minneapolis-St. Paul International Airport.

"Mommy!" she cried. She ran into Lisa's outstretched arms.

"Are you Lisa DiSanto?" Dee Huntington asked.

"Yes, I'm Lisa."

"I'm Ms. Huntington from the L.A. Child Protection Services." She smiled. "I'd like to see your identification."

Lisa pulled out her driver's license and showed it to the woman.

Instantly, a barrage of camera flashes and questions erupted from newspaper and TV reporters.

Ms. Huntington gave a look of disdain at the crowd of reporters. "Let's step over here."

But, it was impossible to escape the commotion as they pressed together for close-up shots of Maddy reunited with her mother.

"Are you happy to be home?"

"Did you miss your mother?"

"Did you try to run away from your daddy?"

"Were you able to call for help?"

Maddy cried and clung to Lisa's hand.

"It's been a terrible ordeal for both of us," Lisa said looking into one of the TV cameras.

"I need you to sign the Receipt of Custody," Ms. Huntington said. She handed a clip board with a triplicate form, along with a pen to Lisa.

Lisa signed the paper. "Is that it?"

"Yes, that's it. Congratulations on getting your daughter back. I'm sure you must be thrilled." She separated the papers and handed one copy to Lisa and placed the other copies in her brief case.

"Of course, I am. Thank you for bringing her back."

"Can we get a picture of the three of you?" one reporter asked, loudly.

The two women smiled briefly, but Maddy tried to hide behind Lisa. Flashes dotted the air like the fireworks on July 4th.

Two men in gray suits approached. "Lisa DiSanto?"

"Yes?"

"We're Agents Driscoll and Gregg. FBI." They flipped open their badges for Lisa to see. "We're here to escort you back to Litchfield."

"That isn't necessary."

"Yes, it is," Driscoll said with a stern smile.

Reporters fired questions like shells from a machine gun.

"Are you going to push for the maximum penalty against your ex-husband?"

"Did you ever feel your daughter was in danger?"

"I'm going to let you handle this," Ms. Huntington said and nodded toward the mob of reporters, "but you're better off not to say anything." She extended her hand to Lisa.

Lisa clasped her hand. "Thank you, again."

Lisa's former divorce lawyer waited nearby. "Hello, Madison." His thin lips didn't seem to move.

Maddy looked at him for a puzzled moment and wiped her tear stained cheeks. She mumbled something nobody seemed to understand and clung to Lisa.

The trio left the airport followed by a shiny, black sedan with the two FBI agents and several other cars with newspaper and TV stickers plastered on the outside.

Turning to Maddy Lisa asked, "Are you happy to be home?"

"I threw up."

"What!"

"I threw up."

"John, pull over. Are you sick?"

"I don't know. My tummy hurts."

"Do you have to throw up again? John, stop the car!"

John pulled onto the shoulder. The convoy of cars followed.

"What's wrong?" Driscoll asked, running to John's side of the car.

"Madison's sick."

Lisa opened the back door and helped Maddy out. "Give me your hankie," she said holding her hand out to John. She wiped the front of Maddy's outfit. "Do you get sick when you ride in cars?"

Maddy shook her head.

"Well, then, what's wrong?" Lisa felt Maddy's forehead with the back of her hand. "You don't have a temperature."

Maddy shrugged and brushed more tears from her eyes.

"Are you all right now? Do you want to get back into the car?"

She nodded and climbed into the back seat.

They drove past groves of elm, maple, and oak trees that separated pasturelands dotted with black-and-white cows swishing their tails over their backs.

The silence in the car was a welcomed relief from the commotion at the airport. Each of the car's three occupants were entwined, as they were, like the hair of Maddy's single braid tied with a tiny, white bow.

"Who fixed your hair?" Lisa asked.

"Daddy."

"Humph."

"Do you remember living here?" Lisa asked, as John pulled into the driveway and tooted the horn.

Maddy nodded, but then brightened when she spied colorful balloons bobbing crazily from the posts on both sides of the steps.

The front door opened. Bruce and Betty Barrett stepped out.

"Grandma! Grandpa!" She ran to her grandparents.

"Oh, my, my! You've grown like a weed," Betty said squeezing her tightly.

Bruce scooped her into his arms. "How's my little flower girl? Only you're not so little anymore," he said juggling her up and down.

"I have supper all ready," Betty said as Lisa and John walked hand in hand up the steps.

The two FBI agents stepped from their car. Everyone quickly introduced themselves. Then, several cars of reporters converged on the scene.

"Can we get a statement?"

"We hear your ex-husband is being returned tomorrow. Do you plan to see him?"

CHAPTER 38

Mike's Return Trip

Mike felt like he was under a spotlight as he sat in a window seat of the 747 jet—handcuffed to a police officer, who sat in the middle seat.

Nearby passengers noticed the handcuffs and stared at Mike with fear and suspicion. Flight attendants glared accusingly at him—their looks plunged the spike of guilt deeper into his soul.

"We had to alert the crew we're transporting a prisoner," the officer explained. "Regulations, you know."

Mike pursed his lips, nodded absently, and turned to the window. He agonized over Maddy. He forced his mind to shut out the sound of her awful screams. Was it only yesterday?

He thought about his first night spent in the county jail. His cell mate reeked of alcohol and vomit. His shirt hung out from dark stained pants and he wore brown, untied shoes with no socks.

The man yelled several times throughout the night. "You ain't gonna take my bottle no more." He scratched his round, protruding belly and rolled over in his bunk.

"Why did you do it?" The words of Sergeant Holloway rang over and over in Mike's ears.

Why? It seemed like the right thing to do at the time. That's why. But as he thought through reasons for doing the right thing for Maddy, he realized it netted far more disastrous results than he could have imagined. *I took a risk and lost. And now, Maddy would suffer for my reckless concern, and my need for justice! Man! What a blind fool! If I could just undo that day,* he reprimanded himself.

He stared out to a blue sky. All trace of his smoldering hope was snuffed out.

"Must have been a bitter divorce for you to take your kid," the officer commented. This was no ordinary small talk. It smacked hard.

Mike didn't answer.

"The courts don't take kindly to kidnapping kids. Most kidnappings are for revenge or ransom. What's your reason? Course, you're assumed innocent until you're proven guilty, but hey, the cards are stacked against you, fella."

"I admit I made a huge mistake—"

"Yeah, that's an understatement."

"I don't want my little girl to feel like all this was her fault. She's innocent."

"Well, you should've thought of that before. Life is about consequences, you know."

"I know. I know. I made her a promise when she was born that I would take care of her." He let out a deep, hard breath. "I really blew it."

"Sorta looks that way."

"My daughter had to go back to Minnesota with a Ms. Huntington. Do you know—"

"Don't know her. But, hey, if she's the one who's supposed to take the kid back, they probably knew she'd get the job done."

An hour passed before either of the men spoke again. Mike thought about Maddy. *Would she be cared for? What if she runs away? What happens if she doesn't remember Lisa? Don't be ridiculous!* He chided himself. *Of course, she'll remember Lisa. It's only been a little over a year. I should've just paid the child support and spent time with Maddy when I could.*

The cop rested his head against the red upholstered seat. His eyes were shut, but he drummed his fingers of his free hand on the armrest.

"Are you married?" Mike asked.

"Yeah, for the third time," he answered, without opening his eyes. "Never had any kids though." He continued to tap his fingers.

Another hour passed.

Mike thought about Stephanie and how unfair life seemed at times. He thought about the times he and Roger talked man-to-man with complete acceptance of each other. He remembered the words Roger had said about Stephanie that intrigued him: "A woman's heart should be so hidden in Christ that a man should have to seek Him first to find her." *I wonder what he meant by that?*

He thought about Rosie. *Poor Rosie. How could I ever make it up to her? I unwittingly left her in the lurch trying to manage the complex, comfort Stephanie, and now, she would have to find another maintenance man.* "Man, you really messed up," he muttered to himself.

"Do you want a little free advice?" the officer asked, opening one eye. He sat forward, hunched his shoulders, and rolled his head from side to side. "Just shove the past into the compost of your life and move on."

Move on? Mike thought. *To what?* He left a path of destruction that needed major repair. But, what could he do? He sat on a plane bound for Minnesota handcuffed to a man who was just doing his job.

There was no doubt the two uniformed police officers at Gate 62 were waiting for Mike. They stood with feet spread apart and arms folded across their chests.

"We're here to pick up Mike DiSanto," the shorter policeman said to the L.A. officer.

"Here's your man." He unlocked the handcuffs, first from his wrist, then from Mike's wrist.

Immediately, the taller policeman tightened handcuffs to Mike and then to his own wrist.

The L.A. officer took a folded paper from his shirt pocket and handed it to the tall one. "I don't think he'll give you any trouble." He looked at Mike, his face a question mark, and disappeared into the crowd.

The two police officers with Mike in tow silently wove their way through the throng of people, down the gray carpeted concourse and outside to their squad car parked at the end of the passenger pick-up area.

They headed west to Litchfield.

CHAPTER 39

A Stir in Litchfield

M ike's return to Litchfield one day after Maddy's arrival caused a stir. People in grocery stores and gas stations, and walking along the streets huddled together in small groups to discuss the latest news. Their small town of 6,000 flashed on every TV newscast and in headlines of several newspapers across the nation.

"On August 15th, a 28-year-old Litchfield man was arrested in Pasadena, California, on charges of kidnapping his daughter, who was just four years old at the time. The man, Michael DiSanto, was returned to Litchfield and taken to the county jail to await his court appearance," Karl Roberts read the article aloud to Katie. He folded the paper and laid it on the kitchen table. "I can't read any more."

Katie sat across from him absently stirring her cereal.

"I know his intention. He's not a criminal. He's a loving father who was just trying to protect his daughter. What father wouldn't?" He picked up the newspaper and smacked it down on the table. "Yeah, he did wrong, but he tried to do right." Karl said.

"Isn't there anything we can do?"

"I'll stop at the jail to see if I can visit Mike. He's going to need a good lawyer!"

***

Karl got his opportunity to see Mike the following day.

In spite of Mike's unkempt appearance, Karl hugged him clapping him on the back. "You look terrible, but a good sight to see!"

"Thanks." Mike looked at Karl with fond affection. "Man! I'm glad to see you!"

Karl's mustache was a bit grayer, but otherwise, he looked the same. His blue eyes still had that glint. He shifted his stance. "Do you have a lawyer?"

Mike lowered his eyes. "No. Do you know any?"

"Yeah." He took out a piece of paper from his shirt pocket and handed it to Mike. "He's good."

Mike glanced at the unfamiliar name and stuffed it in his jean pocket. "Thanks." He looked at Karl. "Man, this seems weird."

Karl nodded. "What else can we do for you?"

"I hate to ask, and if it weren't so important, I wouldn't. Could you contact Rosie Woods at Green Tree Complex and ask her to send our stuff to my folks' house? I'll send her a check as soon as I get my checkbook. And, could you see that Maddy gets her things?"

"I'll be glad to contact Rosie." Karl handed Mike his pocket notebook and Mike jotted down Rosie's phone number. "And, you can store your stuff at my place, if you'd rather."

"Seriously?"

Karl nodded.

"I would really appreciate that, Karl. He inhaled deeply and expelled the air. "I wasn't thinking of consequences."

"Desperate people seldom do." He shook his head slowly. "I'm sorry, Mike."

"Have you heard how Maddy is doing?"

"I've called several times, but—" he shrugged. "Anything else we can do?"

"You can tell me, 'I told you so.'"

"Mike, you know I wouldn't rub your nose in it."

"I know you wouldn't. I deserve it though, and I have no one to blame but myself. I feel like a total failure—as a husband, a father, a son, and even as a construction worker. I am so sorry, Karl." His eyes filled with tears.

"You're not a failure, Mike, until you start to blame others for your mistakes." He put his hand on Mike's shoulder.

Just then, the guard interrupted. "Time's up."

Karl came to see him the following week. I called Rosie the night I left you last week," he said. "She seems like a nice lady."

"She is."

"I hope you don't mind, but I filled her in on what's been happening with you."

"I don't mind at all."

"She shipped all your belongings and they arrived yesterday. Everything was carefully packed and clearly labeled. Katie and I bought Maddy's stuff over to Lisa's last night."

"Man, I miss Maddy. How is she?"

Karl waited before answering, stoking his mustache between his finger and thumb as though trying to find the right words. He cleared his throat. "We didn't see Maddy. Lisa didn't invite us in."

"But, did Lisa say how she was?"

"No. The only thing she said was—" He took a deep breath. "She said, 'You can tell Mike not to bother writing to Madison because I'll make darn sure she never gets the letters anyway.' Those were her exact words."

Mike leaned back in his straight-back chair and folded his arms across his chest. "Figures."

"I'm sorry, Mike."

Mike nodded. "I'll write her anyway. Maybe, just maybe, Lisa will read a letter to her."

"By the way, Rosie wants to know what she should do with your car."

"She can give it to the maintenance man she's going to have to hire. But, I'll write her now that I have correspondence privileges."

"Stephanie sends her greetings."

Mike nodded. "Stephanie is Rosie's daughter. Her husband died last spring."

"I see. Did you hear anything on your court date yet?"

"Yeah. My lawyer contacted me yesterday. It's set for November 14th." He leaned forward clasping his fingers and tapping his thumbs together. "I really screwed up big time, Karl."

Karl nodded. "What does your lawyer say?"

"What can he say?" he said shrugging his shoulders, "Except that he'll do the best he can, but—"

"He's competent and tough, and I know he'll make sure you get a fair shake."

Mike nodded.

Mike had nothing but time on his hands—time to think, and time to replay that awful day he was arrested and Maddy was taken. Time had become an enemy. And yet, time afforded him the opportunity to write to Rosie.

"Dear Rosie," he began, "I cannot tell you enough how sorry I am for all that happened at the complex. It was totally my fault. I have to start at the beginning in hopes you will understand the reason I was not completely honest with you when I came to Green Tree."

"Almost two years after my divorce, Maddy began to show signs of emotional problems. I tried to get joint custody of Maddy, but the courts didn't allow it. I didn't know how else to protect or help her. So, I made the foolish decision to take her. I did not intend to be gone for as long as we were. I am sorry for not being up-front with you when you hired me. I did not intend for you to be stuck with such a mess. I am truly sorry. I wish I could make it up to you. For what it's worth, thanks for all you did for Maddy and for me. Mike"

Strange how nice people cross paths for a short time and nothing comes of it, he thought as he placed the letter in the outgoing box.

Other than his lawyer, Mike's only two other visitors were Karl, sometimes accompanied by Katie. He looked forward to Karl's weekly visits in the jail's crowded visiting area.

But, even with Karl's visits, Mike began to feel isolated. He missed Maddy terribly. He missed working with Karl. Even washing and waxing his truck seemed like something he had taken for granted. In another world. In another time.

Through the barred window, he watched the days grow shorter. If he craned his neck to the right of the red brick building across the parking lot, he could see maple and birch trees—their crimson and gold leaves racing to the ground, as though being stranded on their branches in the face of the stinging autumn wind would be a far worse fate.

He read and reread the letters he received from Stephanie and Rosie. He wrote every chance he had.

Then, the trees became bare and the sky turned gray. Soon, it would snow.

CHAPTER 40

The Trial

N ovember 14th dawned with frost flowers on the window panes. It was brisk outside. It was chilly in his cell. It was cold in Mike's soul.

He showered, shaved, and sat on his bunk to wait.

How absurd, he thought. *I'm sitting in jail attached to the courthouse with such bitter-sweet memories—the place we got our marriage license, and the place Lisa filed for divorce.*

The clank of his jail cell door startled him. "Court time," the officer announced gruffly.

Mike sat next to his lawyer at one of two long tables facing the judge's bench.

"Our objective is to prove your intent was not malicious, but only in the best interest of your child," his lawyer reiterated.

Mike nodded and wiped the sweat from his forehead with his forearm.

Mr. Renshaw filled a Styrofoam cup with water from the pitcher before them on the polished wooden table. He opened his brief case, took out a folder of papers, and spread them in front of him.

Mike sat with his hands clasped together and his arms resting on the cold, clammy table. He looked from the American flag on one side of the judge's high, black leather chair to the Minnesota flag on the other side. The star of the north encircled in a white ring against a blue background reminded him of a simplistic and uncluttered time—something his life now lacked.

He looked at the twelve jurors sitting in two neat rows along the right wall, like magpies on a wire.

He glanced to the other long table just beyond Mr. Renshaw and caught sight of Lisa sitting with her lawyer.

She looked straight ahead except when she bent her head to listen to her lawyer as he whispered to her, covering his mouth with the back of his hand.

Just then, the door to the judge's chamber opened.

"All rise." A tall, gray haired man wearing a black robe swirled in. "The Honorable Judge Jerome Hawkins."

The judge sat down with a flourish.

"Be seated," the court attendant said, and everyone sat down as though on cue.

Mike looked at Mr. Cheatum, the impeccably dressed prosecuting attorney—the attorney who had gained notoriety from several criminal cases he had successfully prosecuted. His every movement was quick and precise.

I'm dead, Mike thought. But, he adjusted his tie and straightened the sleeve of his charcoal gray suit.

"The little weasel," Mr. Renshaw whispered. "He's always got a blank check for somebody to sign."

Mike looked puzzled, but decided not to pursue his lawyer's obvious agitation with the prosecuting attorney. He heard muffled coughs and rustling movements behind him and glanced over his shoulder to a packed courtroom.

Two police officers stationed at each exit punctuated the serious reality of the situation. *I'm on trial for kidnapping*!

The prosecuting attorney, Mr. Cheatum, made his opening statements followed by the defense attorney, Mr. Renshaw.

The first witness to be called was Detective Sherman.

"State your name and place of residence," Mr. Cheatum began.

"Detective Greg Sherman, Green Tree Complex, Pasadena, California."

"Did you, in fact, reside at the same complex during the time the defendant resided there?"

"Yes."

"What drew your suspicions to the defendant's behavior?"

"Nothing."

"How is it that you discovered Mr. DiSanto was a fugitive?"

"I run a make on just about everybody I meet, but, I couldn't find any background information on the defendant, so I became suspicious. His little girl showed agates to a lady by the pool, and I recognized them as Minnesota agates. I checked Minnesota for outstanding warrants. Everything matched—description of defendant and his daughter, the date, and the nature of the crime. I verified the details and notified the police for the arrest."

"Describe the behavior of Mr. DiSanto during the arrest," Mr. Cheatum said.

"He was uncooperative and had to be restrained by two police officers."

"Was he, in fact, belligerent?"

"Not belligerent, but resisting arrest."

"No further questions at this time," Mr. Cheatum said.

Mr. Renshaw stood to cross-examine. He walked toward the witness. "Did the defendant, Mr. DiSanto, make any reference for concern for his daughter?"

"Well, yes," Detective answered hesitantly.

"In what way did Mr. DiSanto show concern for his daughter?"

"He pulled free from the police officers, dropped to his knees with his hands cuffed behind him, and tried to explain what was going on."

"So, could it be that Mr. DiSanto's actions may not have been resisting arrest, but rather trying to protect his daughter?"

"Objection!" Mr. Cheatum bellowed. "Witness could not have known the defendant's intentions."

"Sustained. Stick to facts," the judge ordered.

"What was his four-year-old daughter doing during this time?"

"She was crying."

"Did you hear what Mr. DiSanto said to his daughter?"

"Yes."

"Please relate what you heard."

"He said that she had to go with the lady, and that the lady would not hurt her."

"And who is the lady you are referring to?" Mr. Renshaw asked.

"Ms. Huntington from Child Protective Services."

"At any time, did you hear the defendant express any sentiments to his daughter?"

"Yes, when he was put in the squad car, he called out, "I love you, Maddy.""

"Thank you Detective Sherman. No further questions," Mr. Renshaw said and sat down.

"Witness may step down. The court calls Mr. Karl Roberts. Please approach the witness stand and raise your right hand," the clerk said.

Mike fingered the cleft in his chin and watched with sadness as his boss and friend took the stand on his behalf.

"How long have you known the defendant?" Mr. Cheatum asked.

"Almost seven years."

"He did, in fact, work for you as a carpenter for those seven years, is that correct?"

"Yes."

"Were you aware of the divorce settlement between my client, Lisa Barrett, and the accused, Michael DiSanto?" the prosecuting attorney asked crisply.

"Yes," Karl replied.

"Did the accused ever complain to you of his dissatisfaction with the divorce settlement?"

"Objection!" Mr. Renshaw protested.

"Over-ruled. Witness may answer the question," Judge Hawkins said.

"Yes."

"Did the accused ever complain to you of his dissatisfaction with the divorce settlement on one or more occasions?"

"Yes, but not the amount, just the wa—"

"Answer yes or no," Mr. Cheatum instructed in a monotone.

"Yes."

"He was, in fact, enraged and resentful that he had to pay alimony and child support—"

"Objection!" Mr. Renshaw said jumping to his feet. "Witness could not possibly have known what the defendant was feeling."

"Sustained. Keep your questions to facts," Judge Hawkins warned sternly.

"Did you know of the planned kidnapping prior to the actual abduction?"

"No."

"Are you and the defendant friends outside of work?"

"Yes."

"Close friends?"

"Yes."

"How is it, as close friends, you were not aware of the plans to kidnap his daughter, unless the defendant purposely misled you—"

"Objection. Leading the witness."

"Sustained."

"No further questions," Mr. Cheatum said and seated himself.

Mr. Renshaw stepped forward. "Did Mr. DiSanto ever express his concern to you regarding the well-being of his daughter?"

"Objection!"

"Over-ruled. Witness may answer."

"Yes, he did." Karl sat a little straighter. He repeated the conversation he and Mike had had at his kitchen table—how Mike was most concerned about unusual behaviors that Maddy was displaying."

"What behaviors, Mr. Roberts," Mr. Renshaw said in a mild tone.

"Maddy was wetting the bed, running to hide every time a sitter would come to the house, having nightmares, stomach aches, and crying a lot. Mike said he felt he had to do something to help her, to protect her."

"Objection! Strictly hearsay."

"Change your line of questioning," the judge ordered.

"Yes, Your Honor." Mr. Renshaw faced Karl. "Did Mr. DiSanto ever express his concern for their daughter while they were still married?"

"Yes," Karl answered quietly.

"Would you expand your answer to the court?"

"It was when Lisa was first pregnant." He chewed on his lip.

"Continue," Mr. Renshaw spoke gently.

"Lisa threatened to abort their baby."

Audible gasps and low murmuring came from the spectators.

"Order!" The judge banged his gavel. He turned to the defense attorney. "Proceed."

"How did Mr. DiSanto react?"

"He was very upset and would not sign as the responsible party for their insurance, so the abortion was not done."

"Were you eyewitness to any part of this incident?"

"Yes. We were on a job when Mike received a phone call that Lisa was not at work. He wanted to go home to see if Lisa was there. I rode with. On the way, Mike explained how Lisa had threatened an abortion a couple days earlier. Then, he got a call from the abortion clinic in Camden and I heard him say that he did not agree to the abortion and would not sign."

"Thank you, Mr. Roberts. No further questions."

"Does the prosecuting attorney wish to re-cross-examine?"

"Yes, Your Honor." Mr. Cheatum approached the witness box in a brisk manner. "Mr. Roberts, could it be possible that Ms. Barrett may have been terrified to have the baby, panicked, and under extreme duress wanted to terminate her pregnancy?"

"Objection! Witness does not know what Ms. Barrett was feeling."

"Sustained. Change your line of questioning."

"Is it possible that the defendant used the abduction of their child as a means of revenge against Ms. Barrett for her desire under emotional trauma to want to abort the baby?"

"Objection! Badgering the witness."

"Sustained."

"No further questions, Your Honor."

"Does the defense counsel wish to further question the witness?"

"Yes, Your Honor," Mr. Renshaw said and approached the witness stand.

"Did Mr. DiSanto ever express his concern over the way Lisa Barrett spent the child support?"

"Yes."

"Please tell the court the concern Mr. DiSanto had concerning child support."

"He said that Lisa spent the child support on a lavish lifestyle rather than on clothes and shoes, jackets and other necessities for Maddy."

"Did Mr. DiSanto expound on what he considered a lavish lifestyle?"

"Yes."

"What things did Mr. DiSanto consider to be a lavish lifestyle?"

"Designer clothes, a new car, new landscaping at the house."

"Objection! Second-hand knowledge."

"Sustained. Change your line of questioning," the judge ordered.

"What kind of worker was Mr. DiSanto?"

"Objection! Irrelevant!"

"State your reasons for your line of questioning."

"I am establishing my client's character—that he was not malicious by nature, but rather that he had a conscientious desire to do what was right," Mr. Renshaw said.

"Proceed."

"Mr. Roberts, what kind of worker was Mr. DiSanto?"

"Mike was a hard worker. He had a natural ability to work in construction like no other. He was dependable, honest, and I trusted him."

"As a friend, what one word would describe Mr. DiSanto?" Mr. Renshaw asked quietly.

Karl smiled slightly. "Tenderhearted."

"Please explain your reason for choosing that word."

"Objection! Irrelevant!" Mr. Cheatum said.

"No further questions, Your Honor," Mr. Renshaw said and sat down.

The intense questions, brief answers, and countless objections dragged on throughout the afternoon as Katie Roberts, Irene and Rick DiSanto were called to the witness stand as character witnesses.

Then Bruce Barrett was called to the stand.

"Did you have a good relationship with Mr. DiSanto when he was your son-in-law?" Mr. Cheatum asked.

"Yes."

"What is your relationship now?"

"I'm afraid the kidnapping of Madison caused irreparable harm and emotional damage to our daughter, so of course, the relationship is strained," Bruce said and looked down.

"No further questions."

Mr. Renshaw stepped forward. "Is it true you made excuses for your daughter's habitual late arrivals with Madison for the pre-arranged time in which Mr. DiSanto was to pick up his daughter?"

"I thought she would have good reason—"

"Yes or no, Mr. Barrett."

"Yes."

"No further questions."

Betty Barrett responded to the prosecuting and the defense attorneys in much the same manner as her husband.

Mike glanced at the jurors, but with each volley of questions, answers, and objections, there were no detectable reactions from the jurors.

***

That evening, Mike and Mr. Renshaw sat at a small, round table in the visiting area of the jail.

"The prosecuting attorney is trying to convince the jury that your motive for kidnapping your daughter was malicious—for the sole purpose of causing extreme and irreparable emotional distress to Lisa for what you thought was an unfair outcome of your divorce settlement."

"But, that was not my intention. That never even entered my mind."

"You know that and I know that, but now, we have to convince the jury of it. We're not arguing the fact that you took your daughter—that's already been established, but if we can convince the jury you did it exclusively for the welfare of your daughter—what you intended for her good—we may be able to get a lighter sentence."

Mike nodded.

"Tomorrow is going to be crucial," Mr. Renshaw said.

Mike looked expectantly at Mr. Renshaw.

"Tomorrow, we call Rosie Woods and Stephanie Sterling to the witness stand."

"I hate that they have to come to testify. Is there some other way—"

"They've been subpoenaed, and the U.S. Attorney's office made the travel and lodging arrangements. They may even receive reimbursement for certain travel expenses in addition to their daily witness fee," Mr. Renshaw explained to a hesitant Mike. "And then, you and Lisa will take the stand."

CHAPTER 41

Last Witnesses

The next morning dawned with the sun no more than a rose tint in an opaque gray sky.

Mike finished his shower and wrapped a flimsy towel around himself. He stood in front of one of the four orange-stained sinks of the men's bathroom of the county jail.

Squirting shaving cream onto his fingers, he looked into the dark speckled mirror anchored securely to a dingy tiled wall—same black hair and moustache, and dark eyes. What was different? His reflection looked wavy and contorted in the mirror, but there was something else.

He noticed lines etched deeply into his forehead as he stroked foamy lather against his face and neck. He felt as though he was looking at a stranger. He quickly shaved and dressed.

It was time to go to court.

The clerk called Rosie Woods to the witness stand.

Rosie raised her right hand and was sworn in. She looked kindly at Mike, but lacked her signature big smile.

Mike smiled slightly. *I wish you didn't have to be here*, he thought.

Mr. Cheatum began, "Please state your name and place of residence."

"Rosie Woods, Green Tree Complex, Pasadena, California."

"How do you know the defendant, Mike DiSanto?"

"He was the maintenance man at the complex I manage."

"Do you hire those who do maintenance work at the complex?"

"Yes."

"Did you hire the defendant as the maintenance man at the complex?"

"Yes."

"Did you know the defendant prior to hiring him?"

"No."

Mr. Cheatum paced back and forth. "Mrs. Woods, when you hired the defendant, were you aware that he was a wanted man, a fugitive, for kidnapping his daughter?"

"Objection!" Mr. Renshaw yelled. "Badgering the witness."

"Over-ruled," Judge Hawkins said. "Proceed."

"Did you know the defendant was a wanted man when you hired him?"

"No."

"Would you agree the defendant acted in a deceitful manner in order to obtain employment?"

"Objection!" Mr. Renshaw said. "Witness could not have known the intentions of the defendant."

"Over-ruled. Witness may answer."

Rosie looked down. "No."

"May I remind you, Mrs. Woods, you are under oath? Do you want to reconsider your answer?"

"No."

"Would you state your reason you do not consider the defendant to have deceived you in order to be hired."

"I never asked him if he was wanted for kidnapping," she replied, looking directly at the prosecuting attorney.

Mike smiled ever so slightly.

"What did the defendant do with his daughter while he worked at the complex?"

"He took her with him."

"So, he subjected his daughter to strangers in unfamiliar settings on a regular basis, correct?"

"He always took her with him, so she could be with him."

"I consider the witness to be a hostile witness. No further questions," Mr. Cheatum said.

Mr. Renshaw approached the witness to cross-examine. He smiled. "Mrs. Woods, would you describe the defendant's work ethics as the maintenance man at Green Tree Complex."

"Mike was very capable for whatever task was at hand. He was dependable, and I could trust him to do a good job."

"Do you have any grandchildren?"

"No, but I love children."

"Objection! Irrelevant." Mr. Cheatum said.

"Where are you going with this, counselor?" the judge asked.

"I want to establish her perception of emotional behaviors of children, Your Honor."

"Very well. Proceed."

"Did you love the defendant's daughter?"

"Yes, of course. She was a delightful little girl."

"Did you observe Mr. DiSanto and his daughter inter-act with one another?"

"Yes, all the time."

"Would you describe what you observed?"

"They did everything together, whether it was maintenance, going to the zoo, getting groceries, going to the movies, or coming to my office for meetings. And, they laughed together."

"Did you ever see Mr. DiSanto discipline or become angry with his daughter?

"Once, he raised his eyebrow at Maddy when she didn't use her manners, but that's all I ever saw."

"Thank you, Mrs. Woods."

"The court calls Stephanie Sterling to the witness stand," the clerk said.

"Stephanie was sworn in and took her seat in the witness box.

Mr. Cheatum approached Stephanie with a quick step. "State your name and place of residence."

"I'm Stephanie Sterling and I live at Green Tree Complex in Pasadena, California."

She has gone through so much, and yet, she is so gracious, Mike thought.

"What is your relationship with the defendant?"

He befriended my husband before his death, and he was a tremendous help for my mother, so I consider him a trusted friend."

"Are you romantically involved?"

"No," she said with a smile.

"No further questions," Mr. Cheatum said.

Mr. Renshaw stepped forward. "Mrs. Sterling, how long have you known Mr. DiSanto?"

"Less than a year."

"During that time, have you witnessed the interaction between Mr. DiSanto and his daughter?"

"Yes, on several occasions."

"How would you describe their relationship?"

"Mike was a very caring father, and Maddy was a happy and loving daughter."

"Have you ever noticed Mr. DiSanto to be angry or malicious?"

"Objection!" Mr. Cheatum exclaimed. "Leading the witness."

"Over-ruled. Witness may answer the question."

"No, Mike seemed quite amiable."

"Thank you, Mrs. Sterling. No further questions."

Mike smiled appreciatively and Stephanie smiled back. *I wish I could just say thank you. Thank you for coming. Thank you for being so gracious,* he thought.

"The court calls Lisa Barrett to the witness stand."

Lisa stepped into the witness box and sat on the wooden, straight back chair. Her movements were confluent, her voice concise.

"Did you and the defendant have a stormy marriage?" Mr. Cheatum began the questioning.

"Yes."

"In what way?"

"We argued over financial things mostly."

"Did the defendant have anger issues?"

"Objection!" Mr. Renshaw said.

"Your Honor, I am establishing the defendant's character in adverse situations."

"Objection over-ruled. Proceed."

"Did the defendant display outbursts of anger when you tried to discuss financial issues?"

"He was always angry when we discussed financial matters."

"Did you ever fight over parenting responsibilities of Madison?"

"No."

"Did Mr. DiSanto ever accuse you of being an unfit mother?"

"No." Her small angry mouth drew up into her typical sassy smile.

"Why, then, do you suppose he wanted to abduct Madison and raise her without your influence?"

"Objection!" Mr. Renshaw boomed.

"Rephrase the question, counselor."

"Since Mr. DiSanto apparently considered you a fit mother, could there have been another motive, say revenge, for Mr. DiSanto to kidnap your child?"

"Objection!"

"No further questions." Mr. Cheatum looked smugly to the jurors.

Mr. Renshaw stood to cross-examine. "Ms. Barrett, would you say my client, Michael DiSanto, was a good father?" Mr. Renshaw began.

"Well," Lisa hesitated, obviously disgruntled with the direction the questioning was headed. "Yes, I suppose."

"Did you ever fear for Madison's safety while she was in Mr. DiSanto's care?"

"Of course not."

"'Of course not'? In other words, you had no thought or concern that any harm would come to Madison at the hands of her father, is that correct?"

Mike sat forward in his chair, his fingers clasped loosely.

Lisa tightened her lips into a pout.

"Answer the question," Judge Hawkins directed.

Lisa shook her head.

"May I remind you to state your answers audibly? Did you have concern that any harm would come to Madison at the hands of her father?"

"No." She looked down at the floor.

"Did you consider the alimony and child support to be a fair ruling?"

"Yes. It was adequate only that I didn't have to go back to work."

"Did Mr. DiSanto ever accuse you of misuse of the child support as stipulated in the divorce decree?"

"Objection! Badgering the witness," Mr. Cheatum protested.

"Sustained. Change your line of questioning," the judge said.

"Is it true you were driving a new Camaro at the time of the alleged abduction and in fact, had a new car every year since the divorce?"

Lisa's brown eyes widened, and her thin, dark eyebrows rose in perfect arches.

"Objection! That's irrelevant," Mr. Cheatum spoke loudly.

"Where are you leading?" Judge Hawkins asked.

"Your Honor, I would like to show my client's frustration at Ms. Barrett's flagrant use of the child support money—that it was being used for her own expensive lifestyle and not for clothing, shoes, jackets, medical care, and the well-being of their daughter."

"Ms. Barrett is not on trial here, so what she does with child support money is not relevant to this case as long as there was no indication of child endangerment, and it appears there was none," Judge Hawkins said with a finality that caused even Mr. Cheatum to look up. "Do I make myself clear?"

"Yes, Your Honor. I apologize. I withdraw my question."

"Strike Mr. Renshaw's last question from the record," the judge directed the court reporter.

"Did my client have legal and regular visitation rights to see his daughter?"

"Yes."

"What were the stipulations of those visitation rights as ordered by the court at the time of your divorce?"

Lisa shifted in her chair and adjusted the hem of her dress slightly. "He could see Madison two weekends a month."

"Were these two weekends a month prearranged times?"

"Yes."

"Was Mr. DiSanto ever denied his visitation rights on those designated weekends?"

"Sometimes, but only if I had other plans and couldn't bring her to my parents' house."

"'Sometimes'? On the average, Ms. Barrett, what would you say was the total number of times Mr. DiSanto was allowed to see Madison in the first six months after your divorce? I remind you, Ms. Barrett, you are under oath."

Lisa glared at the defense lawyer. "Probably six."

"And yet, Mr. DiSanto was given the right to see her at least twelve times during that same period. Is that correct?"

"Yes, I suppose."

"Did you contact Mr. DiSanto to make other arrangements more conducive to your schedule?"

"Not really." She looked at her lawyer.

"That would have been, at the very least, a common courtesy, don't you agree?"

"Objection! He's badgering the witness."

"You will refrain from instructing the witness in the rules of etiquette," Judge Hawkins warned.

Mr. Renshaw nodded. "How many times was Mr. DiSanto allowed to see Madison for the following six months?"

"I don't know. Probably about the same," Lisa mumbled.

"Did Mr. DiSanto contact you in order to see Madison at different times when he was denied his prearranged visits?"

Lisa nodded slightly.

"Please state your answer audibly."

"Yes."

"And were mutually agreeable arrangements made for visitation?"

"Sometimes."

"By your own admission, mutually agreed upon visitation rights were sometimes denied the defendant. Is that correct?"

"I guess."

"State your answer either 'yes' or 'no'."

"Yes."

"No further questions," Mr. Renshaw said and sat down.

"The court calls Mike DiSanto to the witness stand."

Mike was sworn in and took his seat in the witness box.

"How long had you been planning the kidnapping of your daughter prior to the actual abduction?" Mr. Cheatum asked, hitting painfully direct.

"A couple of weeks," Mike answered.

Muffled gasps came from the spectators.

"Mr. DiSanto, was it your intent to retaliate for what you considered an unfair divorce settlement?"

"No."

"Was it your intent to cause emotional distress to this mother by abducting her only child?"

"No." Mike stared at the prosecuting lawyer.

"Was it your intent to withhold child support payments in order to defy a court injunction? Because, Mr. DiSanto, that is exactly what you did."

"That was not my intention."

Mr. Cheatum began a slow, deliberate pace in front of the witness stand. "Why did you think you could take the law into your own hands?"

He's trying to make me look like some ruthless man who committed a cold, calculated act of child abduction for the sole purpose of revenge against Lisa and the court system, and I think the jury is buying it, Mike thought. "My intent was to protect my daughter—not revenge against Lisa or defiance against the courts."

"No further questions," Mr. Cheatum said.

Mr. Renshaw walked to the witness box. "Did you ever approach the courts with your frustration and dissatisfaction of denied visitation rights?"

"Yes. I tried to get custody or at least shared custody of Maddy," Mike replied.

"Did you attempt this on more than one occasion?"

"Yes, three different times."

"What were the results of these three attempts?"

"I could not prove that Lisa was an unfit mother. I was also told that because I had a full time job, I would have to provide day care while I was at work. So, it was in the best interest of my daughter to remain with her mother."

"I see." He glanced at the jury. "Did you consider your daughter to be well cared for by Ms. Barrett?"

"No."

"Please explain your answer to the court," Mr. Renshaw said in a kind tone.

"Most times when I picked up my daughter, she wore clothes that didn't fit or didn't have a jacket. I had to buy clothes and shoes and even a hair brush because Maddy didn't have those things, and she was bounced from sitter to sitter on a regular basis."

"How is it that you were aware of your daughter being bounced from sitter to sitter?"

"Numerous times when I called to say good night to Maddy, a different sitter answered the phone."

"About how many nights a week would you say this occurred?"

Mike took a deep breath. "About four or five."

"Did this occur throughout the entire time after your divorce?"

"Not so much at first, but then after a couple of months, it became a regular thing."

"Mr. DiSanto, what was your intention when you left Minnesota with your daughter?"

"I wanted to give her some stability and a chance to know she was loved."

"Did you have any indication that Madison was being traumatized while in the care of Ms. Barrett?"

"Ob-jection! Ms. Barrett was never found to be an unfit mother, to abandon her child, or to put her child in danger at any time," Mr. Cheatum boomed.

"Over ruled," Judge Hawkins interjected. "Witness will answer the question."

Mr. Renshaw faced Mike directly. "Did you have reason to believe that Madison was being traumatized while in the care of Ms. Barrett?"

"Yes."

"Please explain your answer."

"Maddy began to wet the bed. She would run and hide whenever a new sitter came to the house. She had stomach aches, and cried a lot. And, she had nightmares."

"How did it come about that you were made aware of these symptoms of trauma?"

"I received a bill from the clinic where Lisa's mother took Maddy, so I called Lisa to find out why, and she told me what Maddy was doing."

"What did the doctor say the reason Madison was exhibiting these behaviors?"

"Lisa told me the doctor said it was nothing physical."

"How old was Madison when you were made aware of these behaviors?"

"She had just turned four."

"And how old was Madison when you left with her to California?"

"Four."

"So, you had two years after the divorce when you could have taken Madison, and yet, you did not do so until you discovered Madison was exhibiting emotional disorder behaviors, is that correct?"

"Yes."

"No further questions, Your Honor."

The jurors sat motionless as Mike stepped down from the witness stand and returned to his seat at the table.

CHAPTER 42

Closing Arguments

The following day, the two attorneys presented their closing arguments.

"Ladies and gentlemen of the jury," Mr. Cheatum began. "You have before you a man capable, and indeed guilty of, defying the laws of our state. In addition, Mr. DiSanto is guilty of harboring malicious motives in the pre-planned kidnapping of Madison DiSanto." He began to pace back and forth in front of the jurors.

"He was unjustified in his actions to stop court-appointed child support payments when he abducted his daughter and fled the state. He was self-righteous in seeking revenge for what he thought were unfair divorce stipulations. He tried to punish Lisa Barrett by causing extreme emotional distress by kidnapping their only child."

Mr. Cheatum continued his pacing before the jurors as he spoke in a crisp manner. He concluded his closing statements by saying, "I submit to you that his intent was to defy the law and to take revenge against Ms. Barrett were malicious and calculating with absolutely no regard for their daughter's welfare. Therefore, I ask you to find Michael DiSanto guilty of malicious intent in the abduction of Madison DiSanto and that he be given the maximum penalty for his crimes." He looked directly at Mike, clicked his heels, and sat down.

Mr. Renshaw stood. He walked slowly and deliberately toward the jury panel of seven women and five men. "Ladies and gentlemen of the jury, my client, Michael DiSanto, does not deny taking his little girl to California, but he does deny the accusations that he did it out of malicious intent. My client was extremely concerned for his daughter's welfare because of the irregular and erratic care she received when she was jostled from one sitter to another on a constant basis. She was denied the privilege of consistently seeing her father two weekends a month and having no semblance of structure whatsoever."

He looked intently at the jurors. "Mr. DiSanto's intent was to give physical and emotional stability and love to his daughter—something she was denied by her own mother."

"Mr. DiSanto intended the child support be used for Madison's care—basic needs like clothing, shoes, and jackets. Yet, on several occasions, Mr. DiSanto had to purchase such necessities himself. When Mr. DiSanto saw the blatant misuse of the child support money for an expensive lifestyle to which Ms. Barrett afforded herself, he tried on three separate occasions to get custody of his little girl. Ladies and gentlemen, I submit to you that the court system failed him, forcing him to try to rectify the situation by taking matters into his own hands for the sole purpose of the welfare of his daughter."

Mr. Renshaw glanced at Mike and then turned his attention back to the jurors. "I ask that you find Michael DiSanto not guilty of malicious behavior." He paused briefly looking candidly into unyielding faces of twelve people. "I ask you to find my client not guilty of deliberate defiance of the courts to pay child support for his daughter while she was in his care since he assumed full responsibility to provide for her needs. She was in his sole care and not that of several sitters."

***

After court was adjourned, Mike was led back to his jail cell to wait while the jury deliberated. He paced the six-foot area apprehensively. *I wish I could explain my motives for my actions in a way that would give me some credibility. But, I can't explain it—not even to myself,* he thought.

He looked out to gray skies, bare trees, falling snow—and waited.

CHAPTER 43

The Verdict

Meanwhile, the jury instructor gave final instructions to the jury reiterating the importance that a guilty verdict must be beyond any reasonable doubt, and that they were not to discuss the case with anyone outside.

"I must also remind you that according to definition, kidnapping is 'to abduct a person by force or by fraud.' Abduction is 'to carry off or lead away illegally and in secret or by force.' Each is considered a felony and is punishable by imprisonment," he explained.

***

The following day, the jury reached a verdict.

Mike was summoned to the courtroom. He spotted Karl and Katie, his parents, and several friends in the standing-room-only court room. He saw Lisa with her lawyer at her side. He barely breathed.

"Have you reached a verdict?" Judge Hawkins asked.

The spokesperson stood. "We have."

The only sound in the room was the ticking clock. Tick. Tick. Tick.

The spokesperson unfolded a paper and read, "We, the jury, find the defendant, Michael DiSanto, guilty of premeditated abduction, of illegally taking a minor over state lines, and of defiance of a court order to pay child support."

Mike closed his eyes and hung his head.

"The defendant will approach the bench for sentencing," Judge Hawkins said.

Mike walked with stiff legs as he and his attorney stepped forward.

"For abducting and transporting a minor over state lines, I hereby sentence you to a lesser sentence of seven years in prison to be served at Croix Valley State Prison. You will be eligible for parole in four years. I hereby dismiss the charges of non-support of the child for the period that the child was in the care of the defendant. However, monthly payments in full are to resume upon release from prison and all child support in arrears until Madison DiSanto is of legal age."

Justice approved the sentence; mercy pitied the victim.

Seven years! I was going to register Maddy for kindergarten, and now she'll be almost thirteen when I see her again. He agonized in his own thoughts.

Mike's mind tumbled into a pool of darkness that drained the last flicker of hope from his soul. *This can't be happening.* He tried to swallow, but a lump had formed in his throat. His knees felt like they were about to cave in. His chest constricted and his breaths came in shallow spurts. Mike's whole body felt numb.

The judge slammed his gavel.

Mike was handcuffed and led away.

CHAPTER 44

Orientation into Prison

Mike sat in the back seat of the Meeker County deputy's car, his wrists handcuffed to a chain around his waist that connected to ankle shackles. The car pulled out of the parking lot for the two-hour drive to Croix Valley.

The two deputies in front seemed preoccupied with tending to official business. They couldn't possibly have known how desperately a man in shackles riding in the back seat wanted to trade places with them. Never had Mike regretted anything so deeply before.

He spent the first hour lost in thought. He wondered about Maddy. *What would happen to her?* He thought about Karl and Katie. *Oh, Karl would find good help all right, but I feel I let him down. Big time! He tried to tell me, but I guess I was too stubborn to listen,* he contemplated. *And Rosie. Poor Rosie. The heavy burden of finding another maintenance man fell squarely on her shoulders. And Stephanie. It's a wonder she even writes to me.* His thoughts clouded his mind and strangled his heart.

While still several miles from Croix Valley, Mike watched white blinking lights on a towering gray smokestack. It looked like a giant spire, piercing the bright blue sky. A white plume billowed out and suspended itself over the glistening hoarfrost landscape and rooftops. "Is that the prison?" he asked.

"No. It's the electrical company," one deputy answered without looking up.

Trees feathered in ice crystals on the far, steep hillside of Croix Valley and the frozen river some 150 feet below gave the appearance of a white-frosted wonderland, but the reality of prison loomed just ahead.

As their car turned into the twenty-acre prison compound, Mike watched the formidable prison loom closer and closer until they stopped in front of a four-story brown brick building with windows hidden behind iron bars. A twenty foot brick wall with curls of wire on top skirted the entire perimeter of the facility except for an iron gate across the entrance. A single grotesquely gnarled oak tree stood guard in the snow-covered courtyard.

He felt dread tighten around his chest like a python had just coiled itself around him. He walked with short clanking steps between the two deputies. They walked up nine steps. His last splinter of freedom vanished as he entered the Minnesota Prison at Croix Valley. He imagined a neon sign flashing, "All hope abandoned, you who enter here."

The two deputies ushered Mike past polished, tan stone walls to steel doors that opened like an elevator. They stepped inside a small area with another set of steel sliding doors, and a cold quiver slithered down his spine.

The deputies checked their guns with the guard sitting on a stool in a reinforced glass cage. The second door slid open and Mike was led to a windowless processing room. The walls were blank except for a sign that read, "The law is the minister of justice and shall never become the accomplice of injustice."

Mike was fingerprinted and photographed by a stern-faced, blue-shirted guard.

"Look straight ahead. Turn to the left." He gave orders and Mike obeyed feeling like a bizarre mechanical robot—a machine that felt nothing except apprehension and dread.

"Your prints and mug shots are for the alphabet of agencies," one guard spoke, routinely.

Mike looked up in question.

"The FBI and the BCA."

"What's the BCA," Mike asked quietly.

"Bureau of Criminal Apprehension," the man answered as he rolled Mike's inked finger across a designated square on a sheet of paper. "Step over to that desk," he said with a nod. "And take my advice—don't think about home or family or the outside, or this place will be intolerable."

Don't think about Maddy? Don't think about the outside? How else would I keep my senses? This is insanity with concrete walls and iron bars, he thought.

Next, Mike sat opposite the unit director, a bearded man with wire rim glasses.

The man asked several routine questions as he stared intently at Mike as though fixating his face into his mind. "Next of kin?"

"I just have my young daughter."

"Parents?"

"Yes. My mother and stepfather."

"Names?"

"Richard and Irene DiSanto."

"Close friend?"

"Karl Roberts."

"List of potential visitors with addresses and phone numbers?"

"My parents, and Karl and Katie Roberts."

"That's it? You might as well add more now, because they all have to go through background checks and approval before coming to visit—that is, when you can have visitors."

"Rosie Woods and Stephanie Sterling."

Why did I give their names? What are the odds they would visit me? But, the man seemed satisfied with his list of names and their pertinent information.

For the next hour, the man asked questions, and Mike answered.

Finally, the man patted the loose papers into a neat stack. "Orientation takes thirty to forty-five days. During that time, you'll be on isolation status."

"What does that mean?"

"It means you have limited access to phones and minimal visitor time. Sending and receiving mail is unlimited." He seemed calloused to the impact of his own words. "New inmates are housed in a cell hall separate from general prison inmates."

Inmate. Mike mulled the foreign-sounding word over in his mind. *How have I sunk from being a divorced father to a prisoner facing up to seven years locked away from everything and everyone I love?* He wondered, but it was too incomprehensible.

Pointing to the far side of the room with beige-painted concrete blocks, the man commanded, "Step over to that wooden counter."

Another man handed Mike a set of battleship gray sweats, underwear, a blue jacket, and personal hygiene articles. "You can keep your watch and address book. Put your wallet and everything else in this brown bag until you can make arrangement to have your stuff picked up." He handed Mike a small paper sack.

Mike dropped his wallet containing forty dollars and his driver's license into the sack. But, he kept out one photo of Maddy taken while in California and put it in his shirt pocket. "You'll be given a physical and a dental exam. You'll be tested to see what makes you tick and how many smarts you've got. Any questions?" he asked and nodded to the door marked "shower."

Mike shook his head, accepted the meager stack of his worldly possessions, and started for the shower.

"Hey."

Mike stopped and turned around.

"Make yourself an island," he said in a low voice. "Know what I mean?"

Again, Mike shook his head.

"Don't get involved. Mind your own business and do what you're told."

He nodded once and entered the dank-smelling shower area followed by an ever-present guard.

That night, the darkness that cowered in corners and beneath the bunks now gathered itself unashamedly everywhere. Darkness melted into darkness until everything was black.

CHAPTER 45

Prison Life

After thirty-five days of isolation status, Mike felt the full impact of being locked up in prison, and his stomach churned. He barely managed to keep his insides intact. His breaths were shallow. He forced himself to breathe slowly, forcing air into and out of his constricted lungs.

Iron bars confined his body physically, but it was the utter despair that gave true meaning to who he was—a prisoner locked in his own emotions. Anger rose over the debilitating hopelessness that clutched his mind and suffocated his soul.

He lay on his bunk and stared into the darkness. It didn't matter if he closed his eyes or left them opened. He could only guess what time it was when he finally fell asleep.

The next morning, Mike met with the Program Review Team. The room was small and stuffy. He sat at a rectangular steel table opposite a panel of five—an associate warden, an assistant to the warden, the unit director, a security captain, and a female case worker. They sat with polite smiles.

The atmosphere remained casual, yet Mike felt stiff and awkward, resisting the urge to look up at the noisy rattling fan above—anything to divert his attention from the situation at hand.

"We want to help you plan a program during your incarceration so you get the most benefit, and we get the least trouble," said the associate warden, a tall, iron-handed man. "Job openings are posted and inmates

186

must apply. You're subject to hire and fire policies," he said as his right leg bounced up and down. "You work a seven-hour day, six days a week, and you get paid every two weeks—$.50 an hour." He leaned forward tapping his pencil on the yellow note pad in front of him as though expecting a protest.

There was none.

"We have a 1240 prisoner capacity here at Croix Valley," the unit director interjected, "and we're at 1370 now, so you probably won't get the position you choose. We advise inmates to put down a second and third choice." His bushy beard and thick glasses did not hide his straightforward manner, and Mike recognized that he and everyone else would always know exactly where they stood with this man.

"Check over the list of job openings," the director said handing Mike a list. "If you don't get a regular job, you'll be assigned a job in the laundry or the kitchen or wherever else workers are needed. Or, you can sign up for training classes."

Mike looked at the list: no openings in metal shop; no assemblers needed; one machinist needed; one carpenter; and one body man in the auto shop. "I'd like to apply for the carpenter position."

"Second and third choice?"

"Training as a welder or blueprint designer."

He was handed a pencil and filled out the application.

The assistant to the warden, a husky man with bulging eyes, stood up. "You'll be informed later where to report for work. Wake up is at 6:00 a.m., breakfast at 6:30 a.m., and work at 7:00 a.m. Let's go."

Mike was escorted down a long corridor with living units stretched out like arms on each side to a large dining hall at the end. Each unit housed 250 men in single cells. "Inmates live, work, sleep, and eat in their housing units. This keeps the number at any one time small, relative to the number of staff available, that is," the big man said.

"You're on B East Wing," his escort said stopping in front of a cell on the fourth level. "The commissary is open on Wednesday, so stock up when you get the chance." He unlocked the door and waited as Mike entered his six-foot-by-eight-foot cubicle.

"You're lucky. Some of the men on second level have to double up."

Mike nodded.

With the help of fear and echoes of man's inhumanity to man behind bars, the iron-barred door clanked shut.

Mike swallowed hard and surveyed his new surroundings—a steel bunk with a floppy mattress along one dull beige wall, a dingy white toilet and a sink. A small wooden table and chair, and a carved-out niche of a closet filled the opposite wall.

He stacked his prison garb and personal items on the single shelf of the door-less closet area. He looked up at a dull, naked light bulb in a ceiling where patches of peeling paint curled back as though laughing at the absurdity of his life.

He sat down on a scratchy green Army blanket on his bunk, hung his head in his hands, and stared at the gray concrete floor.

He knew he was legally alive. The roster with his name and serial number were proof of his existence, but, his head and heart struggled to grasp his situation. He would soon experience being mainstreamed into general prison life.

Suddenly, a loud bell jangled, and a column of men dressed in gray sweats began filing into their cells. *Like dairy cattle to their stanchions,* he thought. Cell doors slammed shut and locked with a brash harshness of steel against steel.

He was part of a prison microcosm—an isolated, functioning community all its own, like a ship at sea with no port as its final destination.

At 4 p.m., the already detested bell jangled, and the cell doors unlocked. A horde of men, some droop-shouldered, some boisterous, some with angry eyes, filed along the narrow cement walkway into the large mess hall.

A spicy tomato aroma filled the crowded room, and for an instant, the loud din of voices, and the clatter of dishes and spoons banging together made Mike think of his high school cafeteria where there was rowdy laughter, good friends, and purpose.

Here, most inmates had eyes dulled by the monotonous life they led. They swilled in the brine of uselessness, but even that was done without purpose. A gnawing feeling of despair ate into the pit of his gut.

He stood in one of two lines, holding a brown plastic tray. Two inmates worked each line. One heaped a pile of noodles on a plate, and the next one dumped a ladle of hot meat balls in a thin red sauce. A tray stacked with thick wedges of garlic bread sat at the end of the line.

Mike didn't have much of an appetite even for one of his favorite meals. But, he carried his tray and worked his way over to an empty place at one of the many long tables with attached benches. He sat next to a stranger. "Name's Mike," he said.

The man didn't answer, but looked past Mike with a flicker of fear in his eyes.

Mike turned around to see a man about thirty-five years old approaching. He had an ugly jagged scar across his cheek that ran from just below his right eye down to his jaw. Mike looked into dark eyes in pools of yellow, and he wished he knew if this hulk of a man was friend or foe.

"Git yo' white-boy butt outta my spot." His voice rumbled like a growl from deep in his throat.

The other man, taller but thinner, stood up. "Hey, Bo, what'cha wanna do? Git yo' butt thrown in th' stink hole agin? Don't be messin' with some white dude."

Mike stood up to move to another table, but Bo leaned into his chest with his own inflated chest. He stuck his nose with flared nostrils just inches from Mike's face. Mike smelled his stale breath and sweaty body as he sized up the brute of a man who looked like he was itching to fight.

"I'm gonna kick yo' white-boy butt," Bo said in a low, guttural tone.

Mike knew he was no match, and hoped he wouldn't have to prove it.

"Bo!" the thin man warned.

Other inmates stood up waiting for the fight to break out.

"Kick his butt on th' court," the thin man pleaded.

Bo didn't move. Neither did Mike, except for a slight twitch in his jaw muscles.

"Scarecrow, yo' right, man," Bo said without taking his eyes off Mike. "I'll kick yo' butt shootin' hoops," he snarled.

Just then, several guards converged on the inmates. "What's the problem?"

"No problem," Bo said. "Jes' settin' a few rules fo' basketball." He set his tray on the table with a smack.

That evening during open movement, Mike sensed the bitter cycle of prison life—guard over prisoner and inmate over inmate. Mike was fast becoming sucked into its vicious vacuum.

Basketball did not merely pit one team against the other in a friendly competitive sport, it heaved deep-rooted anger, frustration and rebellion onto the floor.

Mike recognized that each sweating man in the gym strove to be dominant for the sake of their own dwindled self-esteem. He knew winning would give each man meaning for his existence. To win on the basketball court was the sole purpose for living tonight.

Mike had always been a strong, athletic competitor, but this night, his adrenaline ran like paste through his veins. To Mike, this resembled a polite gang fight between the Lords and the Dragons, but instead of guns and knives, they used a basketball and hurled it violently from man to man.

Bo stood only an inch taller than Mike, but he was a Goliath when it came to fighting and surviving. Foul verbal jabs between the teams bounced off the walls, and elbows punched ribs with crushing blows. The score was tied 67-67 when the loud buzzer signaled the end of free time.

Turning to Mike, Bo's face twisted into a menacing snarl. "We ain't finished yet."

Mike looked at Bo with unwavering eyes and nodded.

The men streamed into the open shower where steam from the eight showers filled the area like a dense fog.

"Bo's layin' fo' yo'." The voice was low. "Watch yo' back."

Mike turned to see Scarecrow walking past. "Always do," Mike said with a nod. He watched the tall, thin man with a thick crop of hair on the top of his head disappear into the vapor.

Mike knew Scarecrow didn't care about him and wondered why he bothered with the warning.

Back in his cell, Mike jotted a short letter to Maddy in hopes maybe this letter would not come back marked "Return to Sender." Then, lights out.

"Hey." The hushed voice came from the next cell.

Mike crept to the outside corner of his cell. "Yeah?"

"My name's Jesse. I heard about the trouble in the mess hall. 'Glad things worked out OK."

"I don't think it's over yet, but thanks. I'm Mike."

"Stay outta Bo's way," Jesse whispered. "He's a low-down rat with so much anger and hatred that it makes him evil enough to kill children."

Mike grasped the iron bars and leaned against the cold concrete wall. "Do you know why Scarecrow would warn me to watch my back from Bo? Why not just beat me bloody and get it over with? Why the mind games? Why anything?"

"Prisoner accountability. Anyone involved in a fracas goes to the stink hole, and the rest lose privileges. Scarecrow's got a weekend pass coming up, and he doesn't want to lose it."

Mike nodded in the darkness. Tomorrow, there would be no more reason to live other than to survive another day. He did not want to succumb to this end.

CHAPTER 46

Glimmer of Hope

T he winter sky was gray as ashes, bleak and featureless. As the lonely days dragged on, Mike's easy going manner faded into the dreariness of prison life and became like the winter sky.

Finally, winter gave way to spring.

One Wednesday afternoon, Mike walked with Jesse to the commissary located just behind the main prison building. The low, white block structure with brown shingles was a hubbub of activity.

Jesse seemed different from the other inmates, and Mike wanted to know why. "What keeps you going?" he asked, while standing in a long check-out line.

"Hope."

"You mean hope of getting out? Finding purpose? Meaning to life? What?"

"No. It goes beyond that. Hope is something most men here don't have. If I didn't have hope, I would be in despair big time."

"You? Despair? You seem pretty laid back."

"I wasn't always that way, but I have the promise of a better life. I cling to that hope. I also try to steer clear of any trouble."

"Why's that?"

"Because I've been in the stink hole, and I don't want to ever go back. Besides, I see these men in a different way now. I actually have a love for them."

Mike looked keenly at this mild-mannered, sandy-haired man with a deep voice. "You're not weird for other guys, are you?"

"Hardly," he answered with a frown.

"I didn't think so," Mike said laying writing paper, envelopes, stamps, soap, and hard watermelon candy on the counter. "What's it like in the stink hole?"

"It's a dark concrete cell with bare walls and nothing but a bench, a toilet, and a big steel door. You get your meals on a tray shoved through a slot. It's incredibly lonely, and your soul rots from sheer boredom." He shuddered visibly. "If you go berserk, nobody cares. I ended up there the first month I was here." He shrugged. "But that was then, this is now."

Mike vowed to himself that he would do everything in his power to avoid the hole.

"What'd you do?" Mike asked.

"To get into prison or the stink hole?"

"Both."

"I got into prison because I smuggled drugs, sold drugs, took drugs. The answer to everything in life was alcohol and drugs, and I got into the stink hole for trying to smuggle drugs into prison." He looked intently at Mike. "What are you in for?"

"Kidnapping my daughter."

Jesse simply nodded.

"Are you married?" Mike asked.

"No. I was never straight long enough to care about anyone but myself. You?"

"Divorced."

They stepped into warm afternoon sunshine. A morning dove cooed from a nearby jack pine. Suddenly the bird's wings quavered as it flew to the electrical wires attached just under the roof of the auto shop.

Mike popped a piece of tangy, sweet candy into his mouth and watched the bird wing its way to another tree.

Free to fly.

"Do you want to go to chapel after chow? Maybe you'll get some answers to what we were talking about," Jesse asked nodding toward the obscure building tucked among the pine trees.

"Sure. Why not?"

The chapel was a small, white plastered building that housed a square room with thin burgundy carpet and ten rows of twelve chairs split by one center aisle. A dark wood podium stood in front of a white wall with large blue letters. "Psalm 71:5." Beneath were the words, "For Thou Are My Hope, O Lord God."

The chapel was simple and quiet.

"Some men come to sneer at the truth spoken here," Jesse said. "Some come to break the monotony of his life."

Mike nodded, glancing at the small group of men.

"But, some are actually here to be set free from guilt and shame—to walk on streets paved with gold some day," Jesse said with a huge smile.

Mike came because Jesse asked him.

The man speaking from the podium was trim with receding dark hair and blue eyes. Instead of wearing a customary suit of a preacher, this man wore jeans and a white t-shirt with the words Prison Fellowship on it.

His words came fast. "It's good to be here tonight. I tell you, it's a lot sweeter being up here than where you're sitting. I know. I sat on one of these chairs three years ago." He moved from behind the podium.

"I'm Lucas Coleman and if it weren't for Prison Fellowship, I'd probably be robbing a bank somewhere right now."

Mike sat against the chair with his feet apart, his arms crossed casually against his chest. He liked the comfortable style of this stranger. *He's been here. He knows what it's like,* he thought. He leaned forward and rested his elbows on his knees.

"Each man here climbed up fools' hill," Lucas said looking into the faces of the handful of men. "Some made the climb followed by their beast of folly or their mangy mutt, Ego. A few struggled up in stupidity. But, each in his own way and each for his own reason. It doesn't matter. I don't care. What I do care about is where are you going from here?"

Leaning over to Mike, Jesse whispered, "This guy's seventeen-year-old brother was killed on their last armed robbery, and Lucas spent ten years in prison. He changed his life around. Now, he comes back here once a month."

Mike nodded and turned his attention back to the man who now stood within a few feet of the prisoners.

"All men have the capability for good and evil," Lucas said. "It's your choice. There's almost a sanctioned notion that man can do anything if he puts his mind to it. That was once my credo. I wanted to have enough money to pay for my wife's medical bills after eight months of leukemia. My kid brother wanted a new Harley motorcycle. It seemed reasonable to do this one last bank job, but I had gone the way of Cain. The Bible says in Proverbs 14:12, 'There is a way which seems right to a man, but its end is the way of death.' I knew, then, that I needed God in my life."

Suddenly, Mike's spark of interest flamed into a roaring fire. *Taking Maddy to California seemed like the right thing to do. The saying is true. There is a way which seems right to a man, but its end is the way of death. I'm a dead man in a living body.*

He thought about a time at his grandparents' home when he picked up their Bible and leafed through it. The endless genealogies of Adam to Noah, and lists of clean and unclean foods meant nothing to him. But, what Lucas Coleman was saying made sense. He was a godly man in street clothes, and Mike liked that about him.

CHAPTER 47

Trouble

"Hey! White trash boys. Yo' gittin' reeligion now?" Bo jeered, as Mike and Jesse walked from the chapel. Bo shuffled his feet and swung his arms back and forth in his usual strut.

Scarecrow joined in and swaggered around Mike and Jesse. "We been waitin' fo' yo'," he taunted.

Mike stared at him with a look of disdain.

"Oooohh." Bo raised his arms shaking them in feigned fright. "I be scared."

"Cool it," Jesse warned Mike. "They're not worth it."

"Yeah, cool it, white dude." Bo stopped in front of Mike. He stood with legs spread apart, and muscular arms hanging loosely at his side. "Yo' might get yo' white-boy butt kicked up to yo' ugly white face."

Mike stood still—his body taut and his eyes dark as his opponent's. His dad's words flashed through his mind. "Don't ever start a fight, but if one bigger than you comes your way, take your licking like a man."

"Keep walking," Jesse said.

"What'sa matter? Yo' chicken, boy?" Bo asked. "Gotta run to yo' church for yo' sperit'l protection?"

Despite Mike's intentions to keep his emotions under control, anger raced through him. As he stepped around Bo with clenched fists, his jaw muscles twitched like overstretched ropes, but he said nothing.

"What'cha think, Scarecrow?" Bo glanced around nervously. "Should we kick the livin' tar outta these ugly dudes?"

"I say we git 'em." Instantly, he clipped Jesse along the left side of his head with knuckles of steel.

Jesse reeled back. Then, a powerful blow from Bo sent him sprawling to the ground.

Mike grabbed for Jesse, but too late. Jesse lay on his back, his face a bloody mess. Mike bent down and rolled his unconscious friend to his side just as Scarecrow grabbed him from behind. Scarecrow snapped his arms through Mike's arms and locked his fingers together behind Mike's head in a full nelson grip.

Bo drew back his right arm and landed the first solid blow into Mike's stomach. Mike lost his wind in a low grunt as Bo's left fist slammed against his face.

Mike used Scarecrow as leverage as he brought his legs up against Bo's chest sending him staggering backward. Scarecrow lost his grip, and Mike swung around smashing his fist into Scarecrow's jaw.

Bo jumped on Mike's back, and the two fell to the ground like a crashing tree. Arms and legs twisted together, like two ferocious lions, each fighting for the advantage position.

Bo grabbed Mike's shirt, torqued it in a knot and raised his mighty arm, but not before Mike landed a hard, stinging blow to Bo's mouth. Mike scrambled to his feet from beneath Bo and faced the two charging men. He tried desperately to keep his back covered, but Bo and Scarecrow widened their distance between themselves, each trying to get on either side of Mike.

Other inmates gathered around the make-shift asphalt boxing arena—their barbaric shouts egging on the three left standing.

Suddenly high pitched sirens shattered the spring evening, and a mass of guards swarmed the scene.

"All right, boys," one guard shouted to the onlookers. "Break it up."

At the same time, other guards wrenched Mike, Bo, and Scarecrow apart and cuffed them. Great drops of blood spattered to the ground.

Groaning, Jesse tried to get to a standing position. He swayed on his knees trying desperately to clear his head.

Two more guards rushed over with a stretcher and carried Jesse off. He throttled on his own blood.

"It wasn't his fight," Mike yelled, but the plea only brought a guard's club smashing against his side sending a shockwave of pain across his back.

"Shut up," the guard ordered, shoving him toward the isolation section of the prison.

Mike's lower lip began to swell into a grisly mass. His gut felt like a lead ball had lodged deep within.

The guards also dragged Bo and Scarecrow to the wretched stink hole. "We was jes mindin' our own business when these two dudes—"

"I said shut up," the guard said, "and that means you, too!" He jabbed his club in Bo's face.

"A couple of weeks in the stink hole oughta cool you hot heads off," the other guard snarled as each man was shoved into one of three cells.

CHAPTER 48

Released

M ike felt a chill of horror as the steel door thudded shut on the sound-proof cell. A dingy, twenty-watt light bulb barely served its purpose.

The stink hole was everything Jesse described—only worse. The putrid stench of old urine on the cold, damp concrete floor repulsed him. He recoiled at the musty blanket reeking of body odors that lay in a heap on the hard bench. There was no place to get a breath of fresh air. The toilet, like a ghost in a den of demons, sat in mockery of human bodily functions.

He slumped down on the bench as a shaft of pain swept through his knotted stomach, and his gut retched violently as he gagged on his own vomit. He swallowed several times and covered his nose with the crook of his arm. He started inhaling through his mouth so as not to smell the stench of the cell.

When his eyes adjusted to the dimness, he stared at walls of peeling concrete with ugly bumps of exposed rocks.

Running his hand along his jaw, he flinched at its soreness, but moved his jaw back and forth until he felt satisfied that it wasn't broken. He sucked his swollen, bloody lip between his teeth and sat motionless in silence.

Dead silence. The deafening stillness of total isolation, no human beings, no voices, no clanking cell doors, no jangling bell. It seemed even worse than the stench. His ears rang in the absolute silence, and the walls began to close in.

He would not allow himself to become a madman.

He walked the few short steps of his cell cringing at every filthy cockroach that crunched beneath his shoes. "Stay active. Keep moving," he said out loud.

He paced back and forth, forth and back. He stretched out on the bench and did twenty-eight push- ups—two for every day he would sit in this abyss. Turning over, he did twenty-eight sit-ups, forcing his cramping stomach muscles to pull and release, pull and release. Time followed time, days in a monotony of days.

Karl and Katie would come to visit. They would return home a hundred miles away, wondering. He felt like he was in a dark cave, but, he forced himself to think beyond his circumstances.

How is Maddy? Does she get hugs and bedtime stories every night? How is Stephanie? His last unfinished letter to her lay on his desk in his cell.

"Talk out loud," he coaxed himself. "If I keep it all choked inside, I will definitely go insane."

He tried desperately to remember the lists of clean and unclean food found in Leviticus. "Clean foods," he said, "those that chew their cud and have split hoofs or was it divided hoofs?" He couldn't remember for sure.

"Insects—those that crawl, except the long jumping ones. Or, were insects not edible at all?" He paced back and forth.

He repeated Maddy's favorite "Cat in the Hat" story that he had read a hundred times. "The sun did not shine. It was too wet to play, so we sat in the house all that cold, cold, wet day. I sat there with Sally. We sat there, we two, and I said, 'How I wish we had something to do.' All we could do was sit, sit, sit, sit, and we did not like it—not one little bit." But, that was all he could recall.

At night, he dreamed about daylight and work and Maddy and laughter. It wasn't long before he relished dreaming more than being awake. And if he got careless, he dreamed while awake. The nights ran into days and days into nights.

He lapsed into sleep, and dreams turned into nightmares. He saw Maddy alone in a fishing boat drifting further and further out on the dark waters of a big lake. She sat with her head bent over a coloring book, unaware she was floating away from him, away from safety.

Suddenly, she looked up and screamed to him for help. She stood in the boat, arms outstretched. She pleaded for him to hold her. He stood on the shore, struggling frantically, but he could not get his arms untied to swim after the fleeting boat. Then, he, too, was in the water—twisting and turning, but he could not get free.

Maddy's cries became muffled as she sank beneath the water. Deeper and deeper. And Lisa sat on a satin blanket with faceless men and laughed.

He awoke. His blanket was damp with sweat. Night? Day? By the eleventh day, he didn't know any more.

He sat with his head in his hands, not bothering to kick the perpetual onslaught of cockroaches from his shoes. The loathsome roaches crawled up his pant legs, but it was the loneliness and helplessness that tore at his soul. At first, tears trickled down his cheeks and then streamed down as he sobbed unashamedly.

He knew his twenty-eighth birthday had come and gone somewhere in the darkness. Or, was it his twenty-ninth? No, he was in the stink hole for only two weeks, yet each day seemed to take a month to drag by.

What was that saying on the prison chapel wall? Some place in Psalms? "For You are my hope, O Lord God." He had lost all hope.

He felt a desperateness like he'd never felt before. He knelt beside the bench on the cold, damp concrete in the midst of the darkness, cockroaches, and the stench of the hole. "God, if You're real, please show me."

It was a pitiful prayer—a pathetic cry for help—but a plea that came from the depths of his spirit.

Three days later, his cell door opened, and a guard stood, waiting for him to emerge.

Mike's lungs breathed fresh air. He gulped the air like desert animals lap water at an oasis. Light stabbed his eyes, sending a sharp pain through his head. He shut his eyes slightly until he could adjust to the brightness.

The guard escorted him to the showers. "Get cleaned up. The doc will make sure you're fit to go back to your cell."

The first human words Mike heard in two weeks sounded harsh, but they were a welcomed relief from the total silence.

He let the warm water and soap wash over his stiff, aching body in unhurried, gratifying pleasure. He shaved and put on clean prison garb. He brushed his teeth. Never did he think he would appreciate such a simple, mundane task. The guard, then, took him to the infirmary where the prison doctor examined him.

"You seem to be in good enough physical condition to return to work tomorrow," the doctor said in a kind voice.

"Thanks." Mike felt eager to get back to the sound of voices and human contact, and his classes for blueprint design. The hated bell would signal some type of routine, and he would know he was still alive.

The guard took him back to his cell, and the door clanked shut behind him.

He noticed something sitting on the desk. His eyebrows shot up when he realized what it was. A Bible. He opened the cover and flipped through the worn pages. It fell open to Psalm 71. Scanning the page, he read, "For You are my hope, O Lord God."

He remembered his prayer three days earlier—"God, if You're real, show me." Tears welled up in his eyes and began to trickle down his cheeks. He had his answer, the proof he needed. At that moment, he lived and died and lived again.

He sat at the desk in his cell and thought about the words. Reading them again, and again, he began to understand. A light surged into his dark soul. "Lord God, now I know You are real," he said quietly, "and I know You are thinking of me. I feel a love that I've never thought possible." A single tear dropped onto the page of the Bible. "Thank You, God," he whispered. "Thank You."

He couldn't wait to write to Karl, Stephanie, Rosie, and Maddy. *They've got to know what I have found,* he thought.

***

The bell jangled, and prisoners returned to their cells for the afternoon count. Mike walked to the outside corner of his cell. "Jesse?"

"Hey, Mike," came the familiar voice from the next cell. "Glad you're back."

"Me, too. What happened after the fight?"

"I had a broken nose and a concussion, so I ended up in the infirmary for a few days."

"Man, I'm really sorry about that. You took my place for a beating intended for me."

"Just like Jesus did for us, but don't be sorry about what happened to me. It was God's way of keeping me outta the hole. How was it for you?"

"Everything you said it was. But then, if I hadn't been in the hole, I probably wouldn't have prayed."

"You prayed?"

"Yeah. I asked God to show me if He was real."

"And?"

"And thanks for the Bible."

"What Bible?"

"The one in my cell—on the desk."

"I didn't give you any Bible. Mine's right here." And to prove it, he held his Bible through the bars for Mike to see.

"But how did—who put—?"

"You may never know. Maybe it's the Lord's way of dealing with you personally. There's a saying, 'There are no atheists in foxholes and only madmen who deny Christ in stink holes.' Some of us have to hit rock bottom before we see our need for a Savior."

"You've got that right. I never used to think I needed God."

"What man doesn't think that at some point in his life? But without Jesus, I know I'd be dead in more ways than one." He cleared his throat. "Watch who you talk to about this. Talking to the wrong person could get you iced."

"Thanks. I'll remember that." He shifted his stance. "What happened to Bo and Scarecrow?"

"Scarecrow got pneumonia after ten days in the hole and ended up in the infirmary. Bo's back here. And, Mike," his voice sounded stern, "Don't let him hassle you into another fight."

"Not on your life! He may be one angry dude, but not one that's going to get me sent back to the hole."

"I understand Bo's anger," Jesse said. "I know where he's coming from."

"How's that?"

"Bo's dad lived by the bottle and died by the bottle. The story goes that he froze one night in an alley—too drunk to crawl inside. At the funeral, Bo heard his mother say, 'Serves him right. Now the devil can keep him warm.' That could've been me for as many times as I passed out—too drunk to know, or too high to care, that I laid on the threshold of outer darkness myself."

"What pulled you out?"

"Fear."

"What happened?"

"I tripped out one night and stood face-to-face with the most hideous and grotesque demons imaginable. They were clawing their way to me, blood dripping from their mouths—trying to take me to a dark pit teeming with worms. When I came to in the hospital, I vowed I would never do drugs or alcohol again."

"So, how did you end up here?"

"The cops raided the drug dealer's place where I passed out that night. They brought me to the morgue first, but then realized I was still alive, so they brought be to the hospital. I was arrested in the hospital, and I didn't know it for three days!" He laughed. "I had to go to in-house treatment until my court date. That's when I recognized there are some things I can't change, but I can fix the things I can if I'm smart enough to know the difference."

"So how did you find God?"

"Through Prison Fellowship here. I realized that God was seeing to it that I kept my vow to get off the booze and dope and stay off."

"What's Bo so angry about?"

"He's angry at the entire human race and the circumstances that go along with living in a ghetto without a father. Survival of the fittest is what he grew up with. And if fighting and killing is what it took to stay alive, well, that's the rule they lived by."

"So, what's he in here for?"

"Murder."

CHAPTER 49

Loose Ends

T ime marched in one-year increments at Croix Valley Prison. A new warden made changes and improvements—cells and common areas were painted, bathrooms were updated, and even the stink hole was replaced with modern solitary confinement cells. Warden Smith instituted controlled movement which meant that inmates were divided into smaller groups and moved on staggered schedules for meals and free time in order to quell fights and tension. The upsurge of morale for staff and prisoners alike became evident in a short time.

Still, some prisoners claimed, "I don't belong here. This is an injustice."

Mike was reminded of a conversation he had with Jesse. "Try to understand why you had to go through all of this," Jesse had said. "You're not in control. God is."

Mike was quiet for a moment. "Yeah, I see that. But, if Lisa wouldn't have—"

"Mike." His voice was firm. "Bitterness will eat you up."

Mike closed his eyes and nodded. "I guess I had to learn that the hard way. I tell you, Jess, if I wasn't a Christian, it would make no sense at all."

The updated prison transformation may have been like a shot in the arm for inmates, but Mike's greatest morale boost came from the hundreds of letters he and Stephanie had exchanged over the years. They were like an uninterrupted conversation—sometimes intense, other times carefree, but always aware of one another. Stephanie wrote wonderful letters—positive letters, letters of life at Green Tree, and letters of her involvement with women's ministries at their church. But, any hint of intimacy was guarded. He accepted that as he considered his circumstances. After all, what could he offer her? She was a virtuous woman worth more than diamonds.

Once, Stephanie wrote, "Time doesn't heal, but it makes the hurt bearable." He knew she was referring to her time of grief when Roger died. Yet, for Mike, time seemed to be his worst enemy. The second hand on his watch would twitch ever so slowly. A year would pass, and then it would twitch again.

Jesse had long since been paroled and had taken a position with Prison Fellowship in the St. Cloud area. He missed Jesse's friendship and the way Jesse taught him about the Bible. He was glad they wrote to each other.

Life took an upswing when Mike received word that he would be meeting with the Program Review Team at the end of the week. The judge had said the earliest possible parole would be four years, and it had been four years, three months, and seventeen days. If all goes well, he just might celebrate his thirty-second birthday as a free man. And that gave him hope.

He whistled softly as he sat at his desk during afternoon count. He glanced at one of his favorite photos that hung on his cell wall. Stephanie had sent it to him. She was sitting on top of a stepladder holding a paint brush in one hand and a plunger in the other.

He tore open the new letter he had just received from her. As he did so, another photo fell onto the desk. He picked it up and grinned. She was sitting alone at a small table on her veranda at Green Tree Complex sipping lemonade and smiling. He noticed another frosted lemonade glass opposite her.

He read, "I've wanted to tell you this for some time now. I'm not sure I should at this point, but here goes. I've met a man who is the most wonderful man on earth."

He stared at the words. A lump began to form in his throat, and sadness filled his heart. He could not read any further. He laid the letter aside. He sat there for a long time in silence. *If I would've told her how I felt about her, how I had wanted to know everything about her, and how I have come to care so deeply for her, might things have been different?* But, he reasoned, *it would not have been fair to her if I told her that I've come to love her.*

He looked at Maddy's picture—the one he had carried with him since their first trip to the LA zoo. Suddenly, he felt a loss like never before—a loss that tore at his heart.

The bell jangled, and the cell doors slid open. Prisoners filed out for chow and free time. He mechanically stepped in line—another link in a human chain of prisoners, but his mind was far from the routine of supper and basketball.

Afterwards, he returned to his cell. He picked up Stephanie's letter and simply held it. He took a deep breath and continued to read, "Since Roger's death, I did not think I would ever be able to feel love again, but here I am falling in love! And it's delightfully wonderful to be able to feel something once more."

"He is sensitive, caring, hardworking, very handsome, and to top it off, he's a Christian! I wonder how God should bless me so, and I am grateful to Him that I know such a man. My heart soars at just the thought of him. Mother is telling me to be cautious, but deep down, I know she likes him."

"What did you expect?" He mumbled to himself. *Did you think these treasured letters from Stephanie would continue forever? Don't be stupid.*

He took her picture down and put it inside the envelope with the letter. He could not let himself think what might have been.

Of course she would meet someone. She has a captivating charm, a loveliness, and an inner beauty that no one could top. What guy wouldn't want to love and be loved by her? What guy wouldn't want to spend the rest of his life with her?

He thought of the words Roger had said about Stephanie, "A woman's heart should be so hidden in Christ that a man should have to seek Him first to find her." Finally, he understood what he meant, but it was too late.

He thought Stephanie was probably relieved she didn't have to write letters to some guy in prison thousands of miles away. But, he did not want to come across as a poor loser, so he scrawled a note to Stephanie.

He opened his Bible, looking for words of comfort before responding to Stephanie's letter. He read from Psalm 42, verse 11. "Why are you downcast, O my soul? Why so disturbed within me? Put your hope in God, for I will yet praise Him, my Savior and my God."

He inhaled and exhaled deeply. He wrote, "I'm glad you found someone to make you smile and laugh and love again. I know it's been hard for you to be alone all these years." He paused. "He's a lucky man."

"I have good news, too. I am meeting with the Review Board the end of this week. I hope it means I will be paroled soon. It seems like half my life has been behind bars, and if it weren't for my faith, I don't think I would have survived intact. The hardest part was not knowing how Maddy is doing. All my letters to Maddy have been returned. I saved them, but I'm not sure why. I also regret having to leave California so abruptly, as you know."

"Karl came last week. He told me Lisa married her former divorce lawyer. I wonder how Maddy fits into the mix. My hope is that someday I'll be able to make all this lost time up to her."

Mike's letter was unusually brief. *Why dribble on to someone who has her own life to lead?* He inserted his last letter to Stephanie into the envelope.

CHAPTER 50

Review Board

The evening before Mike's meeting with the Review Board, he walked to Chapel. He came face-to-face with Bo. They both stopped dead in their tracks. Their eyes locked.

Mike stood motionless, his jaw muscles twitching as dreadful memories of the stink hole raced through his mind. Another fight would certainly send him to solitary confinement, and any possibility for parole would be locked away for the next three years.

Bo's eyes flashed. His lips curled in a savage sneer.

"Bo." Mike gave a curt nod. And then, words escaped his mouth before he knew what he was saying. "Do you want to go to Chapel?"

Am I nuts? Inviting my worst enemy to Chapel?

Bo drew back slightly in surprise. "Bug off!"

"C'mon, Bo. Everyone knows you're mean enough to beat any guy here, but are you man enough to hear what Lucas Coleman has to say?" He nodded towards the white plastered building. Immediately, he wished he could take back his challenge, but now he had to stand his ground.

"Shut yo' white trash mouth or I'll shut it fo' yo'!"

"It's just us this time, Bo. No Jesse with me and no Scarecrow with you. We could beat each other's brains out—for what? To prove one of us is stronger? To end up in solitary? What then?"

Bo raised his fists and planted one foot back slightly. Neither took their eyes off the other.

"I'm gonna kick the livin' tar outta yo," he said in a growl.

"You know, and I know you could whip me. And you know what else, Bo? I'm not half as scared of getting beat up as you are of going to Chapel." Mike stood with his arms loosely at his side, but his eyes remained fixed on the black dots in yellow pools of this angry man—too late to retreat.

"I ain't scared of nothin'!"

"Yeah? Prove it. Go to Chapel with me."

Bo's veins bulged down his muscular arms. "I wouldn't go to my ol' man's grave with yo', you crazy man."

"What if I'm telling you the truth?"

"I don't give a rip!"

"The only ones who lie have something to hide. I'm not lying, but you'll never really know for sure if you don't find out for yourself."

Bo swung his mighty arm. Mike dodged a blow that would certainly have smashed any man's jaw. They faced each other in a standoff— one with fists drawn up, the other with determination to fight for his opponent's soul.

"Hey, Bo!" It was Scarecrow.

A dread flushed through Mike's head and chest, but he didn't waver, nor did Bo.

"We're shootin' hoops, man. C'mon," Scarecrow yelled, motioning toward the basketball court.

Mike waited, barely breathing.

Bo stood motionless.

"Bo! C'mon!" Scarecrow called again.

"Don't prove anything to me," Mike said. "Prove it to yourself." He turned and walked to the chapel.

As he walked, he wondered if a death blow would come from behind, but he neither heard nor felt Bo's presence behind him. He slipped into the chapel and found an empty place in the middle, and breathed a deep breath.

Lucas Coleman nodded to Mike without interrupting his talk. He was speaking on freedom.

In the quietness, Mike heard the chapel door click. He crossed his arms casually across his chest, and grinned. *I hope it was Bo*, he thought.

"…and you shall know the truth, and the truth shall make you free," Lucas was saying.

***

The next day, Mike sat before the Program Review Team in the same stuffy room where he had been orientated into prison. The questions were brief and Mike's answers were just as short.

"Have you learned that consequences follow every choice you make?"

"Yes, sir."

"Have you learned to regard law as something to be obeyed?"

"Yes, sir."

And so it went.

Then came the long awaited decision.

"The prison system is meant to rehabilitate those who have made foolish choices but have learned from their mistakes," the associate warden said in a formal tone. "We reviewed your behavior over the past four plus years, and other than a fight with another inmate, you have shown exemplary behavior. We feel your incarceration has met the standards we try to achieve in rehabilitating offenders."

The Commissioner of Corrections and the Office of Adult Release spoke, "We are recommending your release." He smiled politely. "You will be processed out of Croix Valley State Prison on Monday morning at 9 a.m." He extended his hand to Mike.

Mike clasped his hand in return.

He wanted to jump off his chair and give each one of the Review Team a bear hug. At last, a free man! No more clanking doors. No jangling bell. No head counts twice a day. He would be a free man in four days! Free to go outside—to work at a real job. Free. Free. Free.

"However," the assistant to the warden said, "There's a matter of pending tax fraud charges against you in the state of California."

"Tax fraud?" He couldn't believe what he was hearing.

"Yes. You will be taken by police escort to California to answer these charges before the courts."

Mike's hopes and fears mixed together like oil on water. He slumped in his chair as though the air was sucked out of his lungs. He hung his head and closed his eyes.

He jotted a hasty note to Karl, letting him know of the pending charges and the uncertainty that lay ahead. Then he added, "Thanks again for trying to tell me about the Lord, and for not giving up on me. I look back and I see that I was running from God, and that is a scary place to be."

CHAPTER 51

Pending Charges

The three hour flight from Minnesota to California was uneventful as he sat handcuffed to a police officer.

He had no idea what to expect, but he did know doubt and emptiness—doubt because of his pending charges and emptiness because he missed Maddy and didn't know how she was doing. In the midst of it all, a hollow feeling gnawed at his heart. Stephanie had found someone else.

He reached for his pocket Bible. He read Joshua 1:9. "Have I not commanded you? Be strong and courageous. Do not be terrified. Do not be discouraged, for I the Lord your God will be with you wherever you go."

"Lord, You are always there when I need You," he breathed. "Please watch over Maddy. And, Stephanie, too." His lips moved silently.

Before long, he looked out to the hazy, yellow sky of California as the plane landed at the familiar airport.

The officer brought him directly to his informal hearing at the Orange County Courthouse. The State Auditor, judge, court-appointed attorney, Mike, and the police officer sat in a small courtroom on the third floor. Dark mahogany walls overwhelmed the room. Not even the tall, narrow windows could brighten it.

The judge—a skinny man with rapid blinking eyes was not at all what Mike expected a judge to look like. "You are charged with tax evasion against the State of California, Mr. DiSanto," the judge read.

"How can that be?" Mike asked, frowning.

"Is this your Social Security number?" the judge asked, holding a paper toward Mike.

Mike read the number in the rectangular box. "No. The last four digits are reversed."

"According to your tax returns for the time in question, this was the Social Security number you used. Was it listed correctly or incorrectly?"

"Incorrectly, but I made a mistake. I inadvertently put down 7496 instead of 7946."

"So, you admit to falsifying your Social Security number to avoid paying taxes on income earned?"

"I didn't intentionally falsify it. I did notice that last four digits were inverted, and I intended to correct it, but—"

"But, you got too busy or you forgot about it, or you didn't think you would be caught? Isn't that right, Mr. DiSanto?"

"No, Your Honor. I intended to—"

"You intended to, but then you were arrested for child abduction. We know the story. It just gives additional credibility to your dishonest character," the judge said.

"Your Honor, I did not intentionally—" But, Mike's explanation fell on deaf ears. He swallowed hard. "I know taking my daughter was wrong. I admit that, and I paid for that. But, this was not intentional." He tried unsuccessfully to keep the edge from his voice.

"Let me give you the definition of fraud. It is 'deceit or trickery to gain an advantage' and is considered a serious charge. Young man, did you fill out these forms yourself?" the judge asked, holding up two forms.

Mike looked at the forms. "Yes."

"Is this your signature?"

Mike's jaw muscles twitched. "Yes."

The case continued for another half hour with accusations from the judge and useless defense statements from Mike.

"I hereby find you guilty of tax fraud against the state of California."

Mike pursed his lips and clenched his hands shut.

The court-appointed attorney spoke up for the first time.

"Your Honor, in view of the fact that Mr. DiSanto has already served four years in prison on unrelated charges and was released early because of his exemplary behavior, I ask for leniency in sentencing this man."

The judge looked at Mike like a man who was all discipline and no love. But, he softened his voice. "I am going to give you leniency. Instead of two years, I hereby sentence you to one year in minimum security at Soledad Prison. Do you have any questions?"

"No, Your Honor."

The judge rapped his gavel. "Court dismissed."

CHAPTER 52

Soledad

The next day, a deputy drove Mike to the Reception Center in Chino for processing. More mug shots. More fingerprinting. The deputy then took him to Soledad South, the minimum security section of a 1,000 acre prison compound at the base of the San TaLucia Mountains in Salinas Valley.

As the police car approached the prison, Mike noticed gun towers surrounding the facility. He saw armed guards manning each tower.

"Gives new meaning to minimum security, wouldn't you say?" the guard asked with a dry laugh.

Mike ignored him.

As the iron gate swung open, he stared at a twelve-foot, cyclone fence with razor wire coiled on top that ran along the border as far as he could see. Ten feet away was a second twelve-foot cyclone fence with the same coiled razor wire on top.

"The area between the fences is called 'no man's land'," the deputy driving the car explained. "You don't want to sleep-walk in there."

Mike looked to five long, low buildings of gray cinder block. Bars covered the windows. He exhaled deeply.

The deputy drove exceedingly slow, as though he wanted every detail to carve itself into Mike's mind. "Each dorm is built to house eighty men," he said drearily. "There are about 160 guys in each now. I hear they get real edgy about not having their space, too," he wheezed, sarcastically.

Mike looked at the deputy with disgust.

Mike noticed more than two hundred men in street clothes milling around on what could have been a lawn at one time, but was now trampled into black dirt by those housed at Soledad. He spotted another hundred or so more men at the softball field inside a chain link fence behind the dormitories.

The police car stopped in front of a square, brick building marked "Administration." The officer led Mike through two black steel doors, each with a small square opening covered with steel mesh grille. They came to a small room where two officers sat at separate desks cluttered with papers.

"First off, here's a visitor form," one officer said routinely. He handed Mike a blue sheet of paper. "All visitors must be approved in advance. Visiting day is Saturday from 9 a.m. to 4 p.m.

Mike took the paper, looked at it, and handed it back to the officer.

"It's your call, but I'd put a couple of names down if I were you." He held the form out to Mike.

He took it, jotted down the same names and addresses of those on the visitor form for Croix Valley and handed it back to the officer.

"There are no jobs in any vocation available and since all cleaning, repairing and cooking are done by inmates, you'll be added to the cleaning roster. That means cleaning latrines, dorms, and the grounds. Any questions?"

Mike shook his head—feeling nothing, thinking nothing, saying nothing.

Most of the other paper work had been completed at Chino, so the officer took Mike to a windowless, gray receiving room where he was issued prison clothes with his prison number stenciled in black.

"The commissary has clothes, and it's up to you if you want to buy some or wear these," the officer said, "but it's mandatory you wear these the first two weeks." He pointed to an open shower. "Over there."

Mike knew the routine.

After the shower, the officer led him to the last one story building in a row of five. "This is your assigned dorm," the officer said.

Once past the doorway, Mike looked at the open and overcrowded dorm area with two rows of steel cots bordering the walls and two rows of bunks head-to-head up the center with a four-foot high, block partition in between. A small, metal nightstand separated each bunk.

It doesn't seem like it would matter which bunk anyone sleeps in, he thought, *they're all the same, and those who sleep here are just numbers.*

His mouth felt dry and hot from the dust settling. Little fuzz balls flitted across the wood floor as two large ceiling fans whirled monotonously.

He could easily see the central bathroom from the doorway. A row of twelve grim sinks jammed along one wall, urinals and stalls with no doors lined the opposite wall, and eight showerheads marked the far wall. Black stains from wall sweat covered the concrete walls and the dank smell of mold and mildew hung in the air.

"Everything you do, you do in front of 160 men and three officers," the uniformed man said noticing the look of chagrin spread across Mike's face.

Minimum security came with a high price. The advantage of minimum security over a single-cell seemed remote to Mike at this point.

A piercing whistle shrieked, and a loudspeaker crackled. "All inmates return to bunks for head count."

Pointing to the fifth bunk in the center row, the officer said, "That's your bunk."

Mike put his bundle of returned letters to Maddy and his few hygiene things in the metal nightstand and sat on his bunk for the afternoon head count. He jotted a hasty note to Karl, letting him know he had been transferred to Soledad for a year.

Suddenly, the dorm clamored with the loud voices of 160 men filing into the dorm.

A dark-haired man with olive skin and a hawk nose flopped on to the bunk next to Mike's bunk. He had an arrogance about him that concealed any hint of insecurity. "Sam Ringold is the name, and high stakes is my game," he said to Mike.

"Otherwise known as Silk Sock Sam," the man in the next bunk jabbed icily, "but he's really just a little muckworm." Then, he squinted his eyes, stretched out on his bunk and stared at the ceiling fan.

"Oy! He's a stupid idiot," Sam said and made a dry spitting sound out the side of his lips as though trying to rid his mouth of an unpleasant taste. "Don't listen to him," he said not bothering to look at the other inmate.

Mike eyed Sam loosely. "I'm Mike DiSanto," he said in a flat tone.

"What's your charge and how long's the stay?"

Mike glared at the man like he was a living brillo pad. He lowered his voice, "Tax fraud. One year." Instantly, he wished he would have ignored the man's question.

"Well, well, well. We have a gentleman in the crowd," Sam announced. "Everyone has a little *gonif* in him. Do you know what that means? *Gonif*? It means 'thief.' Do you understand?" he asked tapping two fingers to the side of his head.

Some of the other inmates looked curiously at Mike, others eyed him with blank faces, and a few had flagrant expressions of annoyance bordering on resentment. Mike was, after all, one more prisoner in the already overcrowded dorm.

"If you're looking for sympathy, you won't find it here," the man on the other side of Mike said as he coughed. His teeth were stained brown, and his fingers were yellow. "The only goal for everyone here is to get by, get through, and get out."

Mike had no intention of making his bunk area into a comfortable home either. "Thanks, but I intend to keep my mind alive, too," he said with a tight smile.

"Just don't screw things up for the rest of us."

"Now, Eddy, is that any way to talk to a new inmate?" Sam asked, slyness dripping from his lips.

"Don't mind these idiots," a stocky man with red hair and beard in the third bunk said. "I'm Rusty O'Malley, and this worthless lump of clay between us is Eddy." He reached across Eddy and held his hand out to Mike.

Mike nodded and shook his hand. He noticed a rosary hanging from the head of O'Malley's bunk.

"Is this your first time in prison or are you on your way out?" Rusty asked, sitting on the side of his bunk.

Mike sensed that Rusty was genuinely interested, but didn't want to parade his past in front of Eddy or Sam or anyone else for that matter.

"Well, what is it? First time in or on your way out?" Eddy hacked, his face taking the color of dust.

Sam waited patiently, too.

"Both," Mike muttered. He felt like a piece of raw meat between two hungry dogs.

The noise died down as two officers entered the dorm. They walked down and back the two aisles looking left and right at each bunk while a third officer stood at the door holding a clip board. A few minutes later, the loudspeaker cracked, "Line up for chow."

The prisoners scrambled to their feet at the foot of their bunks. The officers stood aside and 160 men filed out the door and headed for the dining hall—a large cinder block building at the far end of the minimum security section of the compound.

Rusty stood behind Mike in the food line. "Hey, I didn't mean to put you on the spot back there."

"It's not a big deal," Mike said as they headed for one of the long tables next to the wall.

Rusty automatically crossed himself on his forehead, chest, and two shoulders and started spooning what looked like beef stew into his bearded mouth.

Sam suddenly appeared and squeezed between two inmates across from Mike. "So, tell me, Mike, how did you fraud the government on your taxes?"

"It's none of your business," Mike said dryly.

"Sam's always looking for ways to make money where someone else failed," Rusty muttered, stuffing a piece of bread sopped in gravy into his mouth. "He's like a buzzard circling over the spoils of a fresh kill."

"Balderdash!" Sam exclaimed. He made a spitting noise out the side of his mouth.

"Yeah? You'd steal from your own mother, if you could."

"He did. How do you think he wound up here?" the inmate next to Sam smirked.

"I didn't steal from my mother, God rest her soul."

"What do you call it when you shift money from her account to your account?"

"I had power of attorney over her affairs, and I made an investment that went bad. Besides, it was my financial partner who blew it." He made the spitting noise again.

"Admit it. You got caught with feathers between your teeth."

"You swine!" Sudden anger flamed over his face. "That's unfair."

"Fair and unfair exists only if there is God," an inmate said into his plate of stew. Then, he turned to Sam, "Perfect hatred for the likes of you makes judgment a reality."

"Why you—"

"Hold it," Rusty warned, noticing two nearby officers watching their table.

"We all know Ringold's fantasy," the prisoner continued in a low voice. "An orchard of money trees with leaves of hundred dollar bills, blossoms of security bonds, and diamonds dangling like fruit—all fertilized by greedy lawyers." He got up to leave.

"What's wrong with that?" But, the inmate did not answer. Sam turned to Mike. "You know as well as I do that money talks."

"I know. Mine says goodbye," Mike said suddenly disinterested with their arguing.

That night, Mike lay on his cot and stared into the darkness. He listened to snores, weird laughs, and whispers of the sleepless.

Shutting out the annoying sounds of the night, Mike thought about Maddy. *How will I be able to explain why I couldn't see her all these years? Will she even listen? Would she understand or would her heart be filled with hatred for me?* He prayed silently for her and fell asleep. Night had descended, chasing shadows into darkness.

CHAPTER 53

Visitor

F our weeks after entering Soledad, Mike was cleaning one of the two day rooms in the recreation building. It was Saturday morning. The room had one wall of barred windows facing east allowing the morning sun to throw streaks of orange against the opposite block wall.

Several round tables, piled high with outdoor and car magazines, sat along the walls. "Time" and "Newsweek" were stacked in a corner to make room for a slightly used chess board and dog-eared decks of cards.

The other day room had a large flat-screen TV and several black vinyl chairs set up like a mini theater.

Methodically, Mike moved a mop back and forth, then back into a bucket of dark, sudsy water leaving a heavy pine smell in the room. He picked up a book that was sitting on one of the tables—"Words for the Wind" by Theodore Roethke. He leafed through it. He read, "I wake to sleep and take my waking slow. I feel my fate in what I cannot fear. I learn by going where I have to go."

He frowned slightly, shrugged, and put the book back onto the table, and went back to mopping the floor.

"Mike DiSanto to the visitor waiting room," the speaker box on the wall boomed.

Mike glanced at the speaker and then to one of the inmates sitting at a table. "What did they say?" he asked.

"Mike DiSanto to the visitor waiting room," the man answered without looking up.

Mike dropped the mop into the bucket and rolled it next to the wall. He ran across the grassy area to the Administration Building. *Who could be here?*

"I'm Mike DiSanto. I was told to come to the visitor waiting room," he said to the officer at the desk.

"Sign here and go through those doors," he said pointing to double doors.

Mike scribbled his name and pushed open the door. The loud ruckus of happy voices provided an amazing relief from the usual sound of angry male voices.

Scanning the crowd of prisoners and their girlfriends, or wives and families, he spotted a woman sitting alone at a small table next to a window. She was looking out as gold rays of sunshine streamed around her. *It was like watching a Polaroid picture come to life*, he thought with pleasure.

Her chestnut hair was shiny with soft curls—just how he remembered her. She sat with her back straight, as always, and her chin resting in her hand.

"Thank You, God, for having me write her name down on the visitor form," he whispered. *I didn't think she would really come. She is so beautiful sitting there in the sunlight. If only—why would she be here?* His thoughts tumbled together.

"Stephanie."

She turned and looked up at him. She smiled so big, her eyes seemed to dance on the crescents of her cheeks. She stood, her slender figure silhouetted against the bright sunshine. She wore no make-up except for a hint of eye shadow that emphasized her beautiful green eyes. "Hi Mike," she greeted, warmly.

He wanted to pull her close to himself, hold her, touch her soft hair, tell her of his love for her. But, he could not. She belongs to someone else. She said so in her last letter. So instead, Mike asked, "What's a nice girl like you doing in a place like this?" He couldn't help but smile broadly as he looked at her.

"I wrote you after I received your last letter telling me about your parole hearing. You had already been released, so my letter was returned. It took me this long to find out where you had gone." She looked into his eyes with her own eyes filled with tears.

He brushed her tear from her cheek and quickly withdrew his hand. "I'm really glad you came. It is so good to see you." He stood back. "What are you doing here?"

"I was about to ask the same thing of you," she said with a smile.

He wanted to hug her, to capture this moment permanently in his mind. "It's a long story. Let's go outside to the visitor area."

She stooped to pick up a large cloth bag.

He took her hand and led her through the crowded room. He wished he didn't need a crowded room as an excuse to hold her hand.

The visiting area looked peaceful. Tall trees shaded the fenced area. Several metal tables and chairs were arranged in jumbled rows.

Mike led her through the cool grass to a vacant table. The sun shone through the leaves casting small reflections, like miniature spotlights, on the tables and the ground.

She sat down, and he sat opposite her. The crowd of nearby prisoners with their visitors melted away from sight and sound. The ugliness of prison faded. The whole world seemed to dissolve except for Mike and Stephanie.

"Mike, I don't know where to start." She hesitated. "Well, here." She pulled a letter from her bag and handed it to him. "Just read this."

Eyeing her for a hint of its contents, he took the letter. He couldn't tell anything except whatever was in the letter made her smile. *Maybe she's getting married?* He opened it.

"Read it out loud," she coaxed.

Mike wet his lips and read, "Dear Mike." He looked at her.

"Go on," she urged.

"When I said I met the most wonderful man on earth and was falling hopelessly in love," he looked at her curiously before continuing, "Remember? Well, that marvelous man is YOU."

He gazed tenderly at her. He could hardly believe what he had just read.

She nodded.

A slow smile spread across his face as the meaning of her words flooded through him. He swallowed hard, and his eyes filled with tears.

Their eyes locked for a moment in an exchange that sent electrical charges everywhere.

"I didn't know how you would feel—"

"Stephanie, this is the happiest day of my life!"

He stood, pulled her to her feet, and kissed her tenderly. They embraced, and he kissed her again. The words to an old song sprang to mind, "She has kisses sweeter than wine."

He stood back and smiled at her. "All of your letters over the years— you never said—I thought—I mean, I didn't know. If you only knew how many times I wanted to tell you how I felt about you."

"I didn't know how you felt, either," she said smiling up at him. "Why didn't you tell me?"

"Because you deserve better." He shrugged. "I'm a divorced man and a felon."

"You are also a godly man and forgiven."

They looked at one another for a long moment.

He smiled and drew her close.

"Your letters showed me who you are, and I just couldn't let any more time go by without telling you how I've come to love you so." She smiled up at him through liquid eyes. "What is desirable in a man is his kindness. That is one of the first things that attracted me to you."

He kissed her again, afraid that if he opened his eyes, he would realize it was all a dream. But it wasn't a dream. Stephanie was here—in his arms.

"I'm glad you listed me as a visitor," she whispered.

"I didn't think you would really come. I just put you and Rosie down because the officer suggested I fill the blanks," he said softly.

"Let's sit on the grass," she said.

He leaned against a tree. She sat facing him with her arms hugging her drawn up knees. They talked quietly.

He told her again, but with more detail, about the stink hole, and how he had come to believe in Jesus Christ as his Savior and Lord. They talked about Jesse and Lucas Coleman, and how these godly men helped him to understand the truths of God's Word.

He told her how he mistakenly inverted his Social Security number on his income tax form, and how it led to fraud charges. He left out the sporadic times of feeling near despair and hopelessness.

She told him about the delightful maintenance couple at Green Tree. She spoke about the church she and Rosie attended where Rosie taught women's Bible studies, and where she was involved in Titus 2 weekly mentoring of young women. "I have come to love these women. They are so eager to learn how to love their husbands, their children, to be sensible and pure," she said. "They are a delight."

"What does Rosie think about you driving four hours to come up here?"

"Mother? She came with!" she said with a laugh. "We're staying at a motel in town. She said she'd come with me if I go with her to Carmel on Sunday. We plan to drive back home tomorrow afternoon." Suddenly, she grabbed the bag. "Oh, I almost forgot. I brought a picnic lunch. I didn't know if I would be able to share it with you, but I was hoping."

"What if I had another date for lunch?" he teased.

"She wouldn't get to eat."

They laughed.

She pulled out a red checkered cloth, shook it open, and spread it on the grass. She took out a white, hobnail bud vase with a single, red rose and set it in the center of the cloth.

Mike watched with pleasure in his eyes. "Can I help?"

"Absolutely not." She smiled as she took a round loaf of Italian bread from her bag. She bought out barbequed chicken wings, cubes of cheese, green grapes, and a bottle of water. "I was told no silverware or alcohol, so I brought food we can eat with our fingers."

"This is a feast!!" He reached over and stroked her hand. "Thank you, Stephanie, for making everything so special. Do you mind if I pray?"

"I'd love that."

"Our Father in heaven, thank You for this godly woman. Thank You for bringing us together. Thank You for our lunch. Please join us and bless this food."

"Our first face-to-face prayer," she said smiling.

"Lucas Coleman said something that stuck in my mind." Mike took a bite of a chicken wing.

"What's that?" she asked.

"He talked about the destruction of Sodom and Gomorrah, and how Lot's wife looked back to where all the people and houses had been. He said we are all a little like Lot's wife because we're so human. She was turned to a pillar of salt for looking back, and Stephanie, I was like that pillar of salt—until today."

"I agree with him. I did the same thing after Roger died. But, Mother reminded me that when we experience the death of a loved one, it changes us to the core. We learn to live as the new person we have become. I really believe that the Lord wants us to learn from our past, but not to stay there. We must wrap our arms around the future in trust with our backs to the past of regrets," she said smiling. "For life goes not backward nor tarries with yesterday." She laughed. "I'd like to claim those words, but actually they belong to Kahlil Gibran."

"He makes a good point." He nodded. "I want to look to the future, but I've left some pretty muddy footprints." He set his chicken wing down and looked at Stephanie. "I can't ask you to—"

"Wear dirty boots?"

"Something like that."

CHAPTER 54

Truth

Mike thought about Stephanie's smile. It reminded him of warm summer afternoons and the fragrance of vanilla orchids blooming in the tropics. The weeks between Stephanie's monthly visits dragged on, but he lived for those precious few hours together. They fueled him each morning and gave him purpose to face another day.

Mike smiled every time he read her letters. Her joy radiated outward, no matter what the circumstances. Even when she grieved for Roger, she emanated an inner joy. "A woman who fears the Lord is to be praised," he read in Proverbs 31:30. *How true*, he thought.

"Father God, please don't let anything bad happen to her. To us," he whispered, while sitting on his bunk during afternoon head count one summer afternoon. "And please watch over Maddy, too." He looked at Maddy's picture taped next to Stephanie's. "God, how is Maddy?" he asked.

Mike snapped back to his surroundings when he heard, "Hey, O'Malley. What are ya twirling your beads for this time?" Eddy laughed, showing his brown stained teeth. "Are ya asking for a miracle from a god that don't exist? Maybe to make this prison disappear or maybe make it into a potato field instead?"

"Eddy, you're bordering on blasphemy," Rusty said glaring at the inmate sprawled out on the next bunk. "I'm warning you—"

228

"Blasphemy! Against who? How can ya blaspheme against something that don't exist?"

"Oy!" Sam pounced in. "How can you say God does not exist?"

Mike looked from Sam Ringold to Eddy to Rusty O'Malley, but said nothing.

"Well, the way I figure it," Eddy said, "we're all in prison, and nobody's god is helping us out—"

"God doesn't exist to make our lives cushy," O'Malley began.

"Of course not, you schmuck. He hasn't sent our deliverer yet," Sam interrupted. "But when he does—"

"Yes, He has," Mike said quietly.

Eddy gave a loud cynical laugh.

"What? How can that be?" Sam demanded. "When the Savior comes, we will have peace."

"I'm telling you, He has already come," Mike repeated.

"He's come and gone, and nobody knows it. Great god you guys have," Eddy sneered.

"Listen, you foul-mouthed slob—" O'Malley burst out.

"I know the Savior," Mike said calmly. "I prayed to God and asked Him to show me if He's real—"

"Who do you think you are? The Pope?" O'Malley asked incredulously. He grabbed his rosary and started to chant, "Hail Mary, full of grace, pray for us—"

"All I know is that when I called out one night, I met the Savior," Mike said.

"What do you mean 'you met the Savior'?" Sam asked. "What schmooze! The Savior hasn't come yet. What Savior are you talking about?"

"Jesus Christ, the Son of God," Mike said looking directly at Sam.

"Jesus? Jesus was a Jewish teacher who died a couple of centuries ago. Any history book will tell you that," Sam exclaimed.

"He died for a reason," Mike persisted.

"Of course, He died." O'Malley jumped back in.

"Well, if He died, what good is that?" Eddy asked.

"You moron! Why do you think we have Christmas *and* Easter? Hmmm?" O'Malley grilled.

"I don't celebrate Christmas *or* Easter," Sam boasted haughtily. He made the spitting noise again.

"Ringold, you've got your arrogant airhead screwed on backwards," O'Malley scowled.

"Christmas, Easter, July 4th, it don't matter in prison anyway," Eddy countered.

"Of course, it doesn't matter what day it is. You don't need a special day to pray," Mike said. "You can pray anytime, anywhere."

"Is that right?" Eddy sneered. "To a dead god?"

"God's not dead. He rose again." Mike's tone was firm.

"You think you got all the answers, don't ya?" Eddy accused.

"I don't." Mike held up his Bible. "But, this does."

"What? A book? Big deal," Eddy wheezed nosily.

O'Malley attacked Eddy. "OK, big mouth, where do you think you're going after you die?"

"I ain't going nowhere. Who gives a rip anyway? You?"

"Hardly," O'Malley spurted.

"Then what's it to ya where I go?"

"Eddy," Mike said gently. "Read this." He placed his Bible, opened to John 3:16, on Eddy's bunk. "You're pretty good at figuring things out, so read a little at a time. Alone. Just read it as though it *might* be true. You'll soon figure out that unbelief is not a logical conclusion."

"I don't read books—especially that one!" Eddy looked disdainfully at the Bible as though it was a disgusting piece of trash. "You're beginning to tick me off! Now git that thing off my bunk."

Mike took the Bible back and placed it on his nightstand just as the loudspeaker crackled, calling all inmates to line up for chow.

CHAPTER 55

Joy Comes in the Morning

S ummer faded into autumn, autumn fused into winter, and winter melted into spring. The air felt dry, warm. Skeins of tattered clouds flitted across the horizon the day Mike met with the Parole Board.

"You have met the terms of your incarceration," said the man dressed in a wilted shirt and suit pants. "Do you feel you are rehabilitated?"

"Yes, sir," Mike answered.

"Do you feel you are a changed man?"

Let's see, he thought. *I've lost my daughter, and don't know how she is, I've messed up big time, and I've spent five years in prison. On the other hand, I found grace and forgiveness in my Savior, and I met the love of my life.*

"Yes, sir, I'm a changed man. No doubt about it."

The man eyed him suspiciously. Very well. You will be released Monday at 11 a.m. However, you will be placed on probation for two years, and you must not leave the state of California or you will risk up to two years in prison for parole violation."

Mike felt the joy at being released evaporate like a puff of smoke when he heard he must remain in California for two more years. *Will this never end?*

"Do you know where you will be living?"

"Yes. In Pasadena."

"Here's a card for a probation officer in that area." He handed Mike a business card with the name James P. Freeman in shiny, red letters. "You will report to him every two weeks, and he will be in touch with us after every meeting. Don't try to slip through the cracks. It isn't worth it."

Mike nodded and stuck the card in his wallet.

The man stood. "Good luck." He reached out his hand.

Mike clasped it in a brief handshake.

"Regardless of the months or years locked behind bars, prison life does not equip a man to start a new life on the outside. It must come from within," he said. He eyed Mike with a smile. "I hope you make it."

***

"I'm being released Monday at 11:00 a.m.," Mike said to Stephanie on the phone.

"I'll be at the front gate," she promised. "How will I recognize you?"

"I'll be disguised as a prisoner, except I'll be the one with a grin on my face," he said.

***

The morning of his release, Mike packed his few personal belongings in a brown bag that was already stuffed with the hundreds of cherished letters from Stephanie, the hundreds of letters to Maddy that were returned to him and the one photo of Maddy and two of Stephanie.

There was one particular letter that he had written to Maddy. It said, "Maddy, my little princess, I hope you know about Jesus, but if you don't, I can hardly wait to tell you about Him." He always placed it on top of the stack. *By the time I see her, she'll probably be calling me Dad instead of Daddy, if she calls me anything at all,* he thought with deep sadness.

He picked up his Bible that had traveled from Minnesota to California. Placing the Bible in the sack with the letters, he glanced one final time around his bunk area and headed for the door. But then, he stopped.

He retraced his steps and sat on the edge of his bunk in the strange quiet of the dorm. The only sounds were the humming ceiling fans and the distant muffled voices of prisoners outside. It was the first time in a year that he had a shred of privacy.

He took the Bible from the bag and wrote a note inside the cover. "Eddy, read this for a real change. Hope to see you on the other side. Mike." He slipped the Bible under Eddy's pillow and left.

The sun shone brightly, and a warm breeze ruffled his hair. He breathed deeply and smelled sweet freedom in the air. He could taste the manna.

He stopped at the Administration Building to sign out—his last requirement before stepping through the gate to freedom. Heading down the long, wide driveway, he wanted to run and not look back. Ever!

A red car sat outside the gate. He quickened his pace, past the first twelve-foot cyclone fence with the coiled wire. The gate swung open. Passing the second cyclone fence, he stepped outside the prison gate. This time, the nightmare was really over. *I'm out! I'm free!* The gate clanked shut behind him.

He headed toward the red car, but the woman sitting behind the wheel was not Stephanie. He looked around. He spotted a woman with bouncy chestnut hair and dancing green eyes jump from a car parked across the street. Stephanie's white teeth gleamed in parenthesis of tan cheeks as she ran to meet him.

Dropping the brown paper sack, he hugged her, and together, they twirled around. They clung to one another in a tight embrace. They kissed and laughed and cried and kissed again.

"I've got a brand new start at putting my life back together," he said with a broad grin.

"I do, too, and I don't want to waste another minute of it," she said with a huge smile.

They ran hand-in-hand to her car.

"Do you want to drive?"

"With no driver's license? I'd probably get life." He laughed a hearty laugh. He tossed his bag of belongings into the back seat as she turned on the ignition.

He put his hand over hers. "First things first." He looked into her eyes and knew his own eyes surely must have reflected his deep love for her. "I want to ask you something. I'm not sure if I should of if I even have the right to, but it's something I've been dreaming about for a long, long time."

"Well, ask," she said breathlessly.

"Steph, you know how much I love you."

"Yes, I know." She smiled, and her eyes danced. "I love you, too."

"I don't have a lot of money. I have nothing to my name and nothing to offer you—"

"Mike, it doesn't matter."

"But Steph, I don't want you to say 'yes' unless you really mean it. I want you to be sure."

"I am sure, and the answer is yes. Yes. Yes. Yes!"

"Yes what?"

"Yes, I will marry you," she said with her captivating smile. Suddenly, her face became somber. That is what you were going to ask me, isn't it?"

"Well, no. I was just wondering if we could stop at the Dairy Queen." He laughed.

"What?"

"I'm just kidding." Then putting his arms around her, he said softly. "Stephanie, my love, I want to be the reason you are happy. I want to walk side by side through the good times and the bad. I want to drink a cup of coffee with you every morning. I want to pray together for the rest of our lives." He lifted her chin up. "Would you complete my joy and marry me?

"Hmm. I'll have to think about it."

"What?"

"I'm just kidding. Yes, I will marry you. I want to bring you everything good, and we can laugh together in the days to come."

"Before we make it official, I would like to ask your mom for your hand in marriage."

"She would be pleased at that." She touched his cheek with her fingers tracing down to his lips.

"Would you like to pick out your ring?"

"I'd rather have just a gold wedding band."

He kissed her tenderly.

"How do you feel about moving to Minnesota in a couple of years?"

"Two years? But I thought you wanted to go back as soon as possible—for Maddy's sake."

"I'm on probation for two years, and I can't leave the state."

"It doesn't matter where we live as long as we are together. I will go wherever you go." They smiled at one another with mutual love and respect.

They drove onto the main road and headed south to Pasadena.

"I know Maddy is important to you. She's important to me as well. I want to do whatever I can to help."

"You are a sweetheart, and I love you. What about Rosie?"

"Mother is independent, as you well know. She was like that even before my father died. Besides, she has the neatest couple to help her run the complex. Mother and the Johnstons have become close friends."

"That's good to hear."

"Speaking of Mother, when I graduated from high school, she told me something I will always remember."

"What's that?"

"She said, 'Mothers aren't for leaning on, but to make leaning unnecessary.' I didn't realize she was letting me fly on my own until I went away to college. Of course, I tested her philosophy most of my life," she said with a laugh, "but she patiently loved me anyway. She trained me well, and I will always love her for that. She and my father modeled what it means to love one another. I hope I can be a godly wife to you like she was to my dad."

"You are everything a man could ask for, and I am so thankful God brought us together. Speaking of together, I have to find a place to live, and I need to find work before we can get married." He became serious. "Steph, are you sure you want to be with me?"

"Absolutely," she said with a huge smile. "There's a vacant apartment in Building D, or I could move in with Mother, and you could rent my apartment."

"You'd be too crowded at your mom's. I'll take the one in Building D. Ah, is Detective Sherman still living at the complex?"

"Funny you should ask. As a matter of fact, yes. Right next to your new apartment." She raised her eyebrows and smiled. "Still want the apartment?"

Mike nodded and smiled.

"Actually, I'm glad he discovered me, except for what it did to Maddy. A lot of good came from it. I can look him in the eye now, and that's a good feeling."

"And more good is to come. By the way, Mother did not sell your car so it's still sitting in the car port. I don't think she thought you'd be gone for so long. I tried to start it, but—"

"I told her the new maintenance man could have it, but if the Johnstons don't need it, I'll get it resurrected," he said with a grin.

CHAPTER 56

Finding Work

B y the second week in June, the weather had turned sultry with a hot southwest breeze that blew aimlessly around corners and across streets. The smog hung like a cloud in the San Gabriel Valley. It seemed everyone had stinging, red eyes and tasted exhaust fumes in their throats.

But it didn't matter. Today, Mike would meet with his parole officer.

He walked into a large stucco office building with a red tile roof and took the steps two at a time to the second floor. He sat on the edge of a padded chair in the waiting room, his hands clasped loosely. He didn't think about the meeting—he wondered how long it would be before he found work.

His savings account quickly drained. He began to feel desperate with no job opportunities in sight. He answered ads for carpenters, construction workers, laborers, truck drivers, and even pizza deliveries, but every time he came to the question, "Have you ever been convicted of a felony?" he hesitated before writing down, "Yes." And each time, he would hear the same answer, "We'll call you." But, they never did.

"Lord God, I'm not asking to get rich, but I need to find work. It says in Your word that if a man does not work, he should not eat. Would You help me find a job?"

Just then, a door opened, and a tall man about ten years older than Mike with skin weathered like a sailor's, stepped out.

"I'm Jim Freeman," he said and reached out his hand. He had a ready smile and a confident air about him.

Mike stood and shook his hand. "I'm Mike DiSanto."

"Come into my office." He gestured to one of two chairs in front of his desk. He tilted his chair back, giving his full attention to Mike. "Tell me a little about yourself."

Mike recapped his life starting with his bitter divorce from Lisa, his reckless concern to protect Maddy, and the consequences he reaped for his poor decisions.

Mr. Freeman prodded for more details and sat with his hands clasped together—his chin resting on the steeple made by his two index fingers.

Mike and Mr. Freeman talked for nearly an hour when Mr. Freeman asked, "Have you found work yet?"

Mike looked down. "No, but here's the list of the jobs I applied for." He slid a sheet of paper across the desk.

Mr. Freeman read it carefully, looked up at Mike, and grinned. "I have a good friend who runs a construction company, Integra Builders. Maybe you've heard of them?"

Mike shook his head.

"I'm meeting him for lunch tomorrow. Why don't you join us?"

"Thanks, Mr. Freeman. I would like that."

***

Mike rushed over to Stephanie's apartment to tell her about the meeting the following day.

She gave him a tight hug. "You are such a determined man, and I love you for it."

Mike stood back a bit. "My determination has been known to get me into trouble," he said. "But, I hope I'm learning to think things through now."

***

As Mike drove to the restaurant, his heart beat faster at the prospect of possibly finding work. *Don't count your chicks before they're hatched*, he cautioned himself.

Roberto's Restaurant was crowded with businessmen and blue-collar workers mingled together with no distinction of job class—just people eating lunch together.

"Mike, I'd like you to meet my good friend, Joe Jacobson. Joe, this is Mike DiSanto"

The two men shook hands and sat down. Mike liked the man, but did not want to get his hopes up for a job.

The conversation seemed casual, but more importantly, it was productive.

"I'd like to offer you a job," Joe said as the waitress refilled their coffee cups. "I realize you were just released from prison, and I don't know all the details, but I believe in giving people a second chance."

"Thank you, Joe. I'm mighty grateful for that. I won't let you down."

Mike was to start the next day. The pay was more than fair, and after thirty days, he would be eligible for full benefits. The big bonus was that he and Stephanie could get married! His hopes began to soar.

He thanked Mr. Freeman for arranging the meeting and thanked Joe.

When he got into his car, he thanked the Lord.

CHAPTER 57

Church on Marengo

Mike liked working for Integra Builders. Joe treated all
the workers with respect. Mike also felt a great sense of
accomplishment as progress on the two-story townhomes
moved forward at a steady pace.

He thought about Maddy. She celebrated six birthdays since he
saw her last and would have two more before he could go back to
Minnesota. But unlike the time that passed quickly for his first thirty
days with Integra, the time until he hoped to see Maddy seemed to
stand still. Then, exhilarating thoughts of his wedding to Stephanie in
one week swirled together with longing thoughts of Maddy in an eddy
of emotions.

***

The chapel connected to the otherwise large church where Rosie,
Stephanie and Mike attended was perfect for a small wedding. Stepping
in the courtyard of the chapel was like stepping back into the nineteenth
century. Gray-green Spanish moss draped the branches of cedar trees
like a soft feathery sheet. Tall yucca plants with pointed leaves, like
raised bayonets, and white, waxy flowers towered above Mike as he
dashed up the timeworn marble steps of the chapel.

Inside, colorful glass in arched windows cast a vivid mosaic on
rough textured walls. The deep fragrance of sweet lavender from vases

near the altar permeated the chapel. A quiet reverence cast a soothing charm everywhere, although the wooden benches creaked with every movement of the thirty guests.

Mike, in a dark blue suit, stood at the back of the chapel. His heart pounded. Finally, he would be able to share his life with his beloved.

The door to the dressing room door just off the foyer opened, and Rosie emerged. "She's ready." She smiled so broadly, her signature gold-capped tooth showed. She gave Mike a kiss on the cheek and said, "God bless you."

Mike returned the kiss to her cheek. "Thanks." He escorted her to her seat and returned to the foyer.

Just then, Stephanie stepped out from the dressing room wearing a soft pink dress that stopped just below her knees. She carried a small bouquet of white orchids with green ivy. Mike's eyebrows raised, and a grin spread across his face. "You look ravishingly beautiful," he whispered.

Their eyes met in a mutual exchange of anticipation.

"Thank you, my love. Wait till you see me tonight," she said with a blush. She slipped her hand through his arm, and together they walked down the short, narrow aisle as the violinist played "Love of My Life."

***

That evening, they checked into the Victorian Inn. "I like that," Stephanie said as Mike signed 'Mr. & Mrs. Mike DiSanto' on the guest register.

He smiled, winked, picked up their bags, and together, they climbed the open stairway to the second floor.

"Wait here," Mike said at the door of their room. He set his travel bag and Stephanie's overnight case at the foot of a large, four-post bed. Glancing quickly around the room, he spotted the vase of long stem, red roses he had arranged to be delivered and smiled with satisfaction.

He picked up Stephanie and carried her into the room.

"You are so romantic," she said wrapping her arms around his neck.

"Must be all the time I spent at Soledad Charm School," he said with a laugh, setting Stephanie down.

"Oh, Mike, they're beautiful!" she breathed when she spotted the flowers. She touched a rose lightly, pressing one unfolding bud to her nose. "I got you a little something, but you have to shut your eyes."

She pulled a small box from her overnight bag and held it behind her back. "Ready," she said.

He smiled. He looked around. "Do I have to search for it?

"No, but if you hug me, you'll find it." She teased.

He put his arms around her and felt the small box.

"Should I open it now?"

She nodded with a smile.

He tore the paper off and smelled a rich chocolate aroma even before he lifted the lid. "Bavarian chocolates! You sure know how to get to a man's heart." He grinned broadly.

Then holding her hands, he stepped back and looked at her with open admiration and love before leading her out onto the veranda.

He stood behind her on their private balcony and wrapped his arms around her. She leaned against his chest. They stood there for a long time, gazing quietly at the white lights shimmering from beneath the water as a fountain of three cherubs sent a cool mist into the warm evening air. A gentle breeze carried a sweet, citrusy fragrance to them.

"We must be in heaven," he whispered.

"Mm-hum. I don't want this moment to ever end."

He turned her toward himself, looked deep into her green, dancing eyes, nodded, and held her close. "It won't."

CHAPTER 58

A Promotion and a Surprise

O ne night a few months later as they lay in bed, Stephanie read aloud from their Bible. "Be still before the Lord and wait patiently for Him; fret not yourself over the one who prospers in his way, over the one who carries out evil devices! Refrain from anger, and forsake wrath. Fret not yourself; it tends only to evil. For—"

"Wait. What did you just read?" Mike asked lifting himself up on one elbow. "The last part."

"You mean about not fretting?"

"Yeah, that's it. Read it again."

"Fret not yourself; it tends only to evil. Why?"

"That's exactly what Karl said when I talked to him about my frustration with Maddy's situation. Where is that?"

"Psalm 37." Then, laying the Bible on her chest, she asked, "Are Karl and Katie Christians?"

"They are, but I didn't know what it meant to be a Christian at the time. Now, his words make sense." He laid on his back. "I can't wait for you to meet each other!"

**

The following day, Joe called Mike into his makeshift office of the trailer at the job site.

243

"Mike, you're an asset to this company, and you have the respect of all the guys here," Joe said.

Mike looked puzzled, wondering where this was leading.

"I would like to make you foreman, which means that you will be in charge of the crew. It would take some pressure off me and free me up to do other stuff that needs to be done. You'd be perfect for the job."

Mike raised one eyebrow. "That's quite a compliment, Joe. Thanks. Would I still be able to do carpentry?"

"Absolutely! It will also involve some blueprint modifications when necessary. I know you took a blueprint design class at Soledad, and that's a plus. And Mike, there's a nice pay raise that goes with it," he said with a grin.

"I don't know what to say."

"Say you'll accept the promotion, and we'll both be happy campers."

A huge smile spread across Mike's face. "OK, Joe, I accept."

"Congratulations, Mike, and welcome to management," he said holding out his hand.

Mike grasped his hand in a firm handshake. "I will do my best."

"That's a given," he said slapping Mike once on his shoulder. "Hey, I've got some more good news. I'm hoping to expand Integra into designing and building townhomes to accommodate handicapped folks. I met with the CEO of Green Meadows Assisted Living and Memory Care, and he wants us to submit a bid for a new development they are planning for Pasadena. Who knows where this will lead?"

"That is great news! Congratulations to you!"

"To us. You will play a major part in this, mark my words."

***

On the way home, Mike bought a red rose for Stephanie. As he pulled into the carport late that afternoon, a familiar heavyset man with a big neck and a stone face lumbered through the parking lot. He wore khaki pants with brown suspenders over a clinging t-shirt. Detective Sherman!

Mike hadn't encountered the detective since he moved back into the complex. They eyed one another. Detective Sherman looked icily at

Mike who simply nodded once as he headed to his apartment. Then as an afterthought, Mike turned back. "Um, Detective Sherman?"

The big man stopped and turned to face Mike. "Yeah?"

"I just want to tell you that I, ah, well thanks for doing your job when you arrested me. A lot of good has come since then."

Detective Sherman's stone face softened a bit as he studied Mike. "Glad to hear that."

"I just wanted you to know," Mike said with a shrug.

The detective nodded and continued to walk to his car.

Mike smiled to himself, pleased for the opportunity to talk with Detective Sherman. If only he could talk to Maddy.

When he opened the door to their apartment, he was greeted with the aroma of a pot roast with onions. Stephanie emerged from the bedroom looking exceptionally beautiful in green slacks and a cream colored blouse. She wore her hair swept back with a green head band and matching earrings.

"Wow! This is like the cherry on a DQ sundae, only better!"

He smelled Stephanie's subtle Soft Musk perfume as she greeted him with a tender kiss and hug.

"I like coming home." He held her tight for a moment, then looking around the kitchen, he noticed special touches—a white tablecloth, two candles, Rosie's china dishes with the gold rim, and two goblets filled with ice tea. "Did I forget something?" he asked, looking quizzically at her. "What are we celebrating?"

"You'll see," she said with a mischievous smile. "Dinner is almost ready, so hurry and take your shower."

"Are you going to give me a hint?" he asked, walking to the bathroom.

"Not on your life!"

Mike reappeared in the kitchen just as Stephanie set a platter of roast beef, potatoes, and carrots on the table.

"You outdid yourself," he said with a grin. He thought about his promotion.

As she lit the candles, he asked, "Did you talk to Joe?"

"No. Why?"

"Well, Joe promoted me to foreman and I—" he motioned toward the table with his hand, "thought maybe you had talked to him."

"Oh, Mike, that is wonderful! Good for you! That makes this is a double celebration day!"

"Are you going to tell me what else we're celebrating?"

"Let's pray first."

Mike bowed his head. "Lord, we thank You for my promotion, and we thank You for this meal and the hands that prepared it. And we give thanks for whatever it is that we are celebrating. Thank You for my wife. We invite You to join us at this table and bless this food to our bodies. In Jesus' name, Amen." He looked at Stephanie expectantly. "Well?"

Stephanie smiled a teasing smile. "I took a pregnancy test today, and I'm pregnant."

Mike had never seen her eyes dance quite like this before. He jumped up, pulled her to her feet, and drew her close in a tender hug. "I thought I was happy when I got the promotion, but this is deep down happy!"

"I'm glad you are so happy, because I'm ecstatic."

"When and how long have you known?"

"I've suspected for the last two weeks. I think we'll have a June baby. I have a doctor's appointment next week."

"Awesome! The baby will be a year old when we go back to Minnesota. And to think, I left with nothing but my little girl, and I will go back with my wife and baby!"

CHAPTER 59

Trials and Triumphs

Three months later, Mike returned home from work. Stephanie's car was in the car port, but when he opened the door, she did not greet him.

"Steph?" No answer. He walked into their bedroom and saw her lying on the bed.

"What's wrong?" he asked rushing to her side.

"Oh, Mike, I'm bleeding," she cried.

"Sweetheart, when did it start?"

"After lunch."

"I'm calling the doctor."

"I already called him, and he told me to lie down, but if the bleeding turns bright red or gets heavier, I'm to come in. I'm not bleeding much, and it's not bright red."

"I don't care. I'm taking you in."

"Maybe we should just call him, again," Stephanie urged.

Mike ran into the kitchen and grabbed his phone. "My wife's three months pregnant and started bleeding!"

"Stay calm," the receptionist coaxed. "What is your wife's name?"

"Stephanie DiSanto."

"Who is her doctor?"

"Doctor Andersen."

"Is she cramping?"

Mike called to Stephanie. "Are you cramping?"

"No," she called back, walking to the kitchen. "Mike, my bleeding is very light." She sat down on a chair. "It's not an emergency."

Mike spoke into the phone. No, she's not cramping."

"That is a good sign, but why don't you bring her in, and Dr. Andersen will check her."

"Great. We'll be right there."

He turned to Stephanie. "I'll carry you."

"No, no. I can walk." She stood up, then swayed toward him.

He grabbed her shoulders.

"I'm fine. I just got up too quickly."

He put his arm around her waist and helped her to the car.

"This seems ridiculous," Stephanie said as Mike pulled into the clinic parking lot.

"It's not ridiculous. Now, c'mon," he said opening the car door for her and helping her out.

The receptionist looked up and smiled politely. "The doctor is with his last patient. You both can come on back, and the doctor will be with you shortly." She ushered them to an examining room.

A few minutes later, Dr. Andersen entered. He asked Stephanie several questions and did a short exam.

"I don't think there's anything to worry about, but we'll do an ultra sound just to be sure," he said.

Mike hesitated. "Can I stay with Stephanie?"

"Of course. Right this way."

They were taken to a softly-lit room. Stephanie laid on a bed, and Mike sat on a chair next to her. The young woman administering the ultrasound sat on a stool on the other side of Stephanie. She turned the screen so they could see.

Although Mike could not interpret the images, he watched the screen with wide eyes. "We are looking at a miracle in the making."

"How amazing!" Stephanie said.

"The radiologist will read the ultrasound, and then Dr. Andersen will be back in," the young woman said.

"Could you figure anything out?" Mike asked and sat next to Stephanie on the bed.

"Not really. But, I thought I could see the head."

In a short time, Dr. Andersen entered the room. He sat on the recently vacated stool. "When I listened to the baby's heart, I detected something indistinct, but the ultra sound confirmed my suspicions."

"Bad news?" Mike asked. He slipped his arm around Stephanie's waist, and she laid her head against his shoulder.

"Not unless you consider twins bad news!"

"What?" Mike gasped.

Mike and Stephanie looked at each other with wide eyes.

"Twin boys," the doctor said.

"They can tell that?" Mike asked.

Dr. Andersen nodded with a broad smile. "Everything is fine with mother and babies," he assured. We'll see you in two weeks at your regular appointment. "Congratulations!" He held his hand out to Mike and then to Stephanie. He let the door close with a muffled thud.

"Can you believe it? Twins!" Stephanie said. She clasped her hands under her chin with a joyful laugh.

"I was scared you were going to lose the baby, but now we're having twin boys! Wow! That's incredible! Thank You, Lord!"

"Yes, He is blessing us!"

"What about names?" Mike asked sliding behind the steering wheel.

"I don't know. It's so new right now, but Biblical names, for sure. And they have to be manly names. What do you think?"

"I agree."

She thought for a moment. "How about Daniel and David?"

"Daniel and David," Mike repeated. "Yeah, I like them. How about if we give them middle names after the two men who had the biggest influence on me for work?"

"I like that idea. What did you have in mind?"

"How about Daniel Karl and David Joseph after Karl and Joe? Both men took a chance on me, and both men were my bosses."

Stephanie's eyes danced.

"Daniel Karl and David Joseph it is," he said with an emphatic nod.

***

He called Karl the first opportunity he had. "Karl, we're having twin boys!"

"Hey! That's great! Congratulations! Katie, Mike and Stephanie are having twin boys," Mike heard Karl call out.

"Yeah, we named them Daniel Karl and David Joseph."

"Daniel Karl? You don't say?"

Mike detected more than a hint of pride in Karl's voice. "Have you heard anything of Maddy? I know I ask that every time I talk to you, but—"

"No, Mike. I'm sorry."

CHAPTER 60

Double Blessing

Six months later, Mike awoke to the rare sound of June rain pelting the window, as if tiny grains of sand were being flung against it.

Stephanie stirred.

"Are you all right?" Mike asked quietly.

"I've been having dull labor pains all night."

"Why didn't you wa—"

Suddenly Stephanie bolted upright. "Ugh! Oooh! That was intense," she winced.

"But you're not due for two more weeks."

"The doctor said I could go anytime now." She struggled to get out of bed. "I think this could be it."

Mike jumped out of bed and ran to her side, lifting her to her feet.

"I would like to freshen up a bit." She winced again.

"Breathe," Mike coaxed, as he helped her to the bathroom.

He quickly dressed and grabbed her packed bag. He placed it by the door before brushing his teeth. Stephanie grimaced during a hard contraction.

"Every five minutes," Mike said.

"We better go." She rubbed her hand across her large belly.

"Call your mom."

"I will on the way."

Even though it was raining, Mike drove the usual fifteen-minute drive to the hospital in ten minutes. He pulled up at the emergency entrance and ran in returning almost immediately with a nurse and a wheelchair. He helped Stephanie into the wheelchair and wheeled her to the elevator to the third floor maternity ward.

"Don't push," the nurse cautioned.

"I'm trying not to," Stephanie gasped. "The babies are doing a great job all by themselves."

"Dr. Andersen is on his way," the nurse reassured.

Stephanie was in the labor room just long enough to hear that Dr. Andersen had arrived.

"Oooh, Mike. It's a good thing we're having twins. I don't think I could go through this again."

"I know, honey. I'm so sorry for your pain." Mike held her hand. "Remember to breathe," he coached, trying to be calm for her sake when his entire insides twisted into a knot.

Once in the delivery room, Mike took his place at Stephanie's head.

Soon, the first baby was born.

"Congratulations! You have a good-looking boy," Dr. Andersen announced.

Mike watched one nurse wrap the red squalling baby in a blue blanket and whisk him away to be cleaned.

"Why don't mothers tell their daughters what giving birth is really like?" Stephanie gasped breathlessly. "The joy is worth the pain?"

"Just a few more pushes," the doctor said.

After several more pushes, the second baby was born.

"Well, well, you have two fine-looking sons."

Mike cheered. "We have two sons!"

Stephanie nodded, exhausted. She looked up at Mike. "Are they as good looking as their father?"

"Well, they both have dark hair, but I think they look more like you."

Dr. Andersen made conversation as he worked on Stephanie. "Do you have names picked out yet?"

"Daniel and David," Mike said with a huge grin.

A nurse placed one tiny six-pound bundle in Stephanie's arms.

Stephanie and Mike looked into the face of their first born son. They looked at each other. "Daniel," they said in unison.

Then, another nurse placed a five-pound, twelve-ounce baby on Stephanie's other side. "His name is David," she said looking intently at their second son.

"Hey, how are my boys?" Mike asked tenderly stroking each baby on their cheeks with the back of his forefinger. He kissed Stephanie on her forehead. "You did a great job, sweetheart."

They unwrapped the boys and counted twenty fingers and twenty toes. "They're perfect," Stephanie said in admiration.

"Daniel, you will be our courageous one," Stephanie said smiling at their first born. "And little David, you will be our determined boy—just like your daddy," she said softly as David tried to stuff his fist into his mouth.

"Mother was right. The joy is definitely worth the pain. The only pain that would be worse, I think, is to have a child and lose it," she said with tears in her eyes.

Mike nodded. "God is good." And nodded again.

"We'll finish up here if you want to go make some phone calls," Dr. Andersen said without looking up.

Mike jogged to the visitors' area where Rosie stood waiting.

"Two healthy boys!" he yelled, picking her up and twirling her around.

"Is everyone OK?"

"Perfect!"

"Good, then put me down," she said with a hearty laugh.

He called Karl. "Stephanie just delivered!" Mike exclaimed to a groggy Karl.

"Great news! Congratulations! How's Stephanie?"

"She did great! Sorry for calling so early. I didn't realize—"

"This is good news to wake up to!" Karl said with a laugh.

CHAPTER 61

Changes on the Horizon

T he twins were nearing their first birthdays when Joe approached Mike.

"I got a call from the CEO at Green Meadows."

"Is something wrong?"

"On the contrary! Green Meadows is expanding their assisted living and memory care campuses to the Midwest. Says the need is so big all over the country, but he wants to start with the Midwest."

Mike straightened up with a puzzled look.

"They want Integra to do the job! And Mike, they aren't even accepting other bids. Some of the guys from Green Meadows are scouting around right now looking for land, and if they find what they're looking for, it's a go."

"Man! That is great news! What part of the Midwest?"

"You're not going to believe this, but they're looking at Minnesota, and if that works out, they want to expand to the whole five-state area."

"What part of Minnesota and how soon?"

"The Twin Cities. They're hoping to get started by summer's end." Joe looked intently at Mike. "You've done such a fantastic job as foreman, and I know you're from the Midwest," he raised his eyebrows, "so, I'd like to offer you the position of project manager." He wet his lips. "Think about it. As second in command, you could help expand Integra to be a national company."

Mike gulped. "Second in command. Really?"

"Yes, really. The only drawback, though, is that you would have to stay in California a couple months longer than you had planned. That is, if everything works out with Green Meadows."

Mike nodded and ran his hand along the side of his face and across his chin as he thought about the offer.

"If it all works out, you and Stephanie can fly back for a week to look for a house—that is, if you still want to move back to Minnesota." Joe said cocking his head to one side.

"You know I do." Both men laughed.

"Because Tom Smith has been with Integra since day one, I took the liberty of asking him if he would consider relocating to Minnesota. He has family there so he accepted immediately. He'd be in the office as your right-hand man getting paper work filled out, background checks, licensing, and bonding. You know, dotted line stuff. You'd be out in the field. What do you think?"

"Tom's a great choice! He's easy to work with, and that would sure take a lot of pressure off me."

"So does that mean you'll accept?"

Mike grinned broadly and stuck out his hand.

"Great! Then, it's settled." He clasped Mike's hand and slapped him on the back. "Oh, one more thing. Integra will pay any moving expenses. Once you get back to Minnesota, we'll set you up with a company truck that you can have for personal use, as well."

"That's a lot of frosting on the cake, Joe!"

"It may be, but there's a lot riding on this venture for Integra. The guys in the home office and I agree that you're the man for the job."

"Joe, before we go any further, I want to meet with the guys from Green Meadows."

Joe eyed him quizzically.

"I want to be up front with them—who I am, where I've been, what I've done—"

"Do you think that's necessary? After all, they know your work ethics—"

"Joe, the only way I would take this position is if they know me. If they have the slightest hesitation, for any reason, I am stepping aside. The project manager job offer is off. You'll have to switch to Plan B."

"I don't have a Plan B, but if you're that determined about it—"

"I am, Joe. They may not be willing to take a risk on an ex-con the way you did. That's their right, and I have to respect that."

"All right. I'll talk to them."

"No, I'll talk to them."

"OK. OK. I'll set up a meeting. But I want to be there too."

***

"This is almost too good to be true," Stephanie said when Mike told her the news. She tapped her feet in one spot like one doing a victory dance and hugged him tightly, laughing.

"It all hinges on whether or not the guys from Green Meadows are willing to accept me as the project manager. But either way, do you think your mother would consider moving to Minnesota? She'd be a big help with Danny and Davey."

"I would love to have her with us. I've gotten so I really like seeing her every day, but she's pretty independent. However, she's never had grandbabies before so—"

A cloud of uncertainty hung in the air.

After supper, Mike, Stephanie, and the two toddlers walked to Rosie's apartment.

"Mother! Mike has a possible job opportunity with Integra in Minnesota. He would be the—" she turned to Mike, "what's the job title?"

"Project manager." He smiled at her enthusiasm.

"That's wonderful! Congratulations!" Rosie smiled her usual huge smile and hugged Mike.

"We were wondering if you would consider moving, too?" Stephanie looked hopeful.

"I thought I would never move, but these little guys are so precious, I might have to consider it." She stooped down and hugged them both at the same time.

Stephanie and Mike exchanged glances.

"If I did, and that's a big if, I would not be able to move for a few months."

"That's perfect, because Mike's transfer, if it goes through, would not happen until the end of summer."

"Is it for sure?"

"Joe seems to think so," Mike answered confidently, shielding his own insecurity.

***

The following week, Mike and Joe met with the top three men from Green Meadows at Rosario's Restaurant.

The conversation focused on Green Meadows' expansion on a national level, whether it was the right time, how there was such a great need for "quality living at affordable prices"— their motto—and how pleased they were to have such a dependable company like Integra take this leap with them.

Mike set his fork down and looked thoughtfully at each of the three men.

"Gentlemen, I would like to make you aware of a few things before we move forward any further."

Each man stared at Mike. They afforded Mike the opportunity to speak while Joe pushed stroganoff noodles around his plate.

"This sounds serious," the eldest of the three men said.

"It is. You see, I'm not the man you think I am."

"What do you mean?" the tallest man asked, his brows furrowed together.

"Less than two years ago, I got out of prison. I'm still on probation."

The three men looked shocked. "What for?" The eldest man spoke with an edge.

"I was arrested in 1993 for kidnapping my four-year-old daughter. I can't justify my actions other than I wanted to give my daughter a chance to live in a stable environment. I came to California, but was arrested and sent to prison back in Minnesota for almost four-and-a-half years. After that, I was arrested on charges of tax fraud because I inadvertently switched two numbers on my Social Security number on my tax return."

The three men shifted uncomfortably in their chairs, but allowed Mike the opportunity to continue.

"I served one year in Soledad and then got two years' probation. My parole officer connected me with Joe soon after my release, and Joe hired me. He knew my background, but hired me. He agrees with me about this meeting to let you know about my past." He glanced at Joe, who nodded.

"You know my work experience, and I'm confident I could do a good job for you with Integra. However, I want to lay it all out on the table. If you have any hesitation, any at all, let us know. Joe has other guys who could do a good job for you. It's your decision." He looked directly at each man facing him, but each man turned their attention to each other and avoided looking directly at Mike.

"Thanks, gentlemen, for hearing me out." He looked down at his plate and then at the three men who held his future in their hands. "If you decide against me, I totally understand."

The eldest man spoke. "I don't know what to say except thanks for being so transparent. We appreciate your honesty. But as you must realize, we need to discuss the impact this could have on Green Meadows as a reputable company."

"Of course, you do," Joe interjected. "Let us know your intentions and," he nodded emphatically, "we know you'll do what you feel is best for both companies."

They all shook hands and parted company in silence.

***

Later that week, Mike and Joe were in Joe's office going over blueprint details when the phone rang.

After Joe hung up, he turned to Mike and held out his fist to Mike for a knuckle punch. "Nailed it!"

"No kidding?" Mike jumped to his feet.

"Yup! They all agreed. They want you to head the project. They said if I was willing to take a chance on you, then they would, too. They bought two pieces of property—one is on a lake in south Minneapolis and the other is in a woodsy area of St. Paul, which will be their first project. Do you know St. Paul?"

"A little."

"How far is it from where you grew up?"

"About seventy-five miles."

"When can you go?"

"Do you mean when I am off probation?"

"Well, yeah."

"I meet with my probation officer next week. That should be my final meeting."

"That's good. It'll still be a month or so before they get the plans drawn up and all the details worked out. Are you OK with that?"

"I've been gone for almost eight years now, so I guess another month isn't going to hurt. Yeah, I'm good with that."

"This is great! I'll run the west coast division, and you'll run the Midwest division of Integra Builders! Man! Who'da thunk?"

"Yeah, who'da thunk?" Mike mocked good-naturedly.

***

The following week, Mike met with his probation officer.

Mr. Freeman started by saying, "Mike, you have made my job easy. I congratulate you on the accountability you showed and the determination to do what's right."

Mike nodded. "Thanks."

"I am signing off on your case which means that you are free to leave the state. Do you have any plans?"

"As a matter of fact, I do. I've been offered a position to head up a building project with Integra Builders in Minnesota."

"Well, congratulations again. That is good news. I'm going to add that to my final report." He looked soberly at Mike. "I know you will do a good job." He stuck out his hand. "It's been a pleasure getting to know you and working with you as your probation officer."

Mike clasped his hand. "Thanks, Mr. Freeman."

***

One month later, as Stephanie buckled her seat belt and adjusted her head rest on the 757 jet, she asked Mike, "What did you miss most about Minnesota?"

"Definitely not winter," Mike said with a laugh. "Do you think you'll miss California?"

"Hmmm. I don't think so, especially since Mother will be moving too. I was gone for quite a while with Roger—" she slid her arm through Mike's, "but, I have you, and it doesn't matter where we are, just so we are together."

Mike smiled tenderly at Stephanie and squeezed her arm. "Do you have the realtor's info?"

"Yup. Right here in my purse. She has five houses lined up—each with either a mother-in-law apartment or a small bungalow on the same lot." She smiled up at him. "O, Mike, I'm so excited to start this next step of our journey together!" She rubbed his arm with her hand.

Mike grinned and winked. "I'd like to kiss you right now," he whispered.

"Go ahead." She beamed.

He leaned over and kissed her quickly on the lips.

"That's a tease."

"Um-hum. I know."

"It sure is generous of Karl and Katie to let us stay there with them while we house hunt."

Mike nodded. "Karl and Katie would let all of us live in their house. That's the kind of people they are."

"I can hardly wait to meet them."

"And I can hardly wait to see Maddy!"

CHAPTER 62

Meetings

Karl stood on his front porch sipping a cup of coffee when Mike and Stephanie pulled up in their rented car.

Mike jumped from the car, and the two men hugged, clapping each other on the back with hearty slaps.

"Man, it's great to see you!"

"Likewise and more so," Karl said giving Mike another guy hug.

"Karl, I'd like you to meet Stephanie," he said opening her car door.

Stephanie stepped out just as Katie appeared on the porch.

Katie waved and practically leaped off the steps. She hugged Mike. "Welcome back!" Introductions were made, and another round of hugs ensued as they talked like they'd never been apart.

Mike felt a surge of pride to see Karl and Katie greet Stephanie so warmly, as though she was their own daughter. He supposed that if Karl and Katie did have a daughter, she would have been much like the gracious and loving woman who was his wife.

"Supper is almost ready," Katie announced. She smiled broadly at Mike. "And apple pie for dessert!"

"Wait till you taste her apple pie. Mmm-m-mm," he said giving Stephanie a gentle elbow nudge to her side.

After supper, Mike said, "We'd like to stop over at Lisa's. I want to see Maddy before we do anything else. We might be a little late getting back—if all goes well, that is."

"We'll leave the light on for you," Karl reassured.

"Minnesota is beautiful," Stephanie said looking at tree-lined streets and well-kept houses.

***

Mike swallowed hard when he looked at his former house. "It looks exactly like it did when I left."

"It's a beautiful house."

Mike smiled. "Thanks."

"Does this bring back painful memories?"

"A little. I don't know what to say. It's been so long."

"You'll find the right words."

He rang the doorbell. There was no answer. He rang again, but no answer. His shoulders slumped. "I should've called."

"Why don't we stop over at her parents' house. Maybe Maddy is there."

Mike nodded. "I haven't had any contact with them either during this whole time. This is harder than I thought, but it's something I have to do," he said as he drove the short distance to the Barrett's.

He rang the doorbell.

Betty answered. Her eyebrows shot up and her mouth dropped open. "Mike."

"Hello, Betty."

Just then, Bruce appeared at the door with the same reaction Betty had when she saw Mike.

"Bruce," Mike nodded. "I should've called. I know this is awkward and I'm sorry about that."

Betty opened the door wider. "Won't you come in?" Her tone was stiff.

Once inside, Mike introduced Stephanie. She smiled warmly and extended her hand to Betty, who did not reciprocate.

"Please, sit," Betty said. "What brings you here?"

"Two things—Maddy, and I want to apologize to both of you for the hurt I've caused you by taking Maddy. It must have been difficult not seeing your granddaughter for that year."

"The whole ordeal has been very difficult," Betty said.

"I'm really sorry." Mike looked down.

Stephanie slipped her arm through Mike's as they sat on the couch. "I can't imagine the impact that it had on the two of you, and I hope you had some comfort in knowing that Maddy was OK and well cared for," Stephanie spoke quietly.

"Yes, of course," Betty agreed

"Oh, we knew she would be well cared for. It's just that it was such a shock," Bruce said.

"I know it must've been terrible, and I can only say how sorry I am to have caused you such heartache."

Mike looked to the carpeted floor as a thousand memories flooded his mind. Memories of the many times Mike had picked Maddy up from the Barrett's, and how Betty always served him coffee while Bruce made excuses for Lisa's habitual late arrivals or no arrival at all. He thought of Maddy's innocence and naiveté of grown-up problems, anger, and emotions that even the strongest adult can struggle with. *Because of my reckless concern for her protection, I subjected my precious daughter to a side of life that no child should ever have to be exposed to.*

"Mike," Betty spoke calmly. "I can't speak for Bruce, but I understand how desperate you must have felt, and for that I am sorry. I can't count the buckets of tears I cried over Lisa when she was growing up." She waved her hand as though pushing unpleasant memories away. "I thought that when you and Lisa got married, she would find the love she never seemed to be able to find. But I was wrong. I should have said something to you before you two married, but I didn't, and so I feel that I am partly to blame."

Bruce shifted in his chair. "We're not taking sides, mind you, but Lisa had a very troubled past, with her adoption and all. What I mean is that Lisa never seemed to connect, and I, too, hoped you were her rescuer." His tone was gentle.

Mike shook his head. "I don't have that kind of power nor did I have the right kind of love that she needed. She needs unconditional love and only God can give that. Does that make sense?"

"I guess," Betty answered with a vague look.

"The other reason we stopped by was to see if maybe Maddy would be here," Mike said.

"They're on vacation. They left yesterday and won't be back for two weeks."

"How is Maddy doing?"

Betty and Bruce exchanged glances. "She seems troubled, but she never says anything, so, I'm not sure," Betty said softly.

"I see."

***

Back in the car, Stephanie said, "I know you feel badly about them, and I know how disappointed you must be to not have seen Maddy and to hear that she is troubled. Just give it some time."

"This is tougher than I thought it would be."

***

The first house they looked at from Mike's list was a two story house with a sagging front step and a missing shutter.

"No wonder it's priced so low," Mike said in a mumbled voice eyeing the brittle-looking shingles and the peeling paint.

"Mike! You can't be serious!" Stephanie gasped.

"Why not?" he asked stepping out of the car and going to her side to open the door.

"But it's a shambles, and there are weeds a foot high and—"

"Let's just take a look." He gave her a teasing grin.

Stephanie sat quietly and stared at the house with its shreds of lace curtains hanging in the second-floor windows. She made no attempt to get out.

He smiled at her refusal to get out of the car. "I'm just kidding. There's definitely something wrong here. What's the address again?" He slid behind the wheel.

Stephanie checked the lists. "The realtor wrote 1571, but you wrote 1751 on our list."

"Well, that explains it." He looked sheepishly at Stephanie. "Sometimes I have trouble with numbers." He became serious. "It's a thing called dyscalculia."

She looked at him with a blank stare.

"Once in a while I invert numbers," he said looking down at the steering wheel.

Stephanie put her hand on his cheek. "Sweetheart, that's nothing to feel bad about. I used to wear braces."

He looked at her and grinned.

She surveyed the house again, "I'd hate to think the realtor lined up houses that look like Elmer Fudd's."

They laughed, and Stephanie gave a huge sigh of relief.

"Let's check out the house at 1571."

They drove to a pleasant-looking, split-entry house with a mother-in-law apartment on the lower level, but it was too far from where Mike would be working.

They looked at the next two houses, but decided that neither house warranted a walk-through. It was mid-afternoon by the time Mike and Stephanie headed back to Karl's.

Can we drive by your high school?"

"Sure. I'd love to show it to you and the whole town where I grew up, for that matter."

Stephanie turned up the radio as they drove in silence. She laid her head on Mike's shoulder, humming to the tunes on the radio.

***

"Litchfield is a charming town," she said craning her neck to see everything as they drove down Main Street. "Oh, I love the park with the band shelter and the whole small town feel. I've got a suspicion St. Paul is a bit bigger."

"Yeah, about 280,000 people bigger and that doesn't include the suburbs. But, you're a California girl. You'll get it figured out—probably a lot sooner than I will."

Suddenly, she turned to look back. "DiSanto's Hardware! Is that—?"

"Yeah, my stepdad's hardware store."

"Can we stop in?"

"I don't know, Steph. This might not be the right place for a surprise reunion. Let's go by the high school, stop for supper, and then over to their house afterwards."

"Sounds good."

"Looks like the school is still open. Want to walk the halls?"

"Sure!" She grabbed her purse and jumped out of the car before Mike could get around to opening her door.

The halls were empty except for a few kids loitering about. Mike figured they were there for after-school activities. "They look so young!" Mike commented absently.

He and Stephanie strolled past the glass trophy case in the main hallway. Stephanie spied a tall baseball trophy and read the inscription: 1983 STATE CHAMPIONSHIP. On it were the names of the players on the team.

"Mike! There's your name! Oh, wow! This is so exciting!"

Mike grinned. "It's just a trophy. What do you say we grab a bite to eat?"

She sighed. "OK."

Macaluso's had new booths and different colored carpeting, but otherwise it looked the same.

The hostess seated them, telling them about the Tuesday night special—Pasta Primavera. "One of my favorites," Mike said rubbing his hands together.

"I'll have that, too. It looks really good!"

The restaurant was filled to capacity, and the din of mixed voices made it difficult for any intimate conversation.

Mike smiled at Stephanie and shrugged. She smiled back.

Mike noticed several familiar faces. Some nodded in greeting. "Hey! You're lookin' good!" "Welcome back!" "Good to see ya!"

Others looked at Mike with indifference. Still others had judgment written all over their faces towards Mike and Stephanie.

"Maybe this was a mistake," Mike said leaning across the table so Stephanie could hear.

Stephanie simply shook her head and smiled.

What did you expect? He wondered. *A welcome home party with a band? Do these people think I ran out on Lisa or that I took Maddy out of spite? Do I owe the whole town an apology?*

He snapped back with Stephanie waving her hand in front of his face. "Hello?"

"Sorry," he said.

***

They pulled up to his parents' house a little after 8 p.m. just as the garage door closed.

"They just got home." Mike looked toward the house as lights flicked on. He saw his mother close the curtains in the living room. "This isn't going to be easy. I apologized over the phone, but this is face to face now."

"Sweetheart, they're your parents. They love you." She placed her hand tenderly on the back of his neck.

They stood hand-in-hand on the front steps as Mike rang the doorbell. His stepdad opened the door with his mother standing close behind him.

Rick stared in disbelief, his eyes wide. Irene moved past him and immediately broke into tears when she saw Mike. She didn't seem to notice Stephanie.

"Come in," she cried, pulling on Mike's arm.

Rick stepped aside with a perturbed look on his face.

"Mom, it's good to see you." He hugged her as she wept. He looked at Rick. "It's good to see you too," he said and stuck his hand out to Rick.

Rick reciprocated with a weak handshake.

"I'd like you to meet my wife, Stephanie." He brought Stephanie to his side.

"Your wife?" Irene asked noticing her for the first time. "Oh, my! How do you do?" She extended her hand and dried her eyes with her other hand.

Stephanie accepted her hand and smiled warmly. "I am delighted to meet Mike's parents."

Rick seemed to recover from the surprise of seeing Mike. "It's nice to meet you, too. C'mon in and sit down. Why didn't you tell us you were in town?"

Mike shrugged. "We didn't want to disappoint you if plans didn't work out."

"How long will you be here and where are you staying?" Irene asked composing herself.

"We're here till Thursday and we're staying at Karl's."

"The last time we talked, you said something about being transferred back, but we haven't heard any more details," Rick said settling in his easy chair. He looked steadily at Mike. "It is good to see you," he said with a nod.

"Thanks. And thanks again for going to bat for me in court."

"What's your new job?"

"I'll be heading up a building project with Green Meadows in the Twin Cities and Steph and I are looking for a house."

"I hope you're back for good," Irene said with a big smile.

"For now, at least."

"How about some coffee?"

"Sure."

"Do you have pictures of the twins?" Irene called from the kitchen.

Stephanie took a small album from her purse before following Irene into the kitchen to help.

"We stopped by the house to see Maddy, but they're on vacation," Mike said.

"We haven't seen Maddy since before you left. I feel terrible, but every time we stopped over or called, Lisa refused. We gave up trying a couple of years ago," Irene said. Her eyes looked sad.

Mike nodded. "I know, Mom."

They spent the next hour looking at photos and getting to know Stephanie.

CHAPTER 63

Finding a House

E ven though it had been a late night for Mike and Stephanie, they rose early, eager to explore the last two houses on the realtor's list.

Katie made omelets and toast with fruit yogurt for breakfast.

"Katie, you should open your own restaurant," Mike said as he and Stephanie entered the kitchen.

"If I did that, I would probably never have time to enjoy cooking," she said with a laugh. "Now c'mon, you two, sit down and eat before it gets cold."

Karl sat at the table with a folded newspaper next to his plate and a cup of coffee in his hand.

"Karl and Katie, we both are so grateful to you for opening up your home to us, fixing meals, and for being such wonderful friends to Mike," Stephanie said. "How can we ever thank you?"

"We're blessed beyond measure as it is," Karl said as his laugh lines creased his cheeks. Then, he asked a blessing on their meal and for good house hunting for Mike and Stephanie.

"Anything newsworthy in the paper, Karl?" Mike asked.

"Not much."

"Mind if I check the sports section?"

Karl had a serious look as he handed the paper to Mike.

Mike could not believe his eyes when he unfolded the paper.

The front page headline read, "Ex-con Returns to Hometown." He stared at the words, stunned.

"What is it?" Stephanie asked.

Mike slid the paper over to her.

She read the headlines and looked up at him quietly.

Karl stroked his chin and Katie looked at her plate in silence.

Mike took the paper and read, "Mike DiSanto, who was convicted on kidnapping charges and sentenced to several years in prison, returns. After a bitter divorce from Lisa Barrett in 1991, DiSanto kidnapped their then four-year-old daughter and fled to California where he was subsequently arrested, tried, and sentenced to Croix Valley Prison."

Mike continued reading, "DiSanto and an attractive woman were spotted at a local restaurant last night, but did not comment on his reason for returning. He has no prior arrests, and poses no threat to the general public. Yet, many townspeople wonder, 'Did DiSanto return home to start a new life, or will he strike again?'"

Mike swallowed hard, folded the paper, and set it on the table.

"Sweetheart, I'm so sorry," Stephanie said.

"It is what it is." He shrugged.

"Don't let this spoil your day, son. You know who you are in the Lord, and why you are here. So, what some people may think is not important." Karl's voice was gentle.

Mike nodded as Stephanie reached her hand over to his and squeezed it tenderly.

Katie got up. She put one arm around Mike and the other around Stephanie and hugged them, kissing each on their cheeks.

"Thanks, Katie," Mike said patting her arm. "We'll be fine."

"Yes, and I knew all about this before I married him," Stephanie said looking at Karl and Katie. Although speaking to Karl and Katie, she looked at Mike and said, "I will always stand by his side."

***

The drive to St. Paul was too quiet, so Stephanie said, "Let's call Mother and the boys to see how they're doing."

Mike smiled. "It's only 7 a.m. there. Shouldn't we let Rosie have a little more time before all the action with the boys start?"

"You're right. I forgot about the time difference. Well, then, let's talk about that attractive woman you were with at the restaurant last night."

"Her? She's the reason I'm so happy!"

"Really? Well, do happy people smile and talk?"

Mike grinned. "I guess they do." He looked affectionately at her nestled beside him. "What do you think we'll find today?"

"I think we'll find just the right house for us!"

"Think so, huh?"

"Yup." And her eyes danced.

***

The first house they saw was a strong possibility with its large fenced yard and tuck-under garage. "It says there is a mother-in-law apartment on the lower level," Stephanie said.

"Hmmm. This looks like a pretty upscale neighborhood, although the price isn't bad, but let's check out the last house on the list before we decide."

They drove a short distance to Cherokee Heights, high on a bluff overlooking the fast-moving, dark waters of the Mississippi River. St. Paul's sky line crowded the opposite river bank with tall buildings while the towering structures of Minneapolis silhouetted themselves against the western horizon.

Three bridges connected the residential area on the bluff to downtown St. Paul with easy access to freeways to both St. Paul and Minneapolis suburbs.

"This would be the perfect location for work in either city," Mike said as he stretched his arms and arched his back over the steering wheel.

Cherokee Avenue ran along the outside edge of a park. The oak trees stood tall, but the residents who lived across the street from the park could still embrace the beautiful view.

A yellow two-story house with a brick front and white trim sat on an oversized corner lot. It had several windows, a sun porch, and a two-car attached garage. It had a small bungalow off to one side and set back a little. There was a large garden area along the south side of the double lot.

Mike gave a low whistle. "Nice!"

"Mother would love the garden. Let's get out and take a closer look."

The back yard nudged dense foliage just beyond the small bungalow, which was more than adequate for one person. The driveway to the bungalow entered from a side street which afforded the person who lived there a sense of privacy. The driveway for the house entered from Cherokee Avenue.

He surveyed the yard with approval. "What do you think?"

"Oh, Mike, I love it. It would be perfect for the boys and Mother!"

"Do you want to double-check the other house?"

"No, sweetheart, this one is perfect—even without the fenced yard. Let's call the realtor for a walk-through."

Mike was already dialing the number from his cell phone.

"Tomorrow at 10 a.m.," he said with a huge grin.

"Let's drive around, and see if we can find the school, church, shopping, and a doctor's office."

They spent the better part of the afternoon exploring the area. The gloom from the morning had long dissipated, and Mike and Stephanie sang to the music on the radio on the way back to Karl's.

CHAPTER 64

House Becomes a Home

A t 10 a.m. sharp, Mike and Stephanie stopped in front of the two-story house with the charming little bungalow next door, as another car pulled up behind them.

A tall athletic man with blond hair stepped from his car and gave them a friendly wave.

After introductions, Mr. Calloway said, "Let's take a look around the yard before we go inside."

"We've already done that, and we like what we see," Mike said.

"Great. Well then, let's check the inside," Mr. Calloway said heading up the four steps to the front door.

Once inside, Stephanie raised her eyebrows at the attractively decorated large living room and the open stairway. Mike noticed the shiny hardwood floors and the oak trim around the doors and windows and gave a slight nod to Stephanie.

The kitchen had ample cupboards and counter space and a nice-sized eating area. French doors opened to a family room with a wood-burning stove.

"Great for a cold winter's night," Mike whispered.

Stephanie squeezed Mike's hand. "It is beautiful!"

"Move-in ready," Mr. Calloway said.

"This is the guest bedroom/den/office and the main bath, and this is the mud/laundry room," Mr. Calloway pointed out as he guided them throughout the lower level. "If you like what you see now, you'll love the upstairs," he said confidently. "There's a master bedroom with its own half bath and three smaller bedrooms and a bath."

Stephanie looked at Mike and giggled with delight.

The steps sighed with relief to have footsteps tread on them once again. Mike tried to wiggle the banister, but it was solid. The realtor was right about the upstairs. The bedrooms were painted in various neutral shades that blended with the hall carpet

"I love the white woodwork. It looks so fresh," Stephanie said, and her eyes danced.

Mike scrutinized the structure and the materials used. "I like it. What do you think?" he whispered to Stephanie.

"I love it!" she whispered back.

"Does the furniture go with the house?" she asked the realtor.

"No, that's just for staging to give potential buyers an idea of what it could look like. It's been empty for a time, but we've had a lot of interest lately." He looked from Stephanie to Mike. "Do you want to see the basement before we head out to the bungalow?"

"Was the bungalow originally built as a house?" Mike asked, as they followed the realtor to the large, unfinished basement.

"Actually it started out to be an oversized garage, but the last owners bought the lot and re-did it into living space for the husband's parents. I guess they needed assistance with everyday living. Do you have need for it as a bungalow?"

"Yeah, for my wife's mother.

Mr. Calloway nodded. "Perfect."

The one-bedroom bungalow built on a floating slab was small, but had a charm that would be perfect for Rosie.

"Do you mind if my wife and I talk it over?"

"Not at all. I'll wait in the kitchen."

"Oh, Mike. It's exactly what I would want in a house!" She hugged him and looked up into his twinkling eyes. "What do you think?"

"I think we should make an offer," he said with a huge grin.

"Mr. Calloway, we'd like to make an offer. The only problem is that we're leaving tomorrow to go back to California—"

"Hmm. That might be a problem, but let's hammer out some details and see what happens." Mr. Calloway pulled out several papers and spread them onto the table. They discussed their offer, financing, and a closing date that permitted Mike and Stephanie to close on the house while still in California. Everything seemed agreeable so Mike and Stephanie signed the papers. "If there's anything that comes up, I have your number. If you don't hear from me, just know that everything is a go. Call me when you arrive and I'll meet you at the house."

They shook hands, and the realtor left.

"Before we go, let's pray about this again," Mike said once they got into the car.

"Absolutely!"

"Father in heaven, we give praise to You for leading us to this house, and if it pleases You, Father, we ask that everything would work out on the sale of this house. We want to be obedient to Your will."

"Let's call Mother and the boys!"

CHAPTER 65

Leaving California

"I'm glad the movers can tow my car and that you sold yours," Stephanie said on a glorious Monday morning in mid-August.

"Me too. I'm meeting with Joe to wrap up a few details, but I'll be home before the moving van arrives," Mike said.

"And, I'm very glad we decided to fly back to Minnesota rather than drive across country with the boys," Stephanie said.

"What! You don't think the boys would've sat quietly in their car seats and looked out the windows like perfect little gentlemen if we drove?" Mike said with a hearty laugh.

Stephanie looked at the boys fighting over a blue toy truck. "Silly me! What was I thinking?"

Mike grinned and shook his head. He kissed the boys and Stephanie. "I'll be home by noon."

Mike picked his way through the stacked boxes in the living room. Each one was labeled with the contents and room. Their bedroom set and the boys' toddler beds were disassembled and ready to load along with their dressers, tables, lamps and other items they accumulated. Rosie's boxes marked 'Bungalow' sat alongside.

***

Mike arrived at work as though it were just another Monday. But, this was no ordinary day. This would be his last day in California. He would bring with him some horrific memories, others that were happy and carefree, still others that were awesome, pleasant, and cherished. They were the whispers of the past eight years, but, as vivid and tangible as the tools he would take.

"Tom is leaving next week. He'll schedule a meeting with you, him, and the guys from Green Meadows," Joe said.

Mike nodded. "When do they plan to excavate?"

"They're hoping by September 5th." He rubbed the back of his neck. "Yeah, I know. Everything's moving way too fast, but—" he shrugged.

"That'll give us time to settle in. I think hiring enough good workers is going to be the hard part."

"I know, but you don't have to worry about that. Tom will take care of all that. You just let him know how many workers you need to get the job done. By the way, did you know Tom has a degree in business management?"

"No."

"He's chomping at the bit to put his degree to work. And he's excited to work with you."

"Sounds good to me."

"How's everything coming with your moving plans?"

"The moving van is coming this afternoon, and my mother-in-law is taking us to the airport at 4:30 tomorrow morning."

"Good. Good. Speaking of trucks, we ordered your pickup and it should be ready by the end of the week."

"This all seems way too generous, Joe. I—"

"Nonsense. We're confident you can handle the job, and this is just our way of saying thanks in advance."

Mike lowered his head. "Thanks, Joe. I really do appreciate your confidence in me."

"We're not throwing you to the wolves, mind you. We're all in this together, and if any problems arise, we'll work together to resolve them. Fair enough?"

"Fair enough. By the way, did you know we named one of our sons after you?"

"No kidding?"

"Yeah. David Joseph."

"That's really quite an honor," he said with a huge smile. "Nobody has ever honored me quite like that before. Thanks, a lot. It's a good thing I didn't know about that before or it would've looked like a bribe for the promotion," he said with a hearty laugh.

Mike laughed as well.

Mike finished up last-minute details, said his farewells to the crew, and gathered his personal things before stopping back to see Joe.

"Joe, I've wanted to tell you how much it means to me that you took a chance on me. I mean, coming right out of prison and all. It still amazes me that you would hire me—"

"Freeman is a good friend of mine, and I trust his judgment. When he says a guy is a good man, then I believe him. Besides, you might be able to give someone a second chance someday."

"Well, thanks again, Joe."

"We'll talk every Monday morning and see how things are going. Sound good?"

Mike nodded. They shook hands and gave each other a guy hug, slapping the other on the back. "God bless."

***

Danny and Davey squealed with delight as Mike hugged and tickled them before putting them in their highchairs as Stephanie dished up lunch. "This pretty much cleans out the refrigerator," she said.

"Looks good to me." He sat down at the table just as the doorbell rang.

The mailman stood at the door. "I have a certified letter for Mike DiSanto," he said.

"I'm Mike DiSanto."

The mailman handed him a large envelope. "Just sign here that you received the letter," he said.

Mike signed and returned to the kitchen.

"What is it?"

"I don't know, but it's from Karl." He tore open the envelope. Inside were another envelope and a note scrawled in Karl's handwriting that read, "Mike, I received this certified letter from Lisa. She asked me to forward it to you. Have a safe trip, Karl."

Mike stared at an envelope with his name on it. He tapped the envelope against his open palm. *What in the world could this mean? Does this have anything to do with Maddy?* He felt a dread. *If anything was wrong, wouldn't someone have called rather than write a letter?* He reasoned.

"Is everything all right with Karl and Katie?" Stephanie asked carrying a platter of spaghetti noodles and meat balls to the table. "Everything's fine. Karl forwarded a letter from Lisa."

Stephanie stopped in midair with the platter and stared at Mike. "Well, sweetheart," she said setting their meal on the table, "aren't you going to open it?"

Mike took a deep breath and read, "Mike, I heard you were in town looking for Madison." He looked up.

"Well, go on. Unless you would rather not read it out loud. I would certainly understand if—"

"Whatever Lisa says to me, she says to you." He continued reading the note.

"I filed a restraining order against you, so don't even attempt to see Madison unless you want to go to jail. Lisa"

CHAPTER 66

Flight to Minnesota

The alarm jangled at 3:30 a.m., but Mike had been awake most of the night. His stomach churned, and his thoughts jarred through his mind like agates in a rock tumbler. *Why? Why would Lisa do this? Anger? Revenge? Does Maddy think I don't want to see her? Does she know Lisa is behind this? This is all my fault.*

"Stephanie?" he whispered. "Are you awake?"

"Hmm-hum. I've been praying and thinking about the restraining order. Did you sleep at all?"

"No." Mike sat on the edge of the bed. "Stephanie, how do I fight this?"

"I don't know. I'm not defending Lisa's actions, but she may think that because you took Maddy from her, she's going to retaliate. I don't know. Maybe we can hire a lawyer once we get back to Minnesota and get the restraining order rescinded. That's the only thing I can think of."

"This is tearing me apart."

"I know, sweetheart. I wish I could do something to help."

Mike showered first and got the boys up while Stephanie showered. Danny and Davey went through the motions as Mike finished dressing them, but clearly, they just wanted to go back to sleep.

Everything was packed in their overstuffed suitcases and placed by the front door just as Rosie's headlights flashed in their front window.

"Good morning, Rosie," Mike said quietly, putting Davey in his car seat.

"Good morning to you, too. I'm so excited I couldn't sleep all night! How about you?"

"Yeah, I was awake a lot, too."

Stephanie emerged, carrying Danny, who had fallen asleep with his head on her shoulder. She greeted Rosie as cheerfully as she could.

Mike strapped Danny in, loaded the suitcases, and took one last look around the apartment before closing the door.

"We should be there by 5 a.m. That gives us time to stop at a restaurant for breakfast," Mike said. Clearly, his mind was not on what should have been an exciting day for them. He slid behind the wheel of Rosie's car as she took her place in the passenger seat. Stephanie climbed in back between the two boys.

LAX airport buzzed with activity as passengers and families mingled together saying farewells and well wishes to one another. Rosie hugged the boys, and Mike and Stephanie. "God bless you all, and I will see you in a week."

"We'll call you as soon as we arrive," Stephanie said giving Rosie another hug.

Mike and Stephanie checked their luggage, put the boys in strollers, and headed for US Airways at Terminal 3 stopping at McDonalds for a quick breakfast.

Once on the plane, Danny and Davey sat on Mike and Stephanie's laps with their eyes wide with wonderment. Mike thought about the time he and Maddy flew out to California, and how frightened she was as he buckled her seat belt.

Overhead doors banged shut, and passengers squeezed past each other to their seats. Takeoff was smooth and everyone settled into everyday conversations or quietly reading books or magazines.

Mike held Danny with one arm with his head resting on his other hand. His eyes were closed.

She gently rubbed his forearm.

***

Mike called the realtor. "We arrived," he said looking at his watch. "Can you meet us at the house at about 11:45 a.m.?"

"I'll be there with the keys and a couple of papers for you to sign. See you at the house."

***

The realtor's car was parked in front of their house when they arrived. Greetings were exchanged. Mike unloaded the taxi while Stephanie walked the boys up the steps.

The realtor unlocked the door and ushered them into their new home.

"Oh my," Stephanie said in surprise as she looked around the empty house.

"There's a bed and some blankets in the bungalow, but we had to stage another house with the furniture we used here."

"That's not a problem," she said with a smile. "We can sleep in the bungalow until our furniture arrives. It's just for one night."

Mike nodded.

"Well, if you could just sign these papers, I'll let you settle in."

They walked the realtor to the door. "Thanks a lot for all your extra work to make this transition work without a hitch," Mike said and shook the realtor's hand.

"We are very grateful," Stephanie added.

Just then, the doorbell rang. Stephanie opened the door to a young woman with curly red hair, wearing a pink jogging outfit and running shoes. She was holding an armload of kitchen containers.

"Hello," Stephanie greeted.

"Hi, I'm Jennifer. I live next door. I made some chicken vegetable soup and brownies, and an egg bake for breakfast to welcome you to the neighborhood. Oh, and here are some paper products."

"How very sweet of you. I'm Stephanie and this is Danny"

Mike appeared holding Davey. "Hi, I'm Mike and this is Davey."

"Twins?"

"Yeah, identical."

"I'll say they are. How do you tell them apart?"

"I just call out a name, and whoever comes, I figure that's who he is," Mike said.

Jennifer looked wide-eyed. "For real?"

Mike shook his head. "Kidding."

She nodded. "Is there anything I can help you with to settle in?"

"No, thank you so much. You are a godsend with the food!"

"Well, I hope you enjoy. If there's anything you need, let me know."

"Thank you again. Is this the Minnesota nice that I've heard so much about?"

"Could be, but I like to think of it as just being neighborly. Tootles," she said with a wave, and she was off running.

"Can you believe it?" Stephanie turned to Mike. "Everything we need to get us through until our stuff arrives."

"I'll help you unpack, and then I want to call Karl to let him know we arrived. And, see if he might know of a good lawyer."

CHAPTER 67

Restraining order

M ike wasted no time in calling Karl. "Hi, Karl. We arrived and are settling in."

"How was the flight?"

"Good. Our stuff should arrive tomorrow and Green Meadows is excavating the day after Labor Day, so that'll give me some time to get our address changed, bank accounts transferred, and meet the crew Tom hired." He tried to sound upbeat, but his heart was heavy with sadness.

"Did you receive the envelope?"

"Yeah. I did. It was a restraining order against seeing Maddy."

"Oh. I'm sorry. I didn't know. It seemed important—"

"Do you know anything about getting a restraining order lifted? A lawyer? The process?"

"No, but I would think you would have to go to Family Court where the restraining order was signed. Maybe start there?"

"Thanks. I'm at a total loss what to do or where to start."

"It gets complicated, doesn't it?"

"Yeah. It sure does. I'll drive out to Litchfield as soon as I have a vehicle."

"One more thing, Mike. Remember to trust in the Lord with all your heart and do not lean on your own understanding. In all your ways acknowledge Him, and He will make your paths straight."

***

The moving van arrived the following day. Rosie's boxes were unloaded to the bungalow first and then their house. For the next two days, Mike and Stephanie unpacked boxes and put things away while the boys played nearby. Mike and Stephanie set up the kitchen first, followed by the boys' bedroom and the rest of the house. "I love it even though it looks sparse," Stephanie said eyeing their home with pleasure.

"We'll fill it up soon enough," Mike said as he hooked up the TV.

Just then his phone rang. When he hung up, he looked at Stephanie. "My truck is in."

They loaded the boys into Stephanie's car and drove to the truck dealer. Mike gave a low whistle when he saw the new truck with the crew cab and the Integra Builders logo on the doors.

"I don't deserve this," he said.

***

"Are you sure you don't need me to go to the airport with you tomorrow to pick up your mother?" Mike asked after they tucked the boys into bed.

"No, sweetheart. I'm totally fine to go get her. I have the GPS."

"You mean I've been replaced with a talking voice?"

"You could never be replaced, my love," she said wrapping her arms around his waist looking up at him with dancing eyes. I'll help mother get settled while you go to Litchfield."

***

Monday morning at 7:00 a.m., Mike left for the hour and a half drive to the Litchfield courthouse. He scanned the directory for Family Court, but could not find such a listing. He stepped over to the information desk. "Good morning. Can you tell me where to find the department regarding lifting a restraining order?"

"Yes," the receptionist said and smiled politely. "It's located in the Family Services Center on Holcombe. Do you know where that is located?"

"Yes. Thanks a lot."

"Look for Human Services under Social Services."

He nodded and hurried to his truck.

Mike approached the receptionist in Human Servicers. He greeted her cordially and said "I'd like to talk with someone who can help me get a restraining order lifted."

"That would be Val Thompson. What is your name?"

"Mike DiSanto."

"I will let her know you are here."

Mike sat down to wait.

"Mr. DiSanto, she can see you now," the receptionist said after a few minutes and pointed to a glass-enclosed office.

Introductions were made and a middle-aged Mrs. Thompson invited Mike to sit down.

"What can I do for you?" she asked pleasantly.

"I'd like to have a restraining order lifted."

"Is the restraining order against you or have you filed the order against someone else?"

"It's against me. My ex-wife filed the order so I could not see our daughter."

"It is a very difficult, but not impossible, task," she cautioned. Has there been a hearing previously and a final restraining order issued upon a finding of an act of domestic violence?"

"No."

"Child endangerment or child neglect?"

"No."

"Do you possess any firearms?"

"No."

"You will need to file a motion with the court where the order was issued. You will need to obtain the consent of the person who got the original order against you, or else file a motion to vacate the order and give them notice of your motion before you go to court."

"Do I need a lawyer?"

"The process can get sticky, and there are some technical rules to follow for filing a motion to vacate the order, so I would strongly recommend consulting a lawyer."

"Do you have any recommendations?"

"Yes, we have someone who specializes in domestic law in our department. His name is Bob Greene. Would you like to contact him to set up an appointment?" she asked handing Mike a business card.

"By any chance, would it be possible to see him today? I live about seventy-five miles away."

"Let me check." She called his office with the request. "He said he can see you at 10:00 a.m. for about a half hour to set up preliminary information regarding your case, and you will be able to complete the rest of your file over the phone, if that would work for you."

"Yes. Thanks."

***

At 10:00 a.m., a man of medium build and receding hairline approached Mike. "Are you Mike DiSanto?"

"Yes, I am," he said standing up.

"I'm Bob Greene."

They shook hands and Mr. Greene ushered Mike into his office. A large desk and a black leather chair sat in front of a window overlooking the street. "Please, be seated," he said motioning to one of two chairs in front of the desk. "How can I help you?"

Mike explained his purpose for being there while Mr. Greene listened and made notes on a legal pad.

"Are you aware that restraining orders punish you for a crime that might happen, whether a first-time offense or a repeated offense, and if you go against the order, it is punishable by up to two years in prison?"

"No, I didn't know that."

"I just want you to be clear on a couple of basics." He went on to explain the retaining fees.

Mike nodded.

"Please, give me a re-cap for the reason behind the restraining order," He said.

Mike quickly re-capped his concern for Maddy's welfare after his divorce, and that he had made the foolish decision to take Maddy and the bare facts of the consequences that followed.

Mr. Greene sat back in his chair for a long minute as though studying Mike with his lawyer's mind.

Mike stared at the floor.

"This is a very unusual case," Mr. Greene said.

Mike looked directly at Mr. Greene and nodded.

"But, I think I can help you."

Mike smiled gratefully.

"I'll have my secretary contact you tomorrow with all the questions I need answered. She will record your answers, and we'll proceed from there. I will file the motion to vacate the restraining order which can take up to ten business days. At that time, you can present your side and attempt to have the order dropped. Your ex-wife must be notified prior to the court date, but I'll take care of that."

"I sure appreciate everything, Mr. Greene."

"If we are able to get the restraining order vacated, you still may be required to have supervised visitation with your daughter. Are you in agreement with that?"

"There won't be a repeat offense and yes, I'm in agreement."

"Very well. Do you have the retaining fee?"

Mike nodded and wrote out a check for the amount.

***

Mike completed the forty-five minute phone interview with Mr. Greene's secretary the following day. Then he waited.

***

Seven business days later, Mike and Stephanie brought the boys to Rosie's and left to appear at the 10:30 a.m. hearing at the court house in Litchfield.

Mr. Greene met them just inside the courtroom.

Mike introduced Stephanie and they sat down.

"You'll be given an opportunity to present your side and your reasons why you want the restraining order vacated. Answer any questions as completely and honestly as possible. The judge has read your divorce proceedings, so try to be as accurate as possible with your facts."

"Will Lisa be given the same opportunity?"

"No. She did all that when she filed the petition."

Mike nodded.

In just a few minutes, Mike was called to go before the judge.

"I'll be praying," Stephanie whispered.

The hearing lasted a relatively short time. Mike noticed Lisa for the first time as he returned to his seat and waited while the judge read over the papers before him.

Mike held Stephanie's hand and looked down for what seemed an agonizing length of time.

"Mr. DiSanto, please approach the bench," the judge said.

Mike barely breathed as he walked forward.

"I do not find any evidence that the daughter, Madison DiSanto, would be in danger during times of visitation. Therefore, I hereby rescind the restraining order against Michael DiSanto effective this 29th day of August, 2004. Visitation may resume two weekends per month with additional visitation leniency in three months. The court applies no supervised restrictions." You and the petitioner will receive copies of the ruling by mail within five business days. That's all." He smacked his gavel.

Mike let out a deep breath and stood there with his eyes closed momentarily. "Thank you, Judge," he whispered.

He turned toward Stephanie with a huge grin.

She smiled back with tears streaming down her cheeks.

***

"Can you believe it! I finally get to see Maddy!" he said once in the car.

"I know. Isn't it absolutely wonderful? I'm so proud of you for pursuing such a difficult thing!" She leaned over and kissed his cheek.

"Oh, Father God," Mike prayed. "You are an awesome God and I give You all the praise and glory that I can see my daughter. Thank You! Thank You!"

He turned to Stephanie, put both hands on her cheeks and kissed her.

She looked at him with moist eyes. "Maddy is a lucky girl to have a father who loves her so."

"I can't wait until we spend weekends together with the boys— going to the North Shore, hanging out, fixing up a bedroom for her—"

"Sweetheart, rushing is what you do when catching a plane, but it's only for the moment. Relationships are a slow process, but they last a lifetime. You and Maddy have been separated for many years. Take it slow. Do what you do best."

"What's that?"

"Build."

CHAPTER 68

Saturday

The early morning sun stole glances at the St. Paul skyline between racing gray clouds early that Saturday.

Mike got up at 5:00 a.m. to go for his five-mile run before showering and leaving for his first weekend visit with Maddy.

Stephanie poured a cup of coffee for Mike and one for herself and sat down at the kitchen table. "Are you sure you don't want breakfast?" she asked.

"No, thanks." He looked at Stephanie. "You are loved beyond description, you know that?" Mike said holding her hand and rubbing his thumb over the back of it.

She squeezed his hand and smiled her wonderful smile. "Can I pray for today?"

Mike smiled and nodded.

"Heavenly Father, we trust this day into Your hands. We ask that You will guide Mike as he starts to build a relationship with Maddy. Grant both of them grace. We praise you and give thanks in Jesus' name. Amen."

"Besides seeing Maddy and spending time with her, I'm most excited to take her to church tomorrow."

"Me too."

Mike got up to leave. He kissed Stephanie tenderly. "Thanks for being my wife."

"Totally my pleasure."

Rita Kroon

"We should be home about 6:00 p.m."

"I'll have supper ready."

"Invite your mom. Love you."

***

Mike pulled up to his former house at exactly 8:00 a.m. "Lord, give me wisdom for Maddy's sake," he prayed. He rang the doorbell.

Lisa opened the door. She had a disgusted look on her face. She opened the door wider and turned to walk away.

"Lisa." Mike's voice was low.

She stopped and slowly turned to face him. "What." Her tone was angry.

"I'm sorry. I'm sorry for the hurt I've caused you."

"You put Madison through too much upheaval to suddenly show up in her life again."

"I wrote her hundreds of letters telling her that I loved her."

"You call kidnapping love?" Her voice sounded menacing.

"I'm sorry for that. Sorry for what it did to her and sorry for what it did to you."

She raised one eyebrow and turned away. "Madison! Time to go," she called.

Maddy appeared wearing ill-fitting jeans and tie-dyed tee-top. Her hair was in a ponytail. She carried a grocery bag with her overnight clothes. *She could've had on a flour sack and she still would look my little princess,* Mike thought with fatherly pride. "Hi, Maddy," he said softly.

"Hi." She seemed hesitant.

His throat felt dry. *She's a teenager. How did all this time escape us? I wish I could hug her and erase all the years.*

They walked to his truck. "Do you want to go out for breakfast?"

She shrugged. "I guess."

"Do you have a favorite place?"

"The Litchfield Café is good."

"You'll have to tell me where it is."

292

She gave him directions. They sat in the last booth and ordered breakfast.

"You've grown up to be a beautiful young lady," he said.

After a quiet breakfast, Mike asked, "Do you want to go for a walk in the park?"

Again, she shrugged. "I suppose."

They walked through the park and sat down at a picnic table near the band shell. "I don't know where to begin. I know now it was wrong for me to have taken you, but at the time, it seemed like the right thing to do. I don't know how much you remember of California, but I hope you have good memories. I never intended for you to suffer because of my actions. I'm sorry, Maddy."

"You're a stranger to me."

Mike nodded. "I can understand that."

"I had a few happy memories, but then a nightmare happened, and you weren't there anymore. I waited and waited, but you never came. I even kept my hair long 'cuz if I didn't, I thought you might not recognize me."

Father, God, help me, he thought. "I don't know how much your mother told you, but—"

"She told me you didn't want to be with us anymore."

Mike expelled a hard breath. "I couldn't come to you because I was in prison."

"Kids in school laughed because they said my daddy was in prison, but I didn't believe them."

"Oh, Maddy, I'm so sorry. I'm sorry."

"You could've written."

"I did write you."

"I don't believe you. You're just saying that."

"I have all the letters I wrote to you in my truck."

She looked at him skeptically.

"I'll get them. Wait here." He jogged to his truck and retrieved the box of letters. He set them on the table and lifted the lid.

Her eyes widened when she saw the stacks of hundreds of letters tied together with a string and labeled according to year.

She picked through the stacks of letters. She touched a small bundle of letters tied with a pink ribbon and tucked on the side. "What are these?" She picked up the small bundle of letters and looked curiously at them. "There's no address."

"Those are seven letters I found in the desk in the house where you live. A mother wrote them to her daughter—a letter for each year her child lived. The little girl was killed in a school bus accident when she was seven."

"But, why do you have them?"

"They were an inspiration to me that if I ever had a little girl, I would love her and protect her for as long as I lived. And I would tell her so in letters. Little did I know these would be the letters."

"I have a special letter that I always kept on top. I wanted it to be the first letter you read."

"Why?"

"It's a special letter. Do you want to read it?"

She opened the envelope, took out the letter, and read. "Dear Maddy, This is my favorite letter to you. I want to tell you about someone very special. He loves you so much that He died for you. But He didn't stay dead. He came alive again." She looked at him with a frown. "His name is Jesus," she continued. "He died in your place so you wouldn't have to die in sin and not be able to go to heaven. I hope someday we will be able to talk together about Him. He is called the Savior. I love you so much, but Jesus loves you even more. Daddy."

She folded the letter and put it back into the envelope.

"Maybe someday, you'll understand."

She shrugged.

"Tell me about you."

"I don't know what to say."

"Do you like school? Do you have a special friend or do you have lots of friends?"

"What do you care?"

"I do care. I want to hear all about you."

"School is boring and I hang out with my friends mostly."

"Do you like sports?"

"I'm going out for softball next spring, but that's the only sport I like."

"I used to play baseball when I was in high school."

"Really?"

"Really. Look in the trophy case when you go to school Monday. You'll see."

"OK. I will." She looked intently at Mike. "Why did you go to prison?"

"Because I made a bad choice and the consequences for that decision was prison. Every choice has consequences—some good and some not good. You'll learn that, and hopefully, you'll make good choices and think about what could happen before you make bad choices."

"Do you ever talk about prison?"

"I try not to think about it, and I usually don't talk about it. I understood why I was there, but you didn't. And I'm so sorry. If I could take all my tears that I cried while in prison and put them in bottles, there wouldn't be any empty bottles left on earth. I hope you can forgive me."

"I don't know. Part of me wants to for all the happy memories I do have and part of me doesn't for all the sad memories."

"I understand, Maddy. I think I would feel the same way if I were you."

"You would?"

Mike nodded. "It's a lot to understand at your young age."

"How come you took me to California?"

"That's the bad choice I made. We were divorced for two years and you started having problems—

"What kind of problems?"

"Well, you were wetting the bed, crying a lot, running to hide whenever a sitter came, and you had stomach aches."

"How old was I?"

"You were four."

"But why did you take me?"

"I could only see you two weekends a month, and I wanted to give you more stability, a chance to know you were loved and a chance to be happy. I didn't know how else to give you that."

"Would you do it over again?"

Painful questions, but she deserves to know the truth, he thought. "Yes and no."

She looked puzzled.

"Yes, for all the good that came out of it and no for the hurtful consequences that resulted."

"Do you have a job?"

"Yes. I work for a company that builds assisted living places for people who need help to do everyday things. We just moved to St. Paul and started our first assisted living home last week." He wet his lips. "Do you have any ideas what you want to do when you graduate?"

"Not really."

"You have lots of time yet."

They talked unhurriedly for a couple more hours before Mike said, "I'm getting hungry. Do you want to grab a late lunch and head back to my house?"

"Okay."

"Do you remember a lady named Rosie? She had a gold tooth and you told her she had sparkly teeth."

Maddy thought. "Sorta."

"Well, you'll see her tonight and I'm sure you'll remember her. She lives next door to us. I'm married and we have twin boys."

"You're married?"

"Yes. Her name is Stephanie. I know you will like her."

"How old are your twins?"

"They're going on two years old. Do you babysit?"

"Yeah. For one family with two kids. They're three and four."

"Do you like kids?"

"Yeah. They don't yell at me and we can have fun together."

Mike nodded. "That's good."

***

Mike pulled into the driveway at 5:45 p.m. "C'mon in and meet my other family."

Stephanie greeted her warmly. "Hi Maddy. You've grown up to a lovely young lady. You may not remember me, but I first met you in California. You were playing with your friend, Carla. Do you remember her?"

"Yeah, I remember Carla."

Just then Rosie stepped out of the kitchen and smiled her big smile.

"Oh, I remember you," she said surprised.

Danny and Davey came tearing around the corner and stopped abruptly when they spotted Maddy.

"This is Danny and Davey," Mike said picking up each boy in his arms for a hug. "This is Maddy."

Davey squirmed out of Mike's arms and walked to Maddy. He held up his arms to her. She picked him up and he put his arms around her neck.

Mike, Stephanie and Rosie looked at one another, puzzled.

"Aw. How sweet," Maddy said.

Conversation around the supper table was an uninterrupted cacophony of chatter. Mike noticed Maddy seemingly enjoy being part of the family and was thankful for the boys' chatter that somehow took away any uneasiness she may have felt.

CHAPTER 69

Pieces of the Puzzle

M ike helped Stephanie get the boys ready for toddlers' class before knocking softly on Maddy's bedroom door. "Maddy? It's 8:00 a.m. and we have to leave for church in an hour."

A short time later, Maddy appeared in the kitchen wearing jeans and a yellow tee top. She wore her hair down instead of in her usual pony tail.

Mike looked affectionately at his daughter. He felt a surge of pride like the first time when he held her as a baby. "You look beautiful," he said.

"Good morning, lovely lady," Stephanie greeted warmly. "Come, sit down. We're making blueberry pancakes." She took orange juice from the refrigerator and set it on the table. "I hope you like pancakes."

Maddy sat down. "I don't want to go to church."

Stephanie brushed past Mike to get the syrup. "Give her time," she whispered.

Mike sat down next to Maddy. "Princess. Is it all right if I call you that?" he asked cautiously.

She nodded. "I guess."

"Is there a particular reason why you don't want to go to church?" She shrugged.

"As a family, we go to church every Sunday. As part of our family, we include you in going to church as well." He paused briefly. "Do you go to church in Litchfield?"

"No."

"Well, then you are in for a treat. We certainly won't force you, but we really hope you will go with us. Rosie goes too."

She smiled slightly. "OK. I guess."

***

The pastor spoke about the way every person is special because of Jesus. "Even if we don't feel special all the time. It doesn't matter what age we are or where we live or what our name is," the pastor said, "we are loved by the God of the heavens and the earth. He knows each one of us by name and He loves us unconditionally."

Mike shot a glance at Maddy. She had set the bulletin aside and sat forward in her seat. "Lord, help her to hear Your message," he prayed silently.

***

As Stephanie finished lunch preparations, Maddy sat on the living room floor holding Davey in her lap and putting a simple puzzle together with Danny, "Would you like to go shopping for some school clothes?" Stephanie asked as she set a pan of lasagna on the table. "It would be fun to buy girl clothes for a change instead of boy stuff."

Maddy looked up in surprise. "That would be cool."

As Mike grabbed a jug of milk from the refrigerator, he smiled and winked at Stephanie.

"I'll see if Mother can take the boys, so you, your dad, and I can go shopping before we take you back to your mom's. How does that sound?"

"Way cool!" Maddy nodded emphatically.

"Great!" Mike agreed.

Maddy looked from Stephanie to Mike, and a big smile spread across her face.

It was then that Mike realized the outer puzzle pieces—the framework—of a family picture were coming together. A real family— willing and able to reach out to one another, and empowered to reverse the havoc that once ruled their lives.

AUTHOR BIO

Rita Kroon was born in Minneapolis, but raised in St. Paul, MN. She graduated from Sibley High School and received her AA degree in speech/communications from Lakewood Community College.

She is a member of the Minnesota Christian Writers' Guild and an active participant in a writers' critique group. She teaches women's Bible studies and is involved with evangelism and ESL at her church.

Rita has written wildlife magazine articles, children's short stories, devotionals, poetry, and a humorous newspaper column "Rita Raps it Up."

Her most recent books include:

- *Letters from the Past* (historical Christian fiction)
- *You Have Cancer —a Journey Through the Valley of the Shadow of Death* (her personal story of faith during her battle with cancer)
- *Praying the Scriptures* (a collection of prayers based on Scripture)
- *Womanhood—Becoming a Woman of Virtue* (two-in-one Bible study—in-depth and condensed)
- *40 Days in the Wilderness* (devotional)
- *40 Days of God's assurance (devotional)*
- *40 Days of Encouragement (devotional)*

Rita is a seven-year cancer survivor. She and her husband live in Shoreview, MN. They have three married daughters and 17 grandchildren.

CPSIA information can be obtained
at www.ICGtesting.com
Printed in the USA
FFOW02n0608231014
8282FF